THE CHICKEN RESCUE LEAGUE:
A TEXAS TRAILER PARK MYSTERY

Amy Eastlake

BooksForABuck.com

2004

Amy Eastlake

Published by **BooksForABuck.com**

September 2004

ISBN: 978-1-60215-120-8

Chapter 1

Sam Katz leaned closer to me, his deep blue eyes gazing soulfully into mine.

My heart gave a little jump. We'd only started the relationship a couple of months before when Sam had moved into the trailer park I manage, but things had gone pretty fast—hence me lolling naked in his bed.

"Oh, Tina." He ran one large hand down my waist.

I giggled despite the romantic moment. He tickled.

"I wish you could stay," he continued in that same deep romantic voice.

What was that about? I hadn't been hoping for nonsense about deep and eternal commitments. But I definitely hadn't expected to get kicked out of his bed.

"How come?"

"Emily will be up any minute."

Emily was his four-year old daughter and Sam had exclusive custody. None of the guys I'd dated before had been dads, and I guess my ignorance showed because Emily'd had taken one look at me when they'd first moved in, announced to her father that I was a jerk, and since then, had done her best to make my life miserable.

It wasn't that she was comparing me to a perfect mother and I was coming up short. The kid just didn't like me.

But I could live with that. Sam was the real problem.

I thought about slugging Sam, but realized he was just being male. He couldn't help it that I got all romancey when he used that deep soulful tone in his voice.

"How about you come back over around ten tonight," Sam suggested as I pulled on last night's outfit and got ready to slink back to my trailer.

A rooster crow cut off my answer, giving me a chance to catch my breath and not gush something. I didn't want Sam to take me for granted. After all the bad relationships I'd been in, I wanted this one to work.

"Damn chickens," I said instead.

"It does seem strange," he admitted. "You'd think that wild chickens would keep quiet rather than risk getting caught and eaten."

I shook my head. Sam's story was that he'd been a telephone switch installer until the telecom meltdown had eliminated his job. I wasn't so sure I believed him anymore though. About that or a lot of the things he'd told me. He just didn't seem to know the facts of life that anyone with a blue-collar background in Dallas would know. People in the south keep chickens for laying or fighting. I hadn't seen any fresh eggs lately.

I yanked my t-shirt over my head, stuffed my bra in my pocket, and turned to face him.

He looked so cute with his hard-muscled chest and his black hair and blue eyes that I decided not to worry about it. So what if he had a few secrets. Who didn't? I kissed him on the cheek and ran my hand down that perfect chest. "I'll try to make it over tonight, honey."

His gorgeous smile was quite a reward. He had about five miles of straight, bright white teeth.

"And don't forget rent is due tomorrow," I added.

I heard movement outside his door and gritted my teeth. This seemed to happen every morning. Emily would wake up and head to her father's room to check on him. And Tina Anderson, trailer park manager and girlfriend would have to sneak out Sam's bedroom window. Again.

* * * *

The trailer park I manage is in the Oak Cliff district of Dallas-where they put the poor people and minorities and the trailer parks that just aren't suitable in areas where rich people might actually have to confront how much of the population who does the dirty work lives. You'd think that smack in the middle of a city the size of Dallas would mean high-rise buildings and fancy city parks, but that isn't the way Dallas works. Instead we butt up against a little stream that's thick with poison oak and bois d'arc trees. On the other side is the Trinity River floodplain.

The area around the trailer park might be urban, but there was plenty of space for anyone to hide a million chickens down there. It was a health risk, and the idea of fighting cocks grossed me out. If anyone in my park was responsible, I intended to put a stop to it.

I chased one fluffy white chicken for a while, but it didn't seem interested in heading back to wherever its crate might be. So I tried to home in on the sound of rooster crowing.

"You're out early, Tina."

I turned and faced Patrick Adams.

His trailer is pretty much like the rest of the trailers in my park-beat-up and fading. One difference is that he never opens his blinds. As far as I can tell, he sits at home all day with his blinds drawn and looks at dirty pictures on the Internet. Lack of sunlight and Patrick's diet of Twinkies and Ho-Ho's gives him the appearance of a snowman, pale and softly round.

"Hi Patrick. Rent's due tomorrow."

Patrick was one of my few tenants who paid their rent on time. As endearing features went, this one came high. They don't pay, I don't eat.

"Big night last night, Tina?"

"Uh, no. I'm trying to figure out who's keeping the chickens."

"Oh. So that's why you're wearing the same shirt you had on last night." He paused a beat. "You know, Tina, we could make a few bucks if you'd let me take your picture. I mean, you don't have the greatest body in the world, but lots of guys go for the natural look. And there are whole sites devoted to trailer park trash. You'd fit right in."

"How about I just fit into the people who don't do that kind of thing, Patrick."

He looked hurt. "I thought it might help with your financial problems, Tina. All you have to do is say no."

As if I hadn't been telling him no ever since I'd taken this job. "Is that all I have to do? Well, listen carefully. Hell No. How about that."

He held up a pudgy hand. "No problem, Tina. Like I said, I'm trying to help you. I'd be the first guy to understand what happens when the money runs low."

This was the first I'd heard that my financial problems were the talk of the park. You wouldn't think the telecom shutdowns that had happened up in snobby north Dallas would affect real working people down in south Dallas. But crap flows downhill and I'd lost tenants and was having trouble getting rent from a lot of the others. That and my income from my custom programming projects had largely dried up as people started deciding that they didn't really need new software in tough economic times.

"Don't call me, I'll call you. And by the way, do you know anything about all these chickens?"

"Why ask me?" he demanded.

When Patrick doesn't give you an answer, you can bet he's hiding something. "Because you spend a lot of time peeking through that gap in your Venetian blinds," I reminded him.

Patrick thought about that for a few long seconds. "There's been a lot of cockfighting out south," he admitted. "Get some good cocks and you can make some money." He grinned. "Course, being a woman, you can probably get cock any time-"

I held up a hand. "Don't want to hear it, Patrick. But you think somebody is raising fighting cocks here?"

Patrick shrugged.

I had to look away. His gesture sent slow waves of jiggle around his body like a stadium crowd doing the wave.

"Tell you what, Patrick. If you learn anything, let me know."

If the city learned that the Shady Rest Trailer Park actually allowed tenants to raise roosters for illegal cockfighting, they'd shut us down in a minute. For some reason, cities don't treat trailer parks, or the people who live in them, like citizens. We're more like squatters they'd like to get rid of but need at least a hint of an excuse. As excuses went, fighting cocks would be a dandy.

"How about a deal?" Patrick suggested. He was slightly breathless from standing for so long and I caught the strong odor of marshmallow in the wheezes.

"No pictures," I insisted. I'm working-class, and more than one person, starting with my ex-mother-in-law, has told me what a slut I am. But I have my limits. And being jerk-off bait for a few million horny Patrick Adams's of the world crossed those limits in a big way.

He shrugged again. "Those chicken-fighting guys can be rough and you'll be needing all the help you can get. Tell you what, though. I'll give you something for free. Be careful about Sam Katz."

I'd used Patrick's shrug as an excuse to turn away, but that slam on Sam whirled me back around like a punch to the head. "What are you talking about?"

Patrick giggled and took a step toward me. "A guy shows up driving an almost new Winnebago that had to cost fifty thousand. And he's got some story about having sole custody of his daughter. And nowhere on the Internet is there a Sam Katz that is anything close to a match for our artificially handsome tenant. Kind of makes you wonder, doesn't it, Tina? Checked the back of any milk cartons lately?"

I hadn't noticed that Patrick was getting closer as he talked until he made a quick grab and yanked my bra out of my pocket where I'd stuffed it.

"I had you down for the old fashioned white padded numbers." Patrick sounded disappointed.

"Give me that." I snatched it back and shoved it into my pocket. This bra was going into the washer for a long soak before I even thought about wearing it again.

I'd wasted enough time with Patrick that I didn't feel like chicken hunting any more. Besides, what he'd said about Sam left a strange taste in my mouth. I'm not the world's greatest judge of the male of the species. I can get buffaloed by a cute tush or a good line. But Sam had seemed too good to be true and I hadn't wanted to question it.

I'd switched over to a DSL connection a few months before—telling myself that it was essential if I was going to be serious about my custom programming business and about the shareware game programming I enjoyed. It only took me a few seconds to run a quick backgrounder on

Sam Katz.

There are probably two thousand Sam Katz's listed on the Internet. But Patrick was right. None of them was a thirty-three year old unemployed telecom technician with midnight black hair. More to the point, none of them had recently been divorced and been granted sole custody of their four-year-old daughter.

My Sam Katz was a phony.

When I'd been in high school and got into this kind of trouble, I would run to Andy Anderson. Andy was my mentor in high school. He was the guy who helped me fit in with the cool people when everyone else seemed impossibly rich and I had a choice of exactly two t-shirts to wear with my one pair of jeans.

Andy was the one I'd commiserated my botched tattoo with—and the one who'd taken my cherry. But I'd run to him too often and eventually we'd gotten married. Marriage hadn't been a good idea. Andy traveled with the rich set and liked it. I never felt comfortable there, and his mother's antipathy certainly didn't help. Eventually it dawned on me that we were hurting each other. We did a lot better as friends than as spouses.

Andy had taken the software business we'd started and gone on to become one of the first dot-com millionaires in Dallas. Unlike many others, he'd actually found a way to make money from what he did, and had cashed out early enough that he was able to keep most of what he'd earned.

Now Andy moved in circles so high they gave me airsickness. I'd gotten out of the marriage before I'd strangled. Still, Andy was my go-to guy.

I told myself that I should handle this on my own. Andy was getting on with his life and didn't need me running to him with my little problems.

I told myself that as I dialed, and kept telling myself when I heard his deep voice coming over the other end of my cell. "What's up, Tina?"

"Oh, is it you Andy?"

"You called me, remember?"

"Uh, yeah." I headed for my kitchen and rescued a carton of ice cream from my freezer. Nothing like marble fudge ripple to give your confidence a boost.

"Are you okay?" he demanded.

"I sort of might have a problem." I felt about as articulate as I sounded. I'm normally a bigmouth, but when it came to talking to my ex-husband, I sometimes froze more solid than the block of ice cream I dragged out of the freezer.

He didn't sigh. Thank God for that, at least.

"Listen. I've got a meeting in ten minutes and I don't want to cancel if I don't have to," he told me. "Is it an emergency? Or how about we get together to talk about it? Lunch at Norma's?"

"Lunch is good," I told him. "Noon?"

"Noon works for me. See you then."

I stared at the suddenly dead phone, then at the spoon in my hand. Well, the ice cream was ready and it was hours before noon.

* * * *

I demolished most of the carton of ice cream and changed my clothes three times, finally deciding on a ratty pair of jeans and a logo t-shirt I'd gotten when I did booth duty for Andy back when I'd been employee number three in Anderson Software. It wasn't my best look, but I didn't want to look desperate or like I was trying to seduce him. He was my friend, that was all. Sam, not Andy, was my boyfriend. But then again, Sam was the one who just might be a kidnapper.

My Geo Storm wheezed up the hill that gave Oak Cliff its name, a trail of blue smoke following. The Storm and I had worked out a deal. I gave it a quart of oil every week and it didn't complain too much about the other things it wanted. A buck's worth of oil was a lot cheaper than the valve job it really needed.

Andy was just pulling up when I got there. He'd gotten a new car since I'd seen him last—a cute little Mercedes convertible that probably kept the debutante set wet between their legs.

Twist my arm and I'd admit that I lusted after it a little too.

"Hey, doll," he called out.

We went through the motions of air kissing, but Andy's arm around my waist felt pretty good as we walked into Norma's, a Dallas institution of fat grams and serious comfort food.

Pam, the owner, was working the cash register and came over to say hello and bring us our iced tea and a big basket of corn bread and rolls.

In Texas, iced tea is served sweetened, with enough sugar to make your teeth ache, and Norma's tea is even sweeter than the usual Texas mash. Yumm.

I swallowed a long drink of my tea, grabbed the biggest corn bread muffin from the basket before Andy could snag it, and started chewing.

"Want to tell me about it?" Andy asked. "Or did you just need a free lunch?"

I had a flash of genius. I could put off talking about Sam for at least a few minutes if I ran some of the smaller stuff by him first. Since Andy owns the Shady Rest Trailer Park, he's technically my boss and is technically responsible for meeting code. "Have you heard about the chickens?" I was trying to sound innocent and helpful.

He glared at me. I guess I'd run the innocent-and-helpful routine by him a few too many times. "You called me up with a problem and now you want to talk about poultry?"

"Patrick Adams says somebody is raising fighting cocks in the park. I've heard a lot of crowing for several days now. This morning I spotted a hen wandering around loose."

"Patrick?" Andy was trying not to smile. "He's the pervert, right?"

I rolled my eyes. "Not the pervert, a pervert. We have several."

People don't end up in trailer parks on purpose. They sort of drift there. And perverts drift downhill. So I had my share of peeping Toms, problem drinkers, and men who went to family reunions hoping to get hitched. Mixed among them, though, were some of the nicest people I'd ever met. One thing for sure, not one of them was as cold as Andy's mother could be.

"Cockfighting is illegal in Texas," Andy told me. "If I remember right, it might be legal in parts of Oklahoma. I've also heard that there's a lot of illegal cockfighting in parts of Texas. Including in south Dallas. So, it's possible that Patrick is right. It's also possible that someone wants fresh eggs."

He didn't believe that any more than I did, though. You didn't need roosters for eggs. And what I'd heard had definitely been roosters crowing. It was vaguely possible that someone would keep roosters to fertilize the eggs, but not enough to explain the noise. Someone was raising fighting birds.

"I don't want cockfighting birds in my complex," I told him.

"Call pest control," Andy offered.

"Maybe." It wasn't a bad idea, but I didn't want to spend money if I didn't have to. Since he was the owner, it would be his money and I think I was even more careful with that than I was with my own. "I've got a few things to try myself, first."

Andy looked serious. "There's a lot of money tied up in illegal cockfighting. Don't be the Lone Ranger here, Tina. Let's get professional help."

So much for my thinking I'd start with the easy stuff. Now I had two major worries rather than just one.

A waitress came, refilled our tea, and took our orders. Andy got a salad. I ordered the chicken fried steak dinner. I'd already blown my diet when I'd pigged out on fudge ripple so I figured I might as well enjoy my fall from grace.

Andy waited until the waitress went away, then took my hand across the table. "Are you going to tell me what's really going on, or are you just going to sit there and waffle the entire meal away?"

I took a deep breath and plunged in, telling him about Emily who might or might not be a kidnap victim, about Patrick saying that Sam was too perfect, and about what I'd found, or not found, on the Internet.

"No law against using a false name," Andy said. "But it does sound suspicious."

"I did everything I know how on the Internet," I told him. I reached into my purse and pulled out my copy of Sam's rent application. It included a social security number I was pretty sure was fake and a former address that was definitely fiction. Given the clientele I normally get, neither of those minor falsifications was unusual. Of course, normally I don't date the tenants.

Andy jotted down the information, then took the picture I'd had taken when Sam, Emily, and I went to the Weatherford Peach Festival. "I'll have someone look into it."

I nodded. Andy's company does a lot of secure computing work, so his human resources team crunches through background checks in volume. If anyone could get to the bottom of the mystery, it was Andy.

I stuck my fork at an almost polished plate. Now that I'd gotten my problem off my chest, I was ready to eat. Except somehow, while Andy and I had been talking, I'd inhaled my food without noticing. It wasn't fair and I wasn't satisfied.

I looked into my purse and saw that I had three dollars. "Uh, Andy."

He saw my worried look. "My treat."

"In that case, can I have dessert?"

Norma's has some of the best meringue pies anywhere and the chocolate and peanut butter meringue is a masterpiece. I thought about ordering two, one to take home, but decided that would be pushing it.

"I'll order it for you on my way out. I've got to get back to work." Andy stood and grabbed the bill from the table where Pam had dropped it, leaving a five for a tip. "I'll call you tonight and let you know what I find out."

"Thanks, Andy."

He nodded, then bent next to me, brushed his lips against my cheek, and headed out.

I watched him leave.

Andy isn't a hard-body the way Sam is and stays clear of the weights. Still, he goes for long runs most mornings while he thinks about what he wants to do with his company and how he's going to make his next million dollars. His lean body looked damned good. I felt myself getting excited again. Maybe Andy's mother was right and I really was a slut.

Pam caught me watching and dropped into Andy's seat, sliding the pie in front of me. "You two thinking about getting back together?"

"Hey, Pam. Uh-un. He's all yours if you want to give him a shot."

Pam laughed. "I don't think my husband would go for that. You know you were crazy to walk away from him. He's rich, good looking, and he thinks the world turns around you. My opinion is, you couldn't ask for much more from a man if you had to write the ingredient list."

I hadn't asked her, but she was right. The problem wasn't love. I couldn't imagine not being able to call on Andy for help no matter what happened in our lives. The problem wasn't even Andy's mother— although she did her best to make herself one. The problem was that we lived in different worlds, dreamed different dreams.

Unfortunately, I hadn't done any better on the man front since I'd moved on. Certainly Sam and I had no mass of shared interests.

I realized that Pam was waiting for me to answer, so I tried to get my thoughts together in a way where they'd at least sound logical, even if they weren't. "The problem is," I told her, "he's like a big brother to me. We've shared so much of our lives that there isn't any mystery left. I know he'd do anything to help me, to protect me. But it can be suffocating sometimes."

Pam narrowed her eyes. Don't tell me he's stalking you."

The mental picture of Andy using his Palm Pilot to schedule stalking moments was too much. I burst out laughing. "He tries to squeeze in a quick stalk on the third Saturday of each month," I giggled.

"Guess you're right. He's the most on-the-go man I've ever met." She paused a beat. "Hey, want another piece of pie?"

I sucked up my will power and turned it down. Will power comes a little easier after you've had most of a half gallon of ice cream, a chicken fried steak, a serving of mashed potatoes with gravy, a serving of kernel corn dripping in butter, and a big helping of fried squash. And a piece of pie.

I didn't think I'd need to eat again for a week. Which was lucky because my refrigerator was empty and I wouldn't get my next paycheck until then. Unlike with Andy, going out with Sam is usually Dutch treat. Which meant we wouldn't be going out any time soon.

* * * *

I spent the rest of the afternoon working on the Java code for a game I'd been designing for cell phones. The computer game industry had gotten so specialized and so sophisticated that just about every mainstream game takes a huge team of professionals. Any more, it was only the specialty niches where a single programmer can put something together and make a few bucks. At least I hoped I could make a few bucks. The cell phone industry was right down the tubes with the rest of high tech so I wasn't that confident. Still, programming was what I do.

I keep my trailer dark in the summer because my window air conditioning unit has a hard enough time keeping up with the Texas sun and all the heat thrown off by my computers. So I was surprised when I looked at my watch and saw that it was after ten.

My game was coming along pretty well and I was pretty sure that if I pulled an all-nighter, I could wrap things up. On the other hand, I'd promised Sam that I'd stop by. I felt enough like a traitor having Andy investigate him without dumping him at the same time.

Besides, I only had Patrick's word that there was a problem. And Patrick's word wasn't worth much.

I'd put on a halter top and a pair of shorts that barely keep me legal when I'd gotten home from lunch. In my trailer, I'm lucky if the air conditioner just falls behind. I'd done enough sweating back when I'd been a kid and my father would drag the entire family out to pick cotton at the end of the summer.

I thought about putting on a bra, but Sam was a pretty typical guy and liked to see the boobs jiggling. I don't have that much going on in front, but I decided to give him what he wanted. Except when he was in a hurry to get rid of me when Emily was around, Sam was one hell of a lover.

It was dark outside. I'd thought about hitting Andy up for the money to put some lights up through the complex, but most of the tenants liked it dark. Oddly enough, we'd never had any problems with muggings in my complex. Maybe because potential muggers were afraid they'd run into someone tougher than they were.

I'd walked the couple of hundred feet between my trailer and Sam's about fifty times since we'd started dating so I didn't think I needed any light. Until I felt something give under my foot.

I probably would have been all right if it hadn't screamed.

I panicked, tried to twist away from whatever I'd stepped on, and fell flat on my face.

A rooster screeched at me again, pecked once at my bleeding hand, and scooted off in a movement halfway between flying and running.

It took me a few seconds before I could catch my breath and check that I hadn't broken anything. One thing for sure, that was it as far as the chickens went. No more computer programming, no more ice cream orgies until I found where they were hiding and got rid of them. Either they left, or I'd eat them.

The lights were off in Sam's trailer. For a moment, I thought he'd given up on me. Then I saw the flicker of a television reflected through the curtains of Sam's bedroom window.

He was waiting up for me. I felt a little gooey inside. With some of the losers I've dated since Andy and I split up, I would never know whether they would be waiting, or worse, waiting with another woman looking to get into some three-way action. But Sam wasn't that kind of guy. He seemed satisfied with just me-and I liked it that way.

I almost knocked, then smacked myself in the forehead. If I woke Emily up, my chances of getting lucky were close to zero.

I opened the unlocked door and stepped in.

When he watches television after he puts Emily to bed, Sam uses his earphones. So the silence didn't bother me. But something did. I'm not sure whether it was smell, or some psychic sense, but no amount of Texas heat could keep the goose bumps down on my arms.

I managed not to call out his name. Again, fear of waking Emily kept me from doing anything completely insane.

I stepped into his bedroom and stopped.

Sam lay on his bed, propped up on his pillows like a king on a throne as the television flickered through some news show.

The sheets, which had been white that morning when I left, were a rusty red color. Sam's pale face looked even paler in the reflected glow of the television tube. Paler, because he'd lost so much blood. Red lines gouged deep into his throat showed how he'd been killed.

Papers, books from his bookshelf, and other remains of a detailed search lay scattered everywhere.

I couldn't help screaming.

Sam didn't react to my scream. I stood there, caught between the urge to do something and the urge to flee and pretend that I'd never been here, that Sam was nothing to me but another tenant.

The faint buzzing of a fly persuaded me to move.

I reached to try to stop the bleeding, to give him mouth-to-mouth resuscitation or something. But his head flopped slackly to the side.

Sam, my boyfriend of the past three months, lay dead on his bed, his body already cooling to air conditioner level.

I screamed again.

Chapter 2

It took a few minutes of digging through the disaster left by whomever had killed him to discover that Sam didn't have a phone in his trailer and another minute to remember that I had mine in my purse.

My hands were shaking so hard that I had to try three times before I managed to dial 9-1-1. Then the phone rang so long that I wondered if I'd dialed the wrong number.

When the 9-1-1 Operator heard that the dead body was located in the Shady Rest Trailer Park, she sighed and said she'd dispatch a unit. She also got my name and phone number and told me to stay where I was, to make sure I didn't touch anything, and to check and make sure that Sam wasn't still alive.

I'd already touched everything looking for Sam's phone, so I didn't worry about following the operator's instructions to feel for a pulse.

I was pretty sure I wasn't going to find one. I'm not an expert but I was pretty sure that your body doesn't normally cool down like that if you aren't dead. At least it doesn't in Texas where summer cooling is expensive. I was right, too. Sam was a corpse.

I felt sick in my stomach.

I swallowed hard, thought I'd won the battle, then ralphed partially digested ice cream, pie, chicken fried steak, cornbread rolls, and kernel corn all over poor Sam's body.

"Try not to disturb the evidence," the 9-1-1 operator reminded me.

"Sorry," I told her. "I don't think anything's ever going to disturb this guy again. He's dead."

That stumped the operator for a moment. "Is there anyone else in the, uh, residence with you?"

"Ohmygod, Emily." Had the killer gotten her too? I started running through the Winnebego shouting her name.

"Who is Emily?"

"His daughter."

"I see. How old is the daughter?" The dispatcher sounded interested. Maybe she was trying to put together an Oedipal story in her mind.

"Four."

"Oh." Disappointment tinged the operator's voice.

I'd already searched the trailer when I'd been looking for a phone but I checked again. "She isn't here. Where could she have gone?"

I had visions of poor Emily finding her father and wandering off in a daze. After all, I was twenty-seven and my mind wasn't working straight. And Sam hadn't been my father.

"Just relax, Ms. Anderson." The 9-1-1 operator must have thought I was crazy. When I managed to quiet my brain down for a moment, I realized I'd been hearing sirens for a minute or so now. The operator was doing her best to keep me calm, even to the point of encouraging me when I rambled on and didn't make any sense at all.

It was a noble effort, but one doomed to failure. I'd lost my boyfriend and was feeling about as calm as that rooster I'd stepped on a few minutes before.

"Okay. They're here." When I saw the flashes of police light bars through Sam's window, I hung up the cell and opened the door to the trailer.

"Freeze." The electronically amplified shout almost flattened me against Sam's trailer. A bright light shone directly in my eyes.

I froze as well as my shaky legs, weak stomach, and searchlight-dazzled eyes would allow me.

"Put the weapon on the ground," the voice commanded.

Whoever was talking sounded like James Earl Jones doing Darth Vader. Unfortunately, I didn't have a weapon to put down, so I stayed very still.

Doing nothing was a mistake. When I'd been a pre-teen, my father had taken me hunting a few times. For dad, hunting was serious business. I'd learned to recognize the sounds of shotgun shells being chambered. I must have heard that sound twenty times in the next two seconds.

"I don't have any weapons," I tried.

"Whatever you have in your hand, put it on the ground," Darth insisted.

I looked and saw I was still clutching my cell.

When you live in a trailer park, you see a side of the police that rich suburbanites never do. It's the them-against-us, razor's edge side that keeps cops alive when they're in what has to feel like enemy territory. It's also the side that gets innocent people blown away because they asked too many questions or didn't give the right answer quickly enough.

I bent down and laid my cell on the ground trying to move at a fast enough pace that they wouldn't think I was stalling, but calmly enough that they didn't think I was trying anything either. I didn't get shot, so I guessed it worked.

We all breathed a sigh of relief when I stood back up. I even think I heard Darth's breath wheeze over the megaphone.

Two cops shoved me against Sam's trailer wall and patted me down.

"I'm Tina Anderson," I explained. "I called in the 9-1-1. I'm the manager of the park."

"You hung up on the dispatcher," my searcher told me.

I'd been searched before and then I'd gotten some extra pats. This cop didn't bother with that. He was a six foot tall blond with a surfer tan and blue eyes that looked like turquoise stones. He was a doll and probably had women begging him for a strip search.

Fortunately, I wasn't looking. Half an hour ago, I'd gone looking for my boyfriend and this was the result. Men were nothing but trouble and I planned to use this opportunity to put them behind me completely.

"I saw you'd gotten here and came out to let you in," I explained. "The operator only told me to stay on the phone until you got here."

"She was worried that you might have been attacked."

So all of this had been for my protection. Somehow I didn't feel particularly safe.

The cop told me his name was Mike Heath and offered me a drink of lukewarm coffee from a Styrofoam cup.

I turned down the offer. Swapping spit with Sam had been one thing. Doing it by running your tongue over someone else's nubby plastic was something else.

Mike took my name and information, including my cell phone number. He was pretty much just going over the same information the 9-1-1 operator had gotten, so I suspected he was securing the scene until the detectives and crime scene team arrived.

Sure enough, within about twenty minutes, half the cops in Dallas had arrived, filling my parking lot with flashing cop light bars. Mike stayed busy keeping his fellow cops out of Sam's trailer while they all waited for the detectives to show up. Dallas cops were like piranhas. The scent of blood seemed to attract them from miles around.

Mike also kept his fellow cops away from the window I'd used to exit Sam's trailer that morning. I didn't think he believed my story about why I'd left that way, but he definitely spotted my footprints.

Finally, an aging Buick pulled up. An African American female and a graying Anglo male emerged. The woman looked about old enough to be a high school cheerleader with a figure that would have put most dancers to shame. The man had a beer belly and breath that should have gotten more benefit from the steady dose of mints he kept eating. His eyes were heavy, as if he was going to fall asleep any minute. If I believed the look, he wouldn't recognize a clue if it bit him. I suspected it was a big act. The cheerleader, I wasn't so sure about.

The rest of the cops did a little shuffle-step, as if not sure whether they would be praised for their diligence or told to get back to work. Obviously, these two were the heavy hitters.

"You Anderson?" the cheerleader demanded.

I nodded.

"What, exactly, was your relationship to the deceased?"

I'd been wrongly suspected of a murder before and I had a feeling I knew where this was going. It didn't really matter what I said, the cops had their rules and profiles. And rule number one was that the boyfriend, or girlfriend, was always the killer.

"I didn't do it," I explained.

She raised an eyebrow. "Did I ask that?"

"Please. I'm his girlfriend and I found the body. You'd be idiots not to wonder. So I'm making it easy for you.

"You don't seem that broken up about your boyfriend being murdered in your trailer park."

She had a point. I'd been crazy about Sam, making happily-ever-after plans that involved me finally developing a maternal instinct and having babies with him. So why wasn't I boo-hooing all over Dallas?

It was partly my conversation with Patrick, and my research on the web had already made me wonder whether I really had a relationship with Sam or whether I'd simply been someone convenient for him. An instant family to make his outings with Emily look normal. But mostly, I figured, I was in shock. Which wasn't good. It meant that I was just delaying my reaction.

"Shock," I suggested.

"I see." She made a note in a little notebook she kept around her neck on a chain. "What makes you think Mr. Katz's death is a murder rather than an accident?"

I took a deep breath and let it out. "Because his throat was cut a bunch of times and his trailer was ransacked. I've never heard of anyone killing himself that way and then searching their place. Come on, Detective. You're wasting your time with this."

"We'd both waste less time if you'd just answer my questions."

She kept jotting down notes and I was dying to read what she was writing. Probably things like obviously guilty attitude, or witness uncooperative and definitely suspicious. I didn't think she'd share her notes with me, so I got to work answering her questions without any smart feedback. It went against my grain, but getting hauled off to jail would be much worse.

She got personal quickly, demanding information about whether we engaged in kinky sex (none of your business, but it seemed like mostly wholesome man/woman stuff to me), whether there were any other women in Sam's life (just his daughter Emily, as far as I knew), and a detailed schedule of how I'd spent my day and who had seen me when.

Out of the corner of my eye, I could see the crime scene team at work. They'd taken pictures of Sam for a while, exclaiming about the amount of blood that had soaked into the bed (a lot) and the amount of barf on his chest (pretty much of that too).

Finally, they rolled his body out on a gurney, loaded it into an ambulance-type vehicle marked with the Dallas Police Department shield, and went back to work vacuuming up little bits of DNA, smearing black gunk everywhere to find fingerprints, and generally turning Sam's new Winnebago into even more of a dump than it had been after the killers had left it.

Thinking about how Sam's trailer didn't really fit into the park reminded me of my conversation with Patrick that morning.

"Sam claimed he had sole custody of his daughter," I volunteered, "but he was living here under a false name. Maybe you should find out who he really is and talk to his wife."

I'd thought that information would take some of the heat off of me, but my friend the cheerleader didn't seem to agree.

"When did you discover that Sam Katz was married, Ms. Anderson?"

"Married? I didn't say that."

"You suggested I talk to his wife."

"I meant an ex-wife, of course. I assume he was married when he had the kid. Pretty hard to get custody, otherwise."

"I see." The cheerleader consulted her notes. If they were based on what I'd told her, I knew they weren't going to be very helpful. "You mention that Sam Katz was living here under a false name." She paused. "When, exactly, did you learn that?"

I thought about lying. But I'd talked to Andy and Patrick that day, so I knew I'd get caught for sure. "Today," I admitted.

"Right." She snapped her notebook shut. "Would you mind coming down to the station to continue this conversation?"

Rule number one of police investigation. If they want you at the police station, you're in trouble.

"Am I under arrest?"

"Why would we arrest you? You're just doing your job as a citizen and mourning girlfriend, right?"

"Then I'd be happy to answer any questions right here," I answered.

That wasn't the answer she was looking for. "On the other hand, if we have to arrest you—"

"Then I'll call my lawyer," I interrupted. "I'm addicted to true crime shows, detective. I know what happens at the police station."

Her cheerleader smile looked about as phony as last year's Dallas Cowboy offence. "Oh, television."

I didn't bother telling her I'd had my share of personal experience with Dallas's finest. Doing so would only confirm what she already suspected. That Tina Anderson was a low-life whom nobody much would notice, and who probably had killed her boyfriend in some sort of jealous rage over his wife. Unfortunately, it wouldn't take her long to get my records.

"So, do you have more questions for here, or is it lawyer time?"

"Yes, Ms. Anderson. I have another question. Where is the child?"

That was only one of a long list of questions I didn't have the answer to. I hoped that when the police found out, they would lay off on me. I didn't even let myself think that anything could have happened to Emily. She'd been a bit of a brat at first, but she'd started to grow on me. At least she wasn't dead in the Winnebago with Sam. Other than that, I didn't have a clue.

I finally got to sleep at around three in the morning.

My shock was wearing off and I spent about an hour getting my blanket soggy with tears before I calmed down enough to sleep. Now that I knew Sam was a false identity, all of the plans I'd been making sounded a bit silly, but they'd been my plans, my dreams. I missed them and I missed Sam's arms around me in the night.

At least I got to bed in my own trailer. It could have been worse.

* * * *

The next morning, things got worse.

A murder in a trailer park isn't big news, but a missing child is. The place swarmed with reporters, television crews, and onlookers who could only have been looking for gore.

I ignored the frequent banging on my door and logged into my e-mail. Andy had come through.

His human resources guys had done their work quickly. Sam Katz, my ex-boyfriend, was really Sam Goodwin. And Sam Goodwin was the financial genius behind the multi-billion dollar collapse of a Big Cat Telecom, briefly one of the biggest high-tech companies in Richardson, Texas.

As Big Cat's Chief Financial Officer, Sam Goodwin had created a huge financial empire. Later, it had turned out that he'd created that empire using his company's money-stealing everything he could get his hands on. When the bottom fell out of his scam, he'd disappeared with a lot of the money, leaving customers and investors holding the bag.

The story was pretty much par for the telecom industry a few years earlier, but it was another great example of how bad I was at picking out boyfriends.

I'd been crazy about Sam and all the time, he was one of the biggest con-men of the century. He was wanted by several states and by the Securities and Exchange Commission.

Even so, I missed him. My judgment when it comes to men may be suspect, but Sam had mostly been nice to me. I couldn't even blame him for putting Emily first because that was one of the things I liked about him, what had first given me the idea of setting up a family together.

I wanted Sam back. Since I wasn't going to get that, I wanted whoever had killed him to pay. I was pretty sure I wasn't going to get either of those things. Especially not with the cops thinking I'd done it.

The odd thing was, Sam Goodwin really did have legal custody of his daughter. The concern that had pushed me into investigating Sam had been a false lead.

Still, I had launched that investigation. And I got a really nasty feeling that the timing of Andy's investigation and Sam's death had to be connected.

He'd lived in my complex for a couple of months with no trouble. Then, the very day I'd started an investigation, he ended up dead. I didn't think it was a coincidence. It might have been my searches on the Internet, but it seemed more likely to be Andy's human resources people digging into his background. But somehow, the investigation had tipped off someone who wanted Sam dead. So, maybe the cheerleader wasn't such a dim bulb after all. She'd recognized the connection when I was still reeling from shock.

I called Andy's cell and got a recording.

Some vague memory that it was Saturday led me to call him at home next.

Karen Anderson, Andy's mother, answered.

I should have hung up.

Once Karen realized it was me, she let me have it. "You need to let go, Tina," my ex-mother-in-law instructed me. "Move on with your life and let Andy move on with his."

"Yeah, I'd like that too," I agreed. "But right now, I've got police moving in on my life and I'm afraid they'll be moving in on Andy pretty quickly."

"Police?" Karen's nervous laugh didn't give her the confident tone she was looking for. "Andy is friends with the Police Commissioner. He won't have any problems with the police."

I ignored the insinuation that I would have plenty of problems and told her that claiming connections is a red flag for the cops.

That idea made about as much impression on Karen as a marshmallow hitting the deck of a battleship. For Karen, everything was about connections, about who knows whom, and about membership in the elite group of society whose pictures are in the Dallas Morning News and who make everything happen.

"It's really important that I talk to Andy," I concluded.

"Well, you'll just have to learn to live without it," Karen answered, slamming the phone down loud enough to hurt my ear.

I left a message on Andy's office voice mail and then checked back with my computer for information on Sam Goodwin.

There was a lot more on Goodwin than there was on Katz. He'd been a college track star, did a brief stint as an actor, and then rocketed his way to the top of the accounting group in Big Cat Telecom. For three years, Sam had pulled rabbits out of hats every quarter, seen Big Cat's stock price rocket from twelve dollars to two hundred dollars, and earned millions in stock options, bonuses, and, it later turned out, kickbacks from just about everyone who did business with Big Cat.

The only problem was, the numbers had been bogus. When one big customer pulled an order, the company had been forced to restate earnings, its stock price had collapsed, and Sam had disappeared.

Sam's wife had been a beautiful Russian woman he'd met in college. Surprisingly, she seemed almost invisible on the Internet.

When the phone rang, I was sure it would be Andy. Instead, it was a female voice that sounded vaguely familiar.

"Tina Anderson, please."

"Speaking."

"It's Detective Dikens."

My mind whirled. I couldn't remember any Detective Dikens on my fairly lengthy list of cops that lived in, hung out at, or otherwise visited the Shady Rest Trailer Park.

"Yes, Detective."

She must have caught my confusion. "We spoke for several hours last night."

The cheerleader. Just what I needed. "Of course I remember, Detective."

"I wonder if you could spend a few minutes with us talking about your husband."

"I don't have a husband."

"I mean Andy Anderson."

"Oh. But we're divorced."

From the brief sigh on the other end of the phone line, I knew I'd said the wrong thing.

"We've identified the body, Ms. Anderson. I think Mr. Anderson knows Sam Goodwin's real identity. After all, you gave him everything he needed to do the research, didn't you?"

"You're right. Andy knows that Sam Katz is really Sam Goodwin."

Dikens's brief hiss of breath was followed by a profound silence.

"Still there, Detective," I finally asked. I'd read enough to know that I should wait her out, make her talk first. Unfortunately, I've never been able to keep my mouth shut.

"You didn't mention anything about this last night, Ms. Anderson."

"I didn't get Andy's e-mail until this morning."

"I see." I could practically hear her brain cogs twisting.

"We'll come back to that," Dikens finally said. "Were you aware that Anderson Software was a large investor in several Big Cat Telecom partnerships?"

"I don't know anything about my ex-husband's business," I explained. "He bought me out when we got divorced."

"The way it looks to me is that your husband's company lost millions of dollars thanks to Sam Goodwin's shenanigans."

"He's not my husband." I felt like screaming out the words but I knew that would backfire. I should be thankful that Dikens was following other leads at all and hadn't simply dragged me in as the most obvious suspect.

"Sometime, after your lunch date with your husband," Dikens continued as if I'd never opened my mouth, "Mr. Anderson learned that your tenant Sam Katz was really Sam Goodwin. Naturally he decided to confront Mr. Goodwin. Unfortunately, their discussion escalated to violence."

I considered the possibility for all of one second. "I don't see, it, Detective. Andy is only dangerous inside the board room. He doesn't carry a knife, and he has enough money that losing a few millions to some con-man isn't going to break the bank."

"Yeah? How about if that con-man is sleeping with his wife? The woman who left him but whom he's never been able to put out of his mind. We have several witnesses who can swear that they have seen you, together with Andy, on multiple occasions since your divorce. Perhaps jealousy added a spark to his anger."

My laughter sounded about as convincing as the laugh track from a 1960s sitcom on Nick at Night. "I've dated a number of men since Andy and I divorced. He hasn't killed any yet."

"Can you tell me where your husband is now, Ms. Anderson?"

I reminded her I didn't have a husband and told her I had no idea where Andy might be.

She grunted a few words of what sounded like warning, a few more about needing to talk to me again, and hung up the phone.

I slumped down in the ergonomic chair I'd picked up on E-Bay for twenty-five dollars, and shook.

This was all coming too quickly. Sam wasn't really blue-collar Sam Katz, but a Harvard-educated upper class accountant who had left his footprints all over the backs of anyone standing in his way to the top. He'd been killed in my trailer park, within a hundred yards of my home. His daughter was missing. And now my friend and ex-husband appeared to be leading the suspect list while I took a close second.

A rooster crowed outside, adding the ultimate insult to the mess I was in.

I thought I'd gotten all of the boo-hoos out of the way the previous night but I'd been wrong. All of a sudden, my feelings burst through. I grabbed a box of tissues and blew my nose, then started swabbing at the tears that came pouring out.

* * * *

I don't know how long I would have stayed in that funk, sniffling in my chair like a dying soap opera queen, except that I'd killed off the ice cream the previous day and I'd thrown up everything I'd eaten and I was starving with nothing in the trailer to eat.

I still had my three dollars and an empty refrigerator, so I went to Jack in the Box had a couple of tacos and a drink. I even got change.

I felt vaguely human after I got some fat back in my system.

To keep my mind occupied, I wrote everything I knew about the case on the back of a napkin. Sam's secret identity. His daughter. The custody question. Andy's discovering who Sam really was.

Even writing big, I didn't fill more than a quarter of the napkin. As far as clues went, I was clueless.

So I crumpled up my napkin, threw it in the trash, and dug through my purse until I found my cell phone and the card for the court-appointed lawyer I'd once used.

John Halprin was a dweeby type who wore white socks with dress shoes and never left home without his clip-on tie. I don't think he got his law degree from one of those mail-in places, but I suspected he'd only gotten his position as a court-appointed attorney through his father's connections.

John seemed overjoyed to hear from me.

I hadn't thought about him in the year since we'd met, but apparently he'd thought about me a lot. He even described the outfit I'd worn, making me sound like some sort of fashion model rather than a girl who got her dress-up clothes from Wal-Mart.

"I may have a problem," I told him.

"I'm a lawyer. I've got solutions."

If I believed that, I was in serious trouble. "Did you hear anything about the murder in my trailer park?"

I thought the rustling sound was John shifting his newspaper around, but he could have been moving his lunch bag.

"Body found in trailer park. Child missing," he reported.

"Yeah. That's the one."

"You didn't do it, did you?"

With friends like Halprin, who needs the police? "Of course I didn't do it, John. He was my boyfriend. I liked him."

"Oh." I could practically hear the light bulb going on in Halprin's head. It wasn't particularly high wattage, but it seemed to be enough for him. "The police are suspicious of you because they always try to pin it on the boyfriend or girlfriend. Right?"

Apparently Halprin had learned something in the years since I'd seen him last. Back then, I would have sworn that the bulb had burned out.

"Yeah. Except it turns out that he's really Sam Goodwin, and there are a lot of people who would like him dead."

Halprin waited a moment, probably letting that familiar name catch its context. Finally he grunted. "The jerk who ripped off Big Cat Telecom? I'd like to take a swing at him myself."

"John!"

"A couple of years ago I got a call from my father. He told me to put everything in Big Cat Telecom. They were going to make us all rich. I ended up having to sell my condo and moving into an apartment."

At least he hadn't moved into Shady Rest.

"Well, someone beat you to it. But what I don't know is whether I'm off the hook. Little Miss Detective Cheerleader isn't giving anything away."

"Detective Dikens is assigned to your case?" He sounded a little breathless.

All right, Halprin was a lot more on the ball than I remembered. Maybe he'd traded in his clip-on tie and his white socks by now too.

Of course, maybe the sun flamed out and we just don't know yet.

"Dikens is a bulldog," Halprin told me. "She plays young and dumb when she thinks it'll do any good, and she'll wiggle her body and stir up your brain, but it's all a game for her. She's got a sharp mind and she'll rip you to shreds if she can."

"I'd about figured that out." I personally didn't find her body shakes all that distracting, but she hadn't used them on me. I suspect she could have gotten most males to confess to about anything. For sure her young innocent look was a carefully calculated lie.

"John, here's what I need you to do. We need to find out if I'm still a suspect. If I am, I'll see if I can get you as my court-appointed. If not, you're off the hook."

"Court appointed? How about you hire me? You know, like a client?"

"John, I live in a trailer park and try to support myself from what I make programming cellphone games. Where would I get the money to hire an attorney?"

"Well, I'm not doing this for nothing."

What had happened to that young and idealistic John Halprin I'd met years before? "I told you I don't have any money."

"How about a date. Let's say Monday. That way, I'll have a day the courts are open to check on your status."

I'd already decided to steer clear of the world of dating for a while. But I really needed Halprin's help and he wasn't a bad guy.

"I'll have dinner with you if you want, but it won't be a date. Just a couple of friends getting together."

"If you want to look at it that way."

Chapter 3

There weren't any new messages on my machine when I got back to the trailer so I went to see my best friend Angie Jefferson.

Angie went to high school with Andy and me but instead of discovering computers like we did, she discovered men. Sometime in that process, she'd discovered that lots of men would pay her big money to have a little fun. The funny thing is, she always had a great reputation. I was Tina the Tart and she was Angie the Angel. It was high school logic at its most typical. But that didn't mean I didn't love her.

Angie was the only hooker I'd ever met who loved her job. She'd been crazy about sex as a teenager and a lightbulb had gone off in her mind when she realized that men would actually pay her to have a good time. She didn't bring any business home so she was actually one of my more reliable tenants.

After being abandoned by both Sam and Andy, I needed a quick fix of Angie's patented attitude toward men to straighten me up.

"You do Sam?" she asked before I'd even had a chance to get in out of the heat.

I flopped on her couch and raised a quizzical eyebrow. "Of course I did. I mean, I was hearing wedding bells. I didn't even know his real name and I was wondering whether I should change my name to his."

She sighed. "I meant, did you kill him?"

Angie flipped back a blonde braid—she was wearing her hair long again, in a fat rope of a braid that trailed down her back all the way to her butt.

She ate like a horse and drank like a fish, but Angie could still wear the little size four skirts she'd worn in high school. What size she wore on top, I didn't want to guess and she was nice enough not to brag.

"Of course I didn't kill him," I told her. "I thought we had something serious going on. Even if I had wanted to lose him, I would have just told him to haul his fancy trailer out of my park."

She nodded slowly. "I can't believe you spent three months with him. I mean, the guy was a jerk."

"Well I liked him." Sam's body could keep me tongue-tied, and he'd occasionally been generous and even thoughtful. And he was dead now and I didn't really want to hear bad things about him.

"You were making dream-worlds," she said.

"He was nice and we had fun together."

Angie's look just might have been filled with pity. "I was just getting a glass of wine. I'll get you one, too."

Angie's trailer was perfect. Everything was neat and clean. If she had underwear drying anywhere, it was well hidden. Best of all, she always had food handy.

She poured me a glass of the classy foreign wine she drinks, and put out a bowl of peanut M&Ms, then plopped down in the couch next to me. "I want to know all the details."

I told her about Sam's secret identity, about Detective Dikens's theory that Andy had killed him in a fit of jealous rage, and about the missing Emily.

"Emily probably saw too much," Angie decided. "If they'd wanted her dead, they would have left her with Sam. Someone must be keeping her quiet. We find her, we'll find the real killers."

"What's this 'we'll?'"

She shook her head. "You don't really think Andy killed anybody, do you?"

"Of course not." The idea was ridiculous.

"Well, guess what, sister. The cops are going to realize that, too, before long. So, they'll go back to obvious suspect number two. The trashy girlfriend who probably figured that she'd inherit Sam's nice Winnebago."

Maybe. And maybe butting in would just call attention to me. I'd read somewhere that the cops are always suspicious of civilians who offer to help. Too many killers enjoy keeping track of the investigation.

"I already asked John Halprin to check and see if they were investigating me," I admitted.

"Halprin. God, he is such a nerd," Angie reminded me. "I offered him a free quickie one time and he turned so purple I thought he was going to have a heart attack."

"He isn't that bad." But I couldn't help giggling at the picture. Angie can have that effect on men. With her looks, she could have snagged some rich guy, moved to Highland Park, and driven around between shopping malls in a Mercedes SUV. Instead, she lived in Oak Cliff and distracted the local male population something fierce.

"Let's put it this way," Angie said. "If you have to depend on Halprin to keep you out of trouble, you're already in trouble. He couldn't investigate his way out of a Rocky and Bullwinkle cartoon."

She shook her head firmly. "The cops won't help and Halprin can't. Andy would help you if he could, but his lawyers are going to keep him quiet until the police drop him as a suspect. So we're on our own, girlfriend. But don't you worry. Angie Jefferson, alias Nancy Drew, is on the case."

I took a sip of Angie's wine, ate a handful of M&M's, and then drank some more wine. "Okay. What's the plan?"

Angie's plan, as it turned out, was to raid Sam's trailer and discover clues to locate Sam's mysterious ex-wife. "It's got to be her," Angie exclaimed definitively as she poured herself another glass of wine, then carefully refilled my glass so full that I had to bend down and slurp before I could pick it up without spilling. "It's always the ex-wife."

"I thought it was always the girlfriend," I protested.

"Yeah, but in this case we know you didn't do it," Angie reminded me.

* * * *

With every glass of wine, Angie's logic and her plan made more sense. By the time I'd finished my third glass, she was a genius.

For the second night in a row, I headed for Sam's trailer in the dark.

Angie had dug out a black catsuit for herself. She'd tried to get me to wear tights, but I'd gone back to my trailer for a pair of black jeans and a long-sleeved black t-shirt. For Angie, this was an adventure and dressing up was a key part of the fun. For me, this was serious. Sure Andy would hire smart lawyers and would probably get off, but any rumors of his involvement in murder could devastate the company he'd spent his life building. I didn't want that for Andy, and I certainly didn't want the police to turn their attention back my way.

Sam's trailer was tied down with police tape but Angie cut her way through it with a pocket knife, then pulled out a ring of keys and hunted through for the right one.

"How'd you get his key?" I knew I wasn't going to like the answer, but I couldn't help asking.

"It was before you started dating him," Angie explained.

Great. Sometimes I think Angie has a homing instinct on any guy I've ever been interested in. Except for Andy, my love life seemed to be Angie leftovers.

"Just be glad I do have a key," Angie tried to break me from my sulk. "It's not like we want to break anything."

I was still seething when I followed her into Sam's trailer. In three months of dating, Sam hadn't given me a key.

Angie flicked on her flashlight and scanned around his living room.

It was a mess. Papers were strewn over the floor and books had been yanked from the bookcase and cluttered everywhere.

"Looks like a fight," Angie whispered.

"I think the cops made this mess."

"So, why are we whispering?"

It was a valid question. It took me a good two seconds to get the answer. "We always whisper when we're being Nancy Drew."

I suspected that, in Angie's mind, she was Nancy and I was George. Oh, well.

"Look for secret compartments," she urged. "I'll look through the books."

A Winnebago is about as likely to have secret compartments as I was to grow a beard. Still, I peeked under the furniture, looked in the (mostly empty) canisters in Sam's kitchen, and stared into peanut butter jars and soup cans in the refrigerator.

"What's the deal with Sam and the chickens?" Angie demanded loudly.

I was so badly startled I almost banged my head on the door to the cupboard I was looking in.

"Huh?" It wasn't my most brilliant response. Then again, if I'd been brilliant, would I have been here in the first place?

"He's got all these books on chickens. Look at this. God, this is disgusting."

I glanced at the line drawing she was holding out. It depicted the harness for strapping razor blades onto a fighting cock.

"I guess this answers the question about why we had chickens all around here all of a sudden. Sam must have been raising birds for cockfights. I bet nobody wanted to hire him as an accountant after what he did for Big Cat." It was hard to reconcile the gentle man who loved his daughter with a guy who would raise birds for cockfighting, but I already knew that Sam was good at keeping secrets. Despite three months of dating, I really hadn't gotten to know the man.

"I bet Emily hated that," Angie said. Despite her manner, my friend has a soft spot for children.

"Maybe Emily found out and killed him," I suggested. "That's why she disappeared. She knows that the law is after her."

Angie rolled her eyes. "Are you finished?"

I looked at the ground. "I guess."

"Good. Because we don't have time for silliness and there's no way Emily killed anybody. So, why don't you tell me what you've found?"

I held up a half-empty peanut butter jar. "Want some?"

She stuck a finger in and licked it off. "Pretty good. I guess we should do the bedrooms next. You check out Emily's and I'll do Sam."

I'd only taken two steps when the door burst open. "Police. Freeze."

* * * *

"I want to see my lawyer."

I'd been making that point regularly during the three hours I'd been held at the police substation. Detective Dikens had stopped by, distracted the male cops in the area, and gotten disgusted with me when I'd refused to answer any questions.

I could have explained that we were just looking for something that would point to the real killers because they'd glommed onto the wrong suspects. Instead, I asked for Halprin.

John Halprin finally showed up at three in the morning.

The police shoved me into a room that had bloodstains on one wall and a twenty-watt bulb hanging from an electrical wire. Like everything in the substation, there were signs proclaiming this to be a smoke-free zone and clouds of cigarette smoke as thick as the stench off the river.

Halprin sat in a metal chair, his hands cigarette stained and a paper cup of water by his side. His briefcase hardly looked to be much more solid than the paper cup, and I suspected that the bulge I saw in it came from his lunch rather than from some thick stack of evidence he needed to get to the court.

"Hi, John."

"Couldn't wait to see me, huh, Tina?"

Here's the funny thing. Despite the low-rent briefcase and a pallor that would have done Dracula proud, Halprin looked pretty good. Either I'd dropped my standards a lot, or Halprin had made some changes in his life. Possibly both, I mused.

As early in the morning as it was, Halprin had found a pair of socks that weren't white, matched each other and even went with the heather gray of his suit. His tie looked tied rather than clipped, and his haircut no longer looked like something his mother had done with a bowl and a pair of garden shears.

"I like the new look. Make a lot of money lately?"

He looked at himself. "The court keeps sending me cases. I guess it's been all right." He paused a beat. "You look good yourself, Tina. That t-shirt is real pretty."

What the t-shirt was was small. So small it clung to my body and showed all of the curves, not that I'm overly built upstairs.

I'd had that shirt for a while so, now that I looked at it, I realized it was past retirement time. Not only was it small, half of the material seemed to have washed away. What was left behind was practically transparent, especially in the sticky heat of the police substation.

"Enough of the obligatory compliments," I cut in when it looked like he might go on about exactly what looked good about my t-shirt. "Angie and I broke into Sam's trailer to look for evidence about where Emily might be. The police found out and here we are."

"The police found out because one of your neighbors saw flashlights bobbing around. She didn't know about Sam being dead and thought he was being burglarized."

Wonderful. Our Nancy Drew act had come back and bitten Angie and me in the butt.

"How come you couldn't just turn on the lights like normal people?" John demanded.

I decided John deserved the truth no matter how stupid it sounded. "We'd had a few glasses of wine and we were being Nancy Drew."

He pushed his knuckles into his eyes and sighed. "Figures."

"Hey, you're my lawyer," I reminded him. "You aren't supposed to get all depressed. Besides, we had a key, and we didn't take anything. I don't see how they can charge us with anything and make it stick."

Halprin shook his head slowly. "They're going to assume that you went back to cover up any evidence you may have left behind when you killed Sam."

I stared at him. "But I was the one who called the police. If I'd left evidence, why wouldn't I have cleaned it up before I called the police, rather than risk sneaking back in later? And the cops spent hours searching Sam's trailer anyway. Am I supposed to be so stupid I'd hide the evidence after the search?"

Halprin gave me a grin. "I'm telling you what they're going to think, not that it shows any intelligence on their part. Guess they're no smarter than you were with your crazy stunt."

I wasn't sure I liked the new John Halprin. Before, he'd been a dweeb, but at least he'd been humble. Now, that he was turning into a stud-muffin, he'd gotten cocky. "Won any cases yet, Halprin?" I asked.

His face fell. "You know we plead out most cases. Especially where the D.A. doesn't have an iron-clad case."

That was all the answer I was going to get. So, no. The new Halprin hadn't won any more cases than the old one.

Putting John down hadn't helped me, though, and I felt like a rat for doing it. He was right, I had been stupid to search Sam's house in the middle of the night. The last thing I needed was to offend the man I was counting on to get me out of jail.

"That was a low blow and I'm sorry. But how are we going to get me out of here?"

John perked up. "I talked to the magistrate. Your bail is set at five thousand. I tried to get the judge to go on your recognizance, but he didn't seem to think that managing a trailer park gave you strong connections to the community."

"Let him live there and I'll show him some community," I said, getting angry at the misconceptions about the way the poorer half of the population lives. I'd done my suburban stint and the people in my trailer park were a much tighter community than my Plano neighborhood would ever be.

"You'll need to talk to Big Bob about making bail," John told me, ignoring my tirade.

Big Bob makes bail for most of the prostitutes and he and Angie are sort of friends. He wasn't so sure about me, though, although he'd once offered to cut me a special deal on bail in exchange for some close favors of the horizontal kind.

"Want to borrow my phone?" Halprin asked

I nodded. Calling from the pay phones in the substation can be hazardous to your privacy and your health.

If I needed another sign of exactly how far Halprin's law practice had come along, I got it. Big Bob's number was the first one programmed into his cell. Big Bob doesn't make bail for criminals who can pay their bills. He's small time. Same as Halprin. Same as me.

Big Bob remembered me. "Wear a little makeup and use a push-up and I think I could do something for you," he offered.

"How about I write you a check and you bail me out instead," I suggested. I could come up with the five hundred I needed if I was willing to make another month of minimum payments on the credit cards. Mr. MasterCard was pretty used to that by now.

"Hey. I'm trying to cut you a special deal here."

"Thanks, Big Bob. Just get me out of here. That will be plenty special."

"What can you put down for security?"

"How about my car."

He sighed. "Yellow Geo Storm. Blue book of thirteen hundred? Probably worth less."

That put me in my place. "Uh-huh."

"I'm just too soft hearted for my own good. Still, for a friend of Angie's, I guess I'll do it."

The really pathetic part was, I felt grateful. I hung up the phone and turned back to Halprin.

"All right, that takes care of me for now. What about Angie, though? Do we need to work her bail too?"

"Oh, she's out. Big Bob bailed her at the same time as he sprung a bunch of prostitutes. I'm surprised that they didn't put you in the same holding tank."

"They didn't put me in any tank. They've been shuttling me between interrogation rooms."

"That's because they can't believe you'd be stupid enough to break into Sam's trailer just to play detective," John told me. "So they're looking for an ulterior motive. Like maybe a connection to your husband."

"I don't have a husband."

He shrugged. "I'm just telling you what I hear."

"So they really think Andy did it?"

He nodded and lowered his voice. "It turns out that Andy lost millions when Big Cat went belly-up. He'd invested a lot of his own money as well as Anderson Software's money in the company based on the numbers that Sam Goodwin doctored. Bad enough that the man ripped him off, but when he found out that Sam was balling you too, he flipped out."

I slammed a fist down on the table. "That's the dumbest story I've ever heard."

Sam shook his head. "They'll drop the charges against you and Angie, Tina. But only if you cooperate. Let them know all the details and especially what Andy wanted you to look for. Do that and you're home free."

I couldn't believe this. "You think Andy did it, too?"

Halprin had the decency to blush. "They are the police," he mumbled. "They wouldn't be going after him without a good reason."

It didn't take a genius to figure out why Halprin didn't win many cases. With a defense lawyer like this, who needed prosecutors?

"Well they can forget it," I told him. "Andy didn't kill anybody. Even if he lost everything, there are a dozen companies who would love to bring him in as their CEO. He'll never go hungry. But even if he did, and even if he decided Sam needed killing, Andy wouldn't come to me to cover up after him. He'd make sure nobody suspected him at all."

"I can't cut any deals if you don't put your cards on the table, Tina," Halprin reminded me. "I don't want to sound cocky but I'm a lot better at deals than I am at trying cases."

I could believe that much. "If I find anything out, I'll let you know."

His smile exposed a fairly complex set of braces. Kissing him would be like kissing one of the guys I'd dated in high school.

So why was I thinking about kissing him? Gross.

* * * *

The shiny Chevy Suburban didn't fit into my neighborhood. It was too new a model, and it was the high-end version with the leather interior and keyless electronic access.

My first thought was that drug dealers had decided to use my complex as a base. They'd tried it before and they could probably set up an entire lab in the cargo space of that monster.

I moseyed on over.

Black windows reflected my face and didn't give me even a glimpse of what was inside the vehicle.

I knocked on the window. "Anyone in there?"

I didn't really expect an answer and almost had a heart attack when the door slid open.

I'd never seen the woman before, but something about her felt familiar.

She was about thirty, had a great figure, and looked like she worked out all the time. Her silk shorts set was probably all the rage in the rich suburbs, and her hair shown with artfully displayed blonde highlights.

"Are you Tina Anderson?" she asked.

Uh-oh. I took a couple of steps away. "Yeah."

"My brother told me a lot about you," the woman bubbled. "That's how I recognized you. I sort of pictured you as being a little more, you know, intellectual, though. But that's all right. I mean it isn't like I did much in college except drink beer and chase men. Well, one man, really. My husband." She giggled and flashed me a set of teeth even more expensive than Halprin's.

I must have looked as mystified as I felt, because the woman stopped for maybe a hundredth of a second and caught a quick breath.

"You don't even know who I am, do you? Well, I should be offended that my brother didn't tell you all about me, but that was the way he was. Sometimes he acted like he didn't have any family at all. Except Emily, of course."

Click. It had taken me a while, but I'd finally gotten it. This had to be the sister Emily went to visit the few times Sam had wanted undisturbed time with me.

Now that I knew what to look for, I could see that the familiarity I'd recognized at once was a family resemblance.

If I'd been thinking the previous night, I would have remembered her before we'd made that ill-fated raid on Sam's trailer. He'd probably dropped Emily off with his sister. No wonder she hadn't been around.

"I suspect Sam was afraid he'd let his real background slip if he talked too much about himself," I told her. "He never even told me your name."

"Oh. Isn't that silly. Sam was always playing these spy games, but he was never much good at them. I'm Katherine Goodwin Tate."

"Nice to meet you." My mother raised me to have some manners.

"Why don't you come into my house?" I offered. I'll get you a cup of coffee."

Katherine glanced at my trailer and gave her nose an almost invisible squirm, like she was too polite to say what she really thought of trailer parks and the people who lived in them. It was ironic, really, since her SUV was as big as some of the trailers in my lot.

"Is there a Starbucks near here?" Her voice was rich with a cheer as fake as one of the Rolexes you can buy on any Dallas street corner. "I'd be happy to buy you a latte."

I shook my head. "Sorry. The neighborhood doesn't exactly meet Starbucks' demographic profile. But don't worry, I promise I won't poison you. Come on in. I've got some questions for you."

She looked like she was thinking about running, but she managed to control herself and followed me into my home.

Katherine ooed over my trailer and how everything was so cute the way it all squeezed into such a tiny little place. She wrinkled her nose again when she saw the computer and told me that she didn't really see the point in those machines.

I tuned into just enough of her chatter to allow me to nod at the right point while I made coffee and tried to figure out where to start.

A rooster crowing outside made up my mind. "Did your brother ever talk to you about chickens?"

I must have cut her off in the middle of some conversational flow because she looked disappointed in me. "I beg your pardon."

"Tell me about the chickens."

Katherine plucked one of the coffee mugs out of my hand and took a dainty sip. She screwed her face up and set the mug down on my table. "My brother had a number of hobbies."

I tasted my own cup of coffee to see what Katherine had objected to. It seemed fine to me. Apparently it didn't live up to suburban standards.

"And one of them involved chickens?" I prodded when it looked like Katherine had finished.

"Maybe," she admitted. "Sam was a kind and generous man. He was always looking out for the less fortunate, whether they were humans, or other animals."

Which was why he'd ripped off millions of dollars, lied to me about who he really was, and then gotten into cockfighting, I supposed. The more I learned about the real Sam, the more I felt like a complete dupe for falling for him.

"The way he doted on Emily was something to see," Katherine went on as if this was the most natural direction for the conversation to take. "I almost had to beg him to let her spend some time with me. He wanted to keep her with him all the time. I swear, he thought the world revolved around her."

I understood that perfectly. Sam's focus, his willingness to drop everything and really pay attention to you had been one of the things that had made Sam so attractive. And his obvious strong feelings for his daughter simply added to the appeal. Although I was ready to deny the slightest tinge of maternal instinct, a big strong guy taking care of his little kid made me a bit gooey inside.

It was sexy, but more than simply physical. Like this was the kind of guy you'd want by your side no matter what was happening.

"He was super-protective," I agreed.

"That's why I was surprised when he called and left a message that he needed me to take care of Emily."

I just stared at her. The police had been looking everywhere for the poor kid and she'd been with her aunt the whole time? That didn't make sense. Surely they, or the dozens of reporters chasing after a missing child story, would have found her.

"You have her?"

Katherine froze. "I couldn't watch her. He said he was going to leave her with someone else. I just assumed it would be you."

Chapter 4

I got a letter from Katherine authorizing me to search her brother's car and trailer. She was next of kin so it figured to be legal or at least semi-legal. Since I intended to do the searching anyway, A little protection couldn't hurt.

She balked at first when I told her to go talk to the police. I had to physically get in her car and make her drive down to the substation, then made her park and walked her in. She actually offered to pay me twenty dollars to go with her. I could have used the twenty bucks but they would go a lot easier on her if she went in without me. She needed to tell them about Sam's phone call and what she knew about Emily.

After that, I headed back home and faxed a copy of Katherine's letter to John Halprin. It was Nancy Drew time again.

I pulled a coat hanger from my closet and headed for Sam's car. The cops had searched Sam's car, of course, but they hadn't been especially thorough. After all, he'd been killed in his trailer so there was no reason to think his car was involved. But then, they suspected me or Andy. If it wasn't us, there had to be something in Sam's past that could explain his murder-and Emily's disappearance.

The car alarm almost deafened me when I stuck the unbent coat hanger inside, but no one looked. In our neighborhood, loud trucks and heavy trains set off car alarms about twenty times a day.

Once I'd gotten in, I popped Sam's hood, disconnected his battery cables, and listened to the alarm wheeze to nothing.

"Learn anything?"

I almost jumped out of my skin. I whirled around and tried to hide the bent coat hanger behind my back before I realized I recognized the voice.

"What are you doing up?" I asked my best friend. It was barely one in the afternoon. Angie normally sleeps until at least three.

"I got out of jail too late to go to work," Angie explained. "So I went to bed. Your fancy new alarm clock woke me up."

"I thought I'd check out Sam's car since it doesn't have any police tape on it. Uh, his sister gave me permission."

Angie grinned. "Cool. Find anything?"

"You got here just in time. Why don't you look in the back and I'll look under the front seats?"

She went back to her trailer and brought out a couple of grocery bags and we went to work yanking scraps of paper, old maps, McDonalds sacks, and a few condom wrappers from under the seats, in the glove compartment, and from the compartments on the back of the front seats. The condom wrappers pissed me off. I'd never done it in Sam's car and they didn't look very old. The more I found out about Sam, the more it seemed that our relationship hadn't been what I'd imagined it to be. Sooner or later, the cops would figure that out too, and when they did, they'd realize it gave me another motive for murder.

"I feel like I'm working the cheerleader car wash again," Angie complained as she pulled a dirty sock from under Sam's seat.

"Big difference. Here you get to keep your shirt on," I reminded her. She'd been the star of the cheerleader car wash in high school, but not because of how well she scrubbed hubcaps.

"I don't see how an old Burger King crown is going to help us, though," she answered, tossing out the offending item.

I didn't either, but I wasn't giving up hope. Somewhere there had to be a clue.

I reached again under the front seat and felt something tickle my finger.

I reached deeper but whatever it was fluttered away.

"Looking for this?" Angie held up a long, reddish feather.

"A chicken feather," I guessed.

Angie nodded. "Looks like it to me. Add this to the books we found last night and it's starting to look more and more certain that Sam was involved with cockfighting."

My mind finally made the connection. Cockfighting means gambling. "It's gotta mean organized crime."

Angie wrinkled her nose. "You think there's enough money there?"

Where there's gambling, there's money. Money plus illegal spells organized crime.

Since Sam cheated at work, he could well have been a cheater in chickens too. And cheating the mob is high-risk behavior.

Which meant we had an alternative motive for his murder. A motive that had nothing to do with Andy—or me. Now, if we could get the police to look that way, we'd be off the hook.

"Let's look in the trunk," Angie suggested after pulling out the back seat and finding nothing but a few pennies and an old lollipop.

I considered the lollipop but I wasn't that hungry.

It took me a while to find the trunk latch, but finally I popped it open and we went on back.

Unlike the rest of his car, his car, Sam's trunk was almost as clean as his trailer had been. Always before, I'd written his cleanliness compulsion up to habit. Now, though, I wondered if it might not be something more practical. Like covering up evidence. That feather might have just blown in from somewhere he was visiting. If he really was involved in the business, I guessed he would transport the cocks in his trunk.

So, of course he'd vacuum it out and keep it clean.

Angie didn't let the lack of a mess deter her. She went to work yanking back the carpets.

The only thing I saw under the carpet was the spare tire. I wanted to give up then, but Angie was in unstoppable mode, unscrewing the big wing-bolt that holds the tire in place.

A torn sheet of paper was wedged under the tire. When Angie heaved the spare out of place, the wind caught the paper and it swirled around the trunk, then smacked me in the face.

I managed to catch it before it got away.

Caught it, read it, and felt my face grow pale. I thrust it out at her. "Ohmigod, look at this."

Angie dropped the tire on the ground. "What?"

"Read it. It says 'Cockfighting is cruel and evil. STOP now. Or we'll stop you!'"

"What?" She snatched it from my hands.

"It's signed the 'Chicken Rescue League.' I've never heard of them."

Angie started laughing, then couldn't stop. "Chicken Rescue League? Sam got a threatening note from the Chicken Rescue League?"

Angie read it slowly, still giggling, then handed it back. "You wouldn't think a bunch of chicken activists could be dangerous. Wouldn't they be too uh, chicken?"

"No chicken jokes right now, Angie. This is serious." I had to agree that the idea of a bunch of chicken-protecting zealots sounded strange, but cockfighting is disgusting enough that I was more than a little sympathetic to their goals. Killing people to save chickens was extreme, but it wasn't impossible.

"I think this should get Andy and me out of trouble," I told her. "Obviously these Chicken Rescue people found out about Sam and gave him a warning. When he didn't listen, they let him have it. End of story."

Angie had stopped giggling, but she shook her head. "The police aren't going to believe in a Chicken Rescue League and they certainly aren't going to believe that chicken rescuers are hiring hitmen."

"I don't think chicken rescue motive is that far-fetched. Andy's mother is involved in greyhound rescue, cat rescue, and Rottweiler rescue. Some of those people are extreme."

"Everyone likes dogs," Angie reminded me. "But people eat chickens. I mean, have you ever heard of a a hamburger rescue league or a bacon rescue league?"

It might sound ridiculous but I wasn't going to give up on it. "The note says they'd stop Sam and Sam is definitely stopped. It's the best clue we've gotten so far."

* * * *

The police got almost as good a laugh out of the Chicken Rescue League as Angie had.

I got put through to Detective Dikens immediately when I called, but when she learned that I wasn't going to confess or anything, she seemed less interested. Like maybe my phone call had interfered with an important hair appointment or something.

After instructing me not to interfere with an ongoing police investigation and informing me that I was being investigated for Emily's apparent kidnapping as well as Sam's murder, Detective Dikens basically told me to get lost. She did send a uniformed cop out to pick up the flyer, but only after I whined and pleaded. I suspect that Angie was right and the detective had decided I'd printed the thing up myself.

Even Andy was unimpressed with our discovery. He didn't laugh, but he told me that his lawyer wouldn't be able to do anything with the flyer. The fact that I'd discovered it would discredit it as evidence, and the fact that the Chicken Rescue League sounded like a children's movie made it difficult to imagine a positive jury reaction. Since his mother was involved with a number of 'rescue' organizations, the jury might even think it gave Andy another motive to kill, if they gave it any credibility at all.

Andy was a little more interested in the organized crime angle. Interested enough to tell me to stay away from there so I wouldn't get hurt.

Which meant that I was on my own.

I spent an hour researching the Chicken Rescue League on the Internet. Sure enough, there are activists in the movement to stop cockfighting around the world. The CRL website discussed how cruel cockfights can be. According to their site, there was a lot of cockfighting in Texas, a lot of money involved, and it was all illegal.

What I found really interesting were links to a couple of small news reports about CRL activists who had disrupted actual cockfights, liberated fighting chickens, and in one case, hijacked a gaming desk, clearing out the betting proceeds before payouts could be made.

Apparently no police reports had been filed—the holdup had taken place in Texas where cockfighting is illegal anyway—but the implications were clear. The Chicken Rescue League wasn't just do-gooders wringing their hands and signing petitions. They had a hard-core group who didn't mind breaking the law to pursue their objectives. They might have threatened Sam-might even have killed him. But why would they take Emily and what would they do to her?

Although the Dallas CRL chapter website didn't have any information on 'direct action,' it did list their schedule, including a meeting that evening. I took that as a sign we were meant to be there.

I had to suck up to Angie pretty hard to get her to agree to accompany me. She'd already been an entire day without sex and had been looking forward to getting back to the street and to multiple paid gratifications. Only a combination of my whining and the reminder that the Chicken League might include rich men fully capable of paying for a quickie during the coffee breaks persuaded her to accompany me.

We brainstormed the proper attire for a Chicken Rescue meeting, Angie wanting to wear her feather boa in solidarity with the feathered species. I thought we should dress like Andy's mother, all proper and with pantyhose.

We compromised on jeans and tops—Angie's top being something transparent and advertising her merchandise, mine being a T-shirt I'd gotten for attending a free Network World seminar a few years earlier.

The meeting was out in Rowlett which, when I'd been growing up, had been the type of community where semi-rural trailer-park trash would live and raise their families. I'd even spent a summer there picking cotton—the summer I'd decided to become a computer programmer so I could work in air conditioning and never have to suffer like that again.

I'd avoided Rowlett ever since that summer and I was surprised to see how it had changed. Dallas had spread and Rowlett was now part of the metroplex. Where trailer parks and graying plank houses with sofas on front porches had once stood on gravel roads, brick McMansions now lined the concrete-paved streets.

The Chicken Rescue League meeting was held in a Unitarian Church and Angie almost drooled when she saw the lines of Hummers, Mercedes, and Jaguars mixed with Volkswagons and aging Nissans in the church parking lot.

"I'm two hundred dollar a pop, tonight," she told me.

"Be careful," I reminded her. "Just because they're protective of chickens doesn't mean they'll be protective of anyone else. If they killed Sam, they won't mind killing again to cover it up."

"How about I don't tell you how to program your computers and you don't tell me how to whore?" Angie answered.

Put in my place and with my feelings pretty banged up, I opened the

Storm's door and headed for the church.

Angie's high-heels clattered across the parking lot's smooth concrete as she caught up with me. "I was just kidding," she told me. "Of course I'll be careful. And you do the same."

I had overreacted, of course. Of all the people I knew, Angie was among the most obsessed with safety. In her profession, she had to be. Too many men think that hookers are easy prey. Angie had survived ten years on the streets. I suspected she could survive a night at the Chicken Rescue League. I wasn't so sure about myself.

"Thanks. Now, let's feel some concern for those poor chickens. Here we go." I opened the door and stepped into the church.

* * * *

A hundred heads turned and looked at us as we stepped in.

The speaker, a woman who looked like she'd never missed a meal and wasn't about to start today, frowned at us.

Naturally everyone was dressed in suits and fancy cocktail dresses. Pearls and diamonds glowed and sparkled. The smell of money hung heavy on the air.

"Oh, shit," Angie breathed. "You were right about the pantyhose."

My brain froze. If I'd been a normal person, I would have slunk out, or maybe slipped into one of the folding chairs laid out in neat rows. But I'm the kind of person whose mouth works when her brain is frozen.

"Free the chickens!" I didn't shout, exactly, but in the silent church meeting room, my words definitely echoed.

They're going to kill us, the rational part of my brain informed me as it began to thaw. There's no way that they'll hear that as anything other than a joke.

As the echoes of my words died, the silence grew like a palpable thing, menacing and terribly real.

"It sounds simple, doesn't it," the speaker said, breaking through the silence like a sledgehammer breaking through rotten drywall. "Free the chickens." She shook her head, in evident dismissal of my offering.

"Yet," she continued, "what other option do we have? Can we simply stand by, holding protest signs while criminals commit murder and the police look on and wink? No! The young lady is quite right. We must take action."

I thought the murmur from the audience sounded unconvinced. The elegant woman must have felt that too. She grabbed the microphone like a life buoy and cranked up the volume. "We've passed petitions, written letters to the editors of all the local newspapers, called our state legislators, and met with the governor. And what does that get us?"

The small crowd backed off and the muttering sounded more sympathetic.

"Right. Absolutely nothing." She slammed her jewel-incrusted hands on the speaker podium sending waves of feedback through the sound system.

When the shriek died down, she leaned into the microphone and whispered, "Direct action. Direct action drives results."

I found an empty folding chair, sat my butt down, and watched.

I wouldn't have guessed that a middle-aged Anglo woman who looked like she should be selling Tupperware could be so compelling. As she recited the case against illegal cockfighting, my heart started pounding. When she clicked on her PowerPoint presentation and started showing pictures of slaughtered birds—killed by other birds or by their owners— she sucked me in. I wanted to do something to stop the cruelty. I was ready to take direct action. To rid the world of the evil men who could so cruelly abuse innocent avians.

"Free the chickens." She snapped the projector off and ratcheted up the volume of her talk. I figured she was leading to her strong conclusion, her call to action.

"Free the chickens!" she repeated. "Does it sound humorous to you? There is nothing humorous about the cruel slaughter of innocent animals. Does it sound extreme? There is nothing extreme about preventing illegal, immoral, and dangerous activities. Does it sound unlawful? If it is, then the laws protect the criminals.

"Like Carrie Nation, who took an ax to whiskey wherever she found it, we've got to continue to take the fight to the enemy. As long as we stay police, with our petitions and our letters to the editor, we'll be ignored.

"And why shouldn't they ignore us? Those who care so little about their cause that they can do no more than whine will always be treated like the curs they are. Until we take direct action, the police will treat cockfighting like they treat Superbowl betting—by participating themselves." She slammed another fist into the podium. "Yes, indeed. Free the chickens."

I rocked to my feet, applauding like crazy, as did almost the entire room. A room, I noticed, strangely devoid of Angie and a couple of the cutest males.

* * * *

Second only to the speaker herself, I found myself an unwilling center of attention.

With the speaker's thunderous approval behind it, the idea of direct action was suddenly powerful and I was the woman who had brought it up. Sort of.

Oddly, most of the CRL members who approached me were looking for my advice, my guidance on the way that they could act. As if I was the expert, rather than they.

Nobody seemed anxious to whisper that they'd recently murdered a cockfighter.

I tried to direct the conversation, reminding anyone who asked my advice that cockfighting is controlled by men—often men with mob connections. That it will only be stopped if the men were stopped. The reaction was universally a blank stare followed by some sort of economics lesson. If only we could increase their costs of doing business, several erstwhile chicken rescuers assured me, cockfighting businessmen would seek alternate income opportunities.

Either I didn't get it, I was in the wrong place, or the cold-blooded killer segment of the CRL maintained a low profile.

I was willing to bet on the latter.

I sidled up to the speaker.

"I don't know you." She cut off the conversation she'd been having and turned to face me.

"Uh, this is my first meeting."

She narrowed her eyes. "Do you always try to make this kind of stir when you go to meetings?"

I shook my head firmly. "Not really." I meant it, too. It is pure bad luck that meetings seem to deteriorate around me.

"So this was something special, just for us?"

"Cockfighting has been bothering me lately," I admitted, going with as much of the truth as I could. "I've got chickens running around my, uh, complex and I don't think they're being kept for eggs. Too many roosters."

"I see." Her suspicions faded a little, but not much. "So you decided to join us?"

"I wanted to see if you could do anything to help me. If someone is using my complex to raise gamecocks, I want to put a stop to it. But, frankly, I'm afraid to do anything on my own and the police laughed me off and told me to call animal control."

The woman nodded, encouraging me to continue.

I spoke fast, blurting out my thoughts before I chickened out myself. "We all know about the mob involvement in cock-fighting. The last thing I need is for some Mafioso to decide that I'd stepped over a line. You people are the experts so I figured I'd go to the source."

I was walking a tightrope here. If she was directly involved with Sam's death, she'd be suspicious of my story, even though I hadn't said anything about trailers. Somehow, though, I couldn't see this middle-aged, silk-and-linen-clad woman actually sticking a knife in Sam—or ordering someone else to do it. She was a rabble-rouser for sure, but I didn't think she was a murderer. In fact, I was betting my life on it.

She stared into my eyes, as if seeking to read my mind.

Her charismatic glare reminded me of my sixth grade homeroom teacher and made me want to blurt out all of my secrets.

I bit my tongue and managed to stay silent. For me, quiet was always a challenge.

"I see," she finally said. "Perhaps you could meet with me briefly after the meeting."

I nodded. Was I being invited into the action group of the League? Possibly I was. It didn't take a genius to notice that Angie and I were among the youngest of the people here—us and the men that Angie had dragged outside. When older people decide to make trouble, they generally get someone younger to do the job—and take the heat.

* * * *

Angie, accompanied by a couple of the CRL men, reappeared just in time and we all trooped to the kitchen at the back of the Unitarian meeting hall. There, our speaker, another woman who looked vaguely familiar, and three men were huddled over a large calendar.

The speaker was lecturing one of the men who'd snuck back a little earlier—I suspect he was Angie's first conquest—about how to break into the chicken crates without getting hurt by an angry bird. Which figured. The CRL wouldn't be in the murder business long if they let a couple of suspicious characters like Angie and me into all of their secrets the first time we wandered in off the streets. Getting into the action group so quickly was a fabulous start.

"You're going to steal their birds before the fights?" I asked.

The man nodded, giving me a tired smile that told me that Angie had completely drained him of any romantic interest. Which was all right with me. I didn't need another chicken-obsessed Angie leftover. "No birds, no fight, no gambling, no profit. Plus, at least a few of the roosters are set free."

"And nobody calls the police," the familiar looking woman told me, "because they'd just be admitting that they were engaging in illegal cockfighting anyway."

Her East Coast, ever-so-upper crust accent gave her away. Mrs. Heath was a friend of my ex-mother-in-law. I'd met her at one of Karen's greyhound-rescue activities. Apparently she wants to rescue everybody. Except maybe her fellow humans.

"What do you do with them after you, uh, liberate them?" I asked.

Angie smacked her lips. "I don't know about the rest of you but I just lo-oo-ve fried chicken. My mother had this recipe that used corn flakes and ..." she trailed off when she saw the stare of horror that greeted her words.

"You eat meat?" the speaker demanded.

I should have seen this coming. They didn't just rescue chickens so they could eat them.

"She's making a joke," I put in, shooting a glare in Angie's direction. "Of course we wouldn't eat the chicken. Just because they're birds doesn't mean that they're not people."

Angie may be loose but she isn't dumb. She nodded quickly. "Misplaced humor. My mistake."

"Well, I think it's disgusting," Mrs. Heath told me. "I find that kind of humor..." she trailed off looking for just the right word.

I couldn't help myself. "Tasteless?"

"That's it. Completely tasteless." Mrs. Heath nodded. It took a full second before her face started changing expressions in recognition that she'd fallen for another bad joke.

"Enough of this," our speaker decided. "Since the young lady—"

"Tina Anderson," I put in. I'd thought about using a false identity, but I knew that Mrs. Heath would recognize me sooner or later and I didn't want anyone to think I'd tried to pull a fast one on them—especially since I had.

"Since Ms. Anderson is so interested in our work, and since we're currently shorthanded, I thought we'd invite her into the action circle."

"Does she come too?" the man asked, gesturing toward Angie.

"I'll leave that to you, James. Let me know if you have any problems. After the trouble last time, I'm afraid that we'll be running into more security than we have in the past. Heath and I have to run some more flyers."

The speaker and Mrs. Heath headed out the back door, leaving James, Tina, and myself, along with one other man—another of Tina's conquests.

I'd perked up my ears when the speaker had mentioned flyers, but there didn't seem to be any paperwork around. Still, this seemed to indicate that we were on the right track. The action committee was responsible for the flyers—and Sam had been threatened by one. The trouble last time might mean that Sam's murder resulted from his resistance rather than a plan. I was certain I was with Sam's killers now. All I needed was to get the proof. And of course, the little matter of staying alive while I found it.

"I always get tense before an operation," James said, speaking to Angie more than to either of the rest of us. "I was wondering—"

"No free samples," Angie answered. "You know the price of relaxation. Two hundred. No exceptions."

"But—"

"No credit card, no checks, and definitely no IOU's."

"Oh. I guess I can stop by an ATM."

"Are we going to talk about chickens?" I demanded, "Or is this just a boy's night out?"

James frowned at me. "It's too early for a raid. Things won't really settle down until two in the morning. In the meantime, uh, there's an ATM machine at the 7-11 down the block."

* * * *

At precisely two the next morning, Angie was some six hundred dollars richer and I had a sore butt from waiting on the folding chairs while Angie used the couch in the minister's office to entertain her new friends.

James checked his wallet then reluctantly signaled that it was time for our chicken run.

The raid was in Greenville. That town lay just outside the swelling urban ring that surrounds and strangles Dallas. So far, at least, Greenville had maintained its southern lifestyle and small-town ambience. Lots of good-ol'-boys loved cockfighting and they were close enough to Dallas to attract additional crowds.

Nobody said much on the hour-long drive in James's extended bed four-door diesel pickup. James had tried to strike up a conversation with Angie, but she had fallen asleep as soon as James started driving, leaning her head against his shoulder.

Bob, the other guy, sat in the back seat with me. From the way his attention was focused, he wished Angie had chosen his shoulder. Clearly he didn't see me as an adequate substitute. Thank goodness.

We pulled into a dirt alley and James cut off his headlights, drifting slowly toward a building that looked like it hadn't been painted in fifty years.

The structure, a plank warehouse that listed at ten degrees to the south, had lost the steps leading to its loading dock, but the padlock was big and new. The hasp it hung from looked like a huge bar of steel.

"Our informant was dead-on," James whispered.

I shuddered at his word choice. Had he said the same when he'd found Sam in my trailer park?

"Bob, you and Angie take the lookouts," James continued. "Tina and I will handle the chickens."

Bob nodded, clearly pleased that he wouldn't have to dirty his hands with work. Angie rubbed her eyes and headed down the alley.

I hoped she'd stay out of sight. In her sexy outfit, at this time of the morning, the local police would be happy to pick her up on solicitation charges. Since she wasn't a native, they'd come down especially hard.

Once Angie and Bob were in place, James reached into the back of his pickup and grabbed a huge bolt cutter.

He fumbled, clunked it against the lock, and dropped it on the ground. "Oops."

"Haven't you ever done this before?" I asked.

"I meant to practice."

Great. I was out with criminals who'd never criminaled before. Not only was I going to get caught, it didn't figure that James would know anything about Sam's murder. Still, unless I wanted to give up, I had to go through with this, work my way up in the organization.

I grabbed the tool from his hands and lined it up myself, then put a hundred and twenty pounds of solid girl behind the bolt cutter and snipped through the lock.

The snap sounded like a gunshot and I won't deny that I jumped two feet. James peeled off the busted lock and put it on the ground. He was wearing surgical gloves—unlike me who hadn't even considered fingerprints. So I let him open the door while I put the bolt cutters back in his truck.

The chickens raised a fuss as James carried out the first crate. The wooden box was painted black, with gold paint declaring Hector to be champion of all he saw.

I felt a tinge of guilt. Somebody had put a lot of effort into that crate, maybe even love. But I suppressed that feeling quickly. Hector was there to be doped to the gills and killed. Whoever had raised him for this didn't deserve any sympathy.

"How about a hand here," James said, reminding me I was here to take care of business.

I took Hector from him.

The bird looked at me through the metallic mesh, his head cocked to one side. He cooed softly.

"He's kind of cute," I allowed.

Hector was a deep golden red, like the golden retriever I'd always wanted when I'd been a kid, and his feathers looked soft. He pushed his face against the bars that held him captive. I was sure he was telling me something.

It was late and I was tired enough that my mind wasn't working straight. That was my excuse anyway. I'm positive it wasn't any sort of maternal instinct, no matter how much dating a man with a child had twisted me inside.

For whatever reason, I had to pet him.

I only opened the door a little, just enough to stick in my hand.

Roosters are stronger than you'd think.

The bird's scream sounded like something from a cheap science fiction flick.

My own scream when Hector gouged his claws into my arm, climbed my chest, and grasped my hair in his beak, sounded like something from a horror movie.

Fortunately for me, Hector was more interested in getting away than he was in damaging me. He halfway flew down the street, heading toward Bob rather than toward Angie.

"Keep it down," James instructed me as he came out from the warehouse with another crate. "What happened?"

"Hector got away."

"How . . ." he caught himself. "Never mind. Now we've got to hurry."

I would probably have aborted the job right then, so I had to give James credit for guts-or lack of sense.

We ran through the warehouse, loaded the back of the pickup with a couple of dozen crates filled with pissed-off birds, piled into the cab, and tore out of Greenville.

"I've mostly just done the lifting until now," James told me when we hit the city limits. "We had another guy who did the real dirty work."

I looked up from where I was still trying to stop my bleeding. "Yeah? What happened to him?"

James lowered his voice. "I told Mona that she should warn you but she said not. Some of those bastard chicken mobsters must have found out about Sam. His body turned up in a low-rent trailer park the other day."

I froze. "Sam?"

"Sam Katz. He led the action group."

I was glad I wasn't driving. I would have taken out a telephone pole.

My late boyfriend wasn't a mobster, he was a Chicken Rescue leader. He'd probably had the flyer in his car because he'd been distributing them, not because he'd been the target of one. We had chickens in my trailer park because he was setting them free, not because he was raising them.

This changed everything.

Now I had no clue who had killed Sam.

Chapter 5

"I'm going out for fried chicken," Angie told me. "And you're coming."

I didn't look up from my computer, I just tucked the phone into my shoulder and continued clicking through the thousands of hits on Google Search, looking for anything definite that would tie together organized crime and Texas cockfighting.

So far, I'd come up empty.

"Well?" my best friend demanded.

I sighed. "I'm busy, I have seventy-five cents cash and I'm almost out of gas."

Angie's hesitation was long enough to make me uncomfortable. "I'll treat."

Angie was notoriously tight with money. She'd cleared hundreds of dollars the previous evening but she hated to let it go. Angie had lived through too many rainy days not to want to sock away everything she could for the next one.

"You sure?" I asked, looking up for the first time.

She rolled her eyes. "Oh, hell yes. I'll even buy you dessert."

Google could wait. "I'm on my way."

"You're driving," she told me.

"Great. I'll spend my seventy-five cents on gas."

We went to Church's.

Chicken-fried chicken is something of a Texas specialty even though my Yankee friends tell me that the term is redundant and doesn't make much sense anyway. It's a hunk of chicken slathered with a solid fried breading that keeps all the juices in and creates a heart attack in a minute.

Both of us ordered the deluxe along with iced tea for me and Diet Coke for Angie.

I stuck my plastic fork in the chicken and all of a sudden tears were running down my cheeks.

"What?" Angie wasn't big on displays of emotion.

"I don't know," I gasped.

She looked at the white meat of the chicken in front of me. "Don't tell me you feel bad about this bird."

I felt bad about everything. Between getting dragged to the police station and running around on late-night chicken rescues, I hadn't given myself time to think about Sam or Emily. Sam might not have been perfect, and he'd lied to me about who he was and about the chickens, but he'd still been my boyfriend and we'd had some great times together.

Losing him had created a hole inside of me that I'd filled with running around doing things. But that hole had sucked in everything I'd given it and was demanding more.

I truly didn't believe that a woman needs a man to fulfill her, but I wasn't a kid any more and I'd always dreamed of sharing my life and maybe, some day, of having kids of my own. Sam and Emily had been instant family for me. Despite the fact that Emily had been jealous of me for her father's time, losing them had torn up my dream.

"Suck it up," Angie growled.

I dripped tears in my mashed potatoes. "Sorry."

She handed me an extra napkin and looked the other way when I blew my nose. Angie was right. I couldn't afford to fall apart now. If I didn't get to the bottom of whoever killed Sam, the police were going to hang my butt up to dry. Prison wasn't a healthy place for computer programmers.

"I'm okay now," I lied after I'd blown my nose a second time.

"If you say so. Now let's talk about the case. If Sam was in the Chicken Rescue League, then who do you think killed him?"

"James was probably right," I guessed. "Got to be the mob behind the chicken fights."

"They'd kill somebody because he stole a few chickens?"

"Didn't you get the economics lesson? I must have heard it fifty times. The CRL is trying to turn cockfighting into a money-loser. From what I heard, Sam led the action part of the organization. So, yeah, if they thought he was going to kill their golden egg, I'm betting they would kill him before he put them out of business. He was an accountant, after all. He was probably the one who came up with the idea and sold the economics lesson to the CRL. But the mob put him out of business before he could do it to them."

I hadn't found the specifics, but there was definitely organized crime behind cockfighting. Even the Dallas Police Department didn't know which family controlled the business, or at least they hadn't input anything about it into their computer database. I'd hacked the DPD system first.

Angie shook her head. "You can't take on the mob alone. Even with my help. You've got to go to Andy with what you found and let him and his lawyers and his millions of dollars do some of the work here."

"I hate to go to Andy without having things resolved," I admitted. Especially after the way he'd laughed off my theory that the CRL had murdered Sam.

Angie just glared at me. "What's unresolved? You discovered

evidence in Sam's background that gives someone else a motive for murder. Do you really expect to track down an individual hit man and beat the truth out of him?"

When she put it that way, it did sound absurd. "You're right. I'll call Andy."

"Okay," Angie said. "But why do you figure Sam got involved with Chicken Rescue in the first place?"

That was a good question but not one I had an answer for.

* * * *

Andy keeps moving his headquarters to bigger buildings and now has developers spread out over a number of offices in Dallas. Although he'd started the business in Oak Cliff, he'd relocated into downtown Dallas where he'd been able to lock in low lease rates after the telecom crash.

I parked in a visitor spot in the covered parking structure and banged on the locked door until a security guard came and opened it for me.

The guard seemed completely unconvinced that the president of Anderson software would want to see a low-life like me, but finally agreed to call Andy's admin. I thought it was a bit ironic since I was at least as well dressed as most of the coders I knew, but the guard probably only saw sales people who tend to dress better than programmers. Heck, just about everyone dresses better than programmers.

Fortunately, Mitzi knew me and hurried down to rescue me from the rent-a-cop who looked like he wanted to practice his strip-searching technique. "It's been crazy here," Mitzi admitted. "Our stock has been all over the map. When the police leaked that they thought Andy might be behind that murder, we lost fifty percent. You know I've got my entire retirement tied up in Anderson Software."

This wasn't the time to give a lecture on portfolio diversification, so I just shook my head and tsked. "Once the police find out who did it, he'll be free and clear."

Mitzi didn't look consoled. I could sympathize. All I owned was an aging Geo Storm—and Big Bob now held its title, but at least I could count on friends to help me get by.

Mitzi ushered me into the reception area in front of Andy's office suite and got me a cup of coffee. "Andy is meeting with Kevin Franklin," she explained. "His lawyer will be here in half an hour, but he can squeeze you in between them."

I thanked her for the coffee and reminded myself that this was another reason I hadn't stayed with Andy. Our love life had to be squeezed in between Andy's appointments.

Right on cue, Andy stepped out of his conference room. As always, he looked great. "Tina, babe. It's great to see you."

"Hi, Andy."

"You know Kevin Franklin, don't you? Runs what's left of Big Cat after your buddy Sam Goodwin took them to the cleaners."

I introduced myself and shook Franklin's hand.

He was a big man with spikey black hair that looked like he'd had it cut in the past two hours and an infectious grin.

"Nice to meetcha, Tina. Andy's always said good things about you."

"He does that to piss off his mother," I explained.

Franklin shook his head and laughed. "Not our Andy. I've met Karen Anderson. Nobody would be dumb enough to want to piss her off. Especially now that she's learning Tai Chi."

I'd never heard that Tai Chi was supposed to be dangerous but with Karen Anderson, anything is possible.

Kevin seemed like a decent guy. He'd been taken to the cleaners by Sam, but he'd hung on and it looked like maybe Big Cat would make it after all.

"I hear you were another victim of Sam's questionable relationship with the truth," Franklin interrupted my thoughts. "He cost a lot of people a lot of money but I still hate what happened to him."

"No kidding," I agreed. "By the way, did he ever say anything to you about chickens?"

"Chickens?" Franklin laughed. "Sam was more a steak and potatoes kind of guy.

"He seems to have been involved with the anti-cockfighting movement," I told him. "I was wondering how long he'd been active there."

Franklin looked thoughtful. "You know, he lost a boatload of money playing the market, but most of what Sam stole never turned up. So, I suppose it's possible that he lost the rest of it gambling. If the cockfighters took him to the cleaners, I'm not surprised that he'd go after them. Sam wasn't the kind of guy who would let anybody take advantage of him."

What Kevin said matched my reading of Sam, which surprised me. Except for Andy, I haven't met many men who bother with insights about people. They're generally too busy worrying about stuff or sex.

"Hey, I know Andy doesn't have much time before his three o'clock so I'll run." Kevin scribbled his personal cell number on the back of one of his business cards and handed it to me. "You need any help, give me a call."

I stuck the card in my jeans pocket. I doubted that Sam would have shared his feelings with his boss, but you never knew.

"I think I've got everything under control," I said. "But thanks anyway."

"Really?" He looked surprised. "Andy here was telling me that his lawyers haven't found squat."

I nodded but didn't elaborate. I'd give Andy what I found and let him decide whom to talk to.

"Well, I've got to see if I can put out any fires back at the ranch." He turned to Andy. "Good to see you, buddy. We still on for squash this weekend?"

Andy nodded and was glad I hadn't seriously considered Kevin. Squash? It wasn't the kind of game trailer park trash play.

"You doing all right, babe?" Andy demanded after Mitzi had ushered him into the elevator leaving the two of us alone. "You look like hell."

Men can be so good for the ego. "It's been a rough couple of days," I admitted.

"I don't understand why you didn't call me to make bail for you? What were you thinking?"

"We're not married anymore, Andy. "And you're not my daddy."

He patted my arm. "It makes me feel good to help out when I can."

I felt myself get a little sniffly and grabbed a tissue off of Mitzi's desk. Dang, I was turning into the human waterworks. "Forget that. Angie and I figured out who really killed Sam."

Andy shook his head. "I pushed Pelcovitz about your Chicken Rescue theory. Once he stopped laughing, he told me that even if Chicken Rescue people had killed Sam, he'd never been able to convince a jury, the police, or the D.A."

So I told Andy what I'd learned about Sam's role in the CRL and how they'd been working to bankrupt the cockfighting business.

He nodded slowly. "Pinning the murder on organized crime would have to be more convincing than blaming a bunch of do-gooders. Pelcovitz should be here any minute. Why don't you tell him the story and see what he thinks?"

Sid Pelcovitz arrived precisely three minutes before his appointment. He was your classic stereotype lawyer. His suit couldn't have cost less than two thousand dollars and his shoes were shiny enough for me to check out the circles under my eyes. No wonder Andy thought I looked tired. I was a mess.

Sid glared at Andy when I joined them in the conference room. "She's a suspect. You shouldn't have any contact with her."

"Tina didn't kill anybody. Besides, she's learned something about the case—which is more than I can say for the twenty investigators you've got me paying for."

"Yeah?" Pelcovitz assayed a smile in my direction—and failed miserably. "Spill."

I told Sid about my adventures, answered those questions I could, and confessed to having no idea what to do next.

Pelcovitz made a few notes, then shook his head. "Let's assume we can get this James, no last name, to testify. The prosecution is going to make a big deal about how good his word is since he's got to admit to B&E and stress his prejudice against cockfighters. Then they'll accuse us of just trying to confuse the jury. We don't have a suspect, a weapon, or anything else. There's no proof of mob involvement. All you have is a theory."

"We have a motive," Andy said. "I thought we were just supposed to be able to show reasonable doubt."

Pelcovitz's smile looked nasty. "In Texas, reasonable doubt means not a chance in the world. Right or wrong, juries here want to believe the cops, want the assurance that they've got the right guy. I don't want to minimize what you've done, but it isn't close to being enough. The prosecutors will call it a conspiracy theory."

I lived in a section of town that thought of the cops as invaders rather than defenders. That might be why I was so regularly excused when I reported for jury duty.

"So that's it?" I asked. "We just walk away from the evidence because it's too much trouble to find out the truth."

Pelcovitz blinked like I'd thrown something at him. "Andy's got a flock of investigators in retainer. Lord knows they aren't making any progress on finding the ex-wife or Emily. I'll turn them on the mob connection and pray I don't get any of them killed."

I'd been so wrapped up in my own pet theories that I hadn't even bothered with the obvious. The police always suspect the wife or girlfriend. I was the girlfriend and I knew I hadn't done it, but what about the ex-wife? Just because the court had awarded Sam custody didn't mean that his ex-wife was happy about it. And given that Emily had turned up missing, the wife would almost have to be a suspect. Maybe the mob hadn't gotten to him first.

"What do you mean they're not getting anywhere? Does the wife have an alibi?" Not that that would mean anything. She could have hired someone to kill Sam for her.

"We can't find her," Pelcovitz admitted. "Neither can the cops. She's disappeared."

And these were the investigators he was going to turn onto the mob. I wasn't very comforted.

"Can you give me what your investigators found out about Sam's wife?" I asked. "Maybe I can do a little more snooping around."

"That's what the investigators are getting paid to do," Andy reminded me.

"And that's what they haven't done at all," Pelcovitz said. "While this little lady came up with the beginnings of a halfway decent alternate theory all by herself. If it's all right with you, Andy, I'll give Tina the reports."

"Hell no," Andy turned to me. "Whoever killed Sam won't mind killing again, Tina. And I'd just as soon not have them kill you."

I relied on Andy's protectiveness, but this was going too far. "I'm neck-deep in this already, Andy, and I'm sinking fast. If we don't find out who killed Sam, the police are going to hang it on me. Pelcovitz here is smart enough to get you off the hook, but I'm the one they'll go after next. All I'm asking is that you give me the ammunition I need to have a chance.

Andy shook his head but didn't respond.

"So, can I give her the files or not?" Sid was looking for closure. "One thing for sure, she'll be safer going after the ex-wife than taking on the Dallas mob all by herself."

Andy shrugged. "I don't like it, but all right." He reached for my hand and squeezed it. "Be careful, babe. If you need help, don't be too proud to call for it."

I didn't think pride was my big problem but I've been wrong before so I didn't argue with him.

"Right, Tina. I'll get them to you then. It's possible he investigators have missed something obvious." Pelcovitz shook his head. "They're supposed to be the best agency in Dallas, but they've been pure bozo on this."

Pelcovitz stood, shook Andy's hand, then mine. "It was good to meet you, Tina. Good to see you again, Andy."

Mitzi didn't bother to show Pelcovitz out, which, I thought, indicated how often he must have been up here lately.

I started to follow him, but Andy grabbed my arm. "Hang on a second, Tina."

"If Pelcovitz is going to work the chickens, I want to work the wife," I told him.

"You're going to get yourself hurt," he said. "You're out on bail and the first thing you do is burglarize a bunch of mobsters. What if they'd had a guard or dogs?"

"Dogs would have gone crazy trying to get into the coops," I said.

Andy wiped his hand across his forehead. "That makes me feel so much better. Pelcovitz and his investigators can handle it, Tina. And they'll clear you as well as me."

I knew I sounded whiny but I couldn't help it. "I don't just want to get cleared. I want to find out who killed Sam."

Andy looked at his shoes. "You must be pretty broken up about what happened, Tina. I want you to know that I'm sorry."

I looked at him suspiciously. "What are you trying to tell me?"

He looked up, startled. "Oh. Did it sound like I was confessing?" He actually laughed. "No, Tina, I didn't kill your boyfriend in a fit of jealous rage. Or even because he cost me thirty million dollars. I'm just sorry that you've got more stuff to go through."

I nodded. "I'm trying not to get sappy. Doesn't always work."

"You're welcome to come over to the house for a few days," he suggested. "You know, hang out at the pool and let the servants pamper you."

I don't do pamper and Andy knew it. Still, it sounded more tempting than it should have. "Your mother still living there?"

He nodded. "Afraid so."

"I'll take a rain check."

* * * *

A courier got me out of bed at seven the next morning with a fat package from Sid Pelcovitz. Sure enough, the lawyer had sent me a copy of the detective reports dealing with Sam's ex-wife Amber.

The dossier was thick, filled with information I couldn't imagine having any use for—like her high school transcript and a list of the plays she'd had bit parts in. She'd immigrated to the U.S. from Russia when she was only two so she didn't figure to be connected to the Russian Mob. Still, she was a long way from the pristine saint her photos made her out to be. The stack of papers included her police record.

Amber had served two years probation for drug possession and actually spent a couple of months in jail for possessing an unlicensed weapon.

I put together the facts—scorned woman who lost child custody, access to weapons and other criminals, and no particular respect for the law. I could see why Sam had won custody. I could also see why Pelcovitz would be interested in her as a suspect.

The only problem was, any sort of decent lawyer could have gotten her custody of Emily if she'd wanted it. Maybe not when they'd gotten the divorce, but for sure when the truth came out about Sam's embezzling from Big Cat Telecommunications. So why would she murder the man?

* * * *

I checked out Pelcovitz's detective service and learned what I'd suspected. They were a bunch of retired FBI and police types—almost all old, almost all guys, and almost all from professional backgrounds. They would stick out like bankers in a barnyard in Pleasant Grove where Amber lived.

I, on the other hand, had lived in Pleasant Grove when I'd been in elementary school. I knew the neighborhood, and I could fit the white trash image. It was time for trailer-trash Tina to get back to work.

I knew I'd get my head bit off if I tried to wake Angie up now. Besides, she is worthless before noon. I stuck a note in her mail slot, fired up the Storm, and headed east.

The drive to Pleasant Grove took about forty minutes. When I got there, I felt like I'd never left home. Potholes, ratty 1940s apartments scattered among one-story frame houses with fading paint, and aging pickup trucks marked the landscape. There wasn't as much of the furniture on the porch as I remembered, though. Air conditioning had finally arrived in this suburb of Dallas and with it, the neighborhood changed. Before air conditioning, people would hang out on the street, chat from their porches, and work on the cars disintegrating in their front yards. Once they got air conditioning, though, they stayed inside and watched television. It's called progress.

I cruised slowly down Amber's street. A two-story apartment building lifted like a skyscraper above the flat landscape. Across the street, a convenience store and a beauty salon formed the local industry.

Amber's apartment was on the second story of the walkup. Nobody answered when I banged on the door.

I peaked in through a bend in her Venetian blinds and saw about what I expected. A medium sized television dominated the living room, a faded loveseat and an easy chair in front of it. A cheap dinette set made up the entire furnishing of the dining room.

The only thing that I could possibly label as a clue was a copy of the latest Harry Potter book. Since as many adults read Harry Potter as children, I didn't think that meant much, but it could. There certainly wasn't the mess I would have left behind if I'd been taking care of a child.

Of course, if Amber really had killed Sam and kidnapped Emily, surely she'd be smart enough to head out of town.

I knocked on her door again, not because I thought she'd answer but because I didn't have any other ideas. Driving all the way to Pleasant Grove without a plan was starting to sound like one of the less brilliant ideas I'd had that week. Considering my week, that was saying a lot.

I clunked down the steps and headed toward my car when something caught my attention.

A bit of pink showed through the fake brass grillwork in front of apartment 2C's mailbox.

Breaking into a building and setting a bunch of chickens free violates local code. If I remembered my high school civics right, breaking into a mailbox was a federal crime punishable by countless years in jail and probably deportation to some undesirable and anti-female desert nation.

Walk away, I urged myself.

Instead, I made a bargain. If I couldn't find anything to pick the lock with within five minutes, I'd take that as a sign and go have a couple of donuts. If I could, I'd pick the lock.

It took me a couple of minutes but I found a bobby pin and a paper clip. Good enough.

The mailboxes were fastened with cheap locks. Amber's didn't last twenty seconds against paper clip and bobby pin combination.

Her mail slot was filled to overflowing, the last item being a yellow card from the mailman indicating that Amber would have to come down to the post office to pick up the rest of her mail.

Okay, Amber had split. I grabbed the crunched up wad of mail and headed for the park.

I pulled up near where a multi-ethnic crowd sweated around a track.

It was a hundred degrees outside-like most any August day in Texas —but half the people there were wearing sweats or these odd reflective outfits that keep the sweat in and make you feel maximum misery while you're turning into a baked potato.

Every once in a while I got feeling guilty about my lack of exercise. The Pleasant Grove track was an inoculation.

Ignoring the sweating mob, I got down to my loot.

Amber's mail was about as exciting as mine normally is.

I sorted through it quickly, pocketing a coupon for a free pizza at a place Angie and I had been talking about going to, throwing away the neighborhood shopper that nobody reads anyway, and winnowing it down to the bills and the one hand-addressed letter.

The electric bill wasn't likely to be interesting and I put it aside. The phone bill had more potential. Like most of the world, Amber was a cell user, which meant that all of her calls, not just the long distance ones, would be listed.

Pelcovitz's package hadn't included any phone records. Maybe it's harder for private investigators to get these than the movies make out. So already I had something they hadn't found. Cool.

I tried to peel back the envelope without ripping it, but stopped when I felt the paper start to give. I needed to steam the sucker open.

I put my hand on the key, but then stopped. I was here, almost an hour from home, and I hadn't talked to anyone, hadn't tried to find anything about Amber or Emily.

I got out and started walking the loop.

I smiled at every woman in my age range but paid special attention to the children. School would be opening in a couple of days, so this was the last chance for moms to bond with their kids before the bloody wars of homework and after-school activities fired up.

When someone smiled back, I tried to start a conversation.

My first four were dry holes. They didn't live anywhere near Amber or didn't know anyone in the area.

By this time I was dripping wet, completely miserable, and ready to concede that Angie was right and that sleeping until noon would have been the smarter decision.

When I saw the slender blonde woman pushing a red-headed child in a stroller while a kid who looked about Emily-age tagged along, I decided to give it one more chance.

"Sure is hot," I admitted.

"Yeah."

"I like this park, though," I lied, turning around and walking the same direction as the woman. "I'm thinking about moving to the area and so I'm checking out the amenities."

She frowned at my word choice and I castigated myself. When I'd been a kid, I'd read too much and avoided television as my way of rebelling. Amenity wouldn't be a high usage words in this neighborhood.

"I mean, I've seen some really cute guys hanging around."

That got another frown. "Guys are the same everywhere."

"Boy, ain't that the truth."

She smiled for the first time. "I'm Heather."

"Tina."

"Where you moving from?"

"I rent a trailer in Oak Cliff, but my manager doesn't do much. I was trying to save up some money and buy some property out in the country, but—" I shrugged. "You know how that goes."

"What about your old man?"

I shrugged again. "Sort of between guys right now, if you know what I mean. Besides, it always seems like I end up supporting them rather than the other way around."

"Tell me about it."

"Cute kids," I said.

She shrugged. "Wear me out. They're always going. If their dads would help out a little, I could maybe get ahead."

Heather wasn't the most cheerful woman I'd met but I wasn't going to let that discourage me. "My little girl is starting kindergarten next year," I lied. "So I'm wondering about the schools. And I saw an apartment complex over on Paris Street. Just a little place. Two-stories with maybe eight units. You know what they're asking for a unit over there?"

"You're kidding. I've got a friend who has a kid starting kindergarten. And she lives in that same complex. Let me give her a call."

It would have been a great coincidence except it was what I'd spent the past couple of hours looking for. I could only feel relief.

Heather reached into her purse and pulled out a cell, pushing a speed dial number to dial.

I took over the stroller while Heather listened, pushing the little boy back and forth like he was a lump.

"Amber? It's me, Heather. Listen, I'm in the park with Taylor and Freddy and I ran into this chick who wants to know how much your apartment costs. Give me a call. And I get off at eleven. If you don't mind leaving Emily, let's plan on going out and getting ripped."

Finally! If I hung out in this park any longer, I'd be giving a wet t-shirt exhibition.

Heather hung up abruptly and grabbed the stroller from me. "My friend isn't in. How about you give me a phone number and I'll have her call you?"

I reached into my purse, pulled out a pen and a piece of scrap paper, and scrawled my first name and phone number on it.

Heather took it, stared for a minute, then grabbed my arm. "What is this, anyway?"

"Huh?"

"This pizza coupon. It's got Amber's address on it. What kind of game are you pulling?"

Chapter 6

I thought fast and came up empty. Finally, I decided on a modified version of the truth.

"Well, Heather, I sort of lied to you," I admitted.

"No shit."

I sighed. "Okay, here goes. I dated Sam Goodwin for a while."

"That asshole."

"Yeah, maybe. But you've got to admit that he was a complete hunk."

Heather wrinkled her nose. "He dumped Amber like she was yesterday's news and told all kinds of lies to get custody of their kid."

Heather's extreme reaction to Sam's name encouraged me. If Amber was mad enough to tell her friends about it, maybe she'd been mad enough to kill him. "Did you hear he got murdered?"

Heather had been pushing her stroller back and forth but when I said the word murder, her shoulders tensed and her lips narrowed into a thin line.

"Murdered? You're kidding?"

I said nothing, waiting for once rather than blathering.

"Well," she finally continued, "he had it coming. Some woman's husband did it, huh?"

I shrugged. "Nobody knows. Here's the thing, though. From what I could tell, Sam only cared about two things. Himself and Emily. Now we all know where he is. But what happened to Emily?"

Heather jerked when I said Emily's name, which told me I had a bite. She knew something and I needed to figure out how to reel it out of her.

"Want to know the funny thing?" Heather demanded after staring at me for a good five seconds.

"Sure."

"Amber wouldn't have done anything to him even after everything he did to her. She was always making up excuses for him. Always willing to justify whatever it was he was doing, even when she was the one who kept getting hurt."

"But—"

"But nothing. That's the kind of woman she is."

"I didn't mean that. I'm sure she didn't do anything to him." All right, so I was lying again. It seemed like I was doing a lot of that these days.

"Damn right."

"But you know she's got Emily, right? I mean, do you think that the police brought her over? Because I know that she was with Sam earlier in the day."

Heather shook her head. "I think Taylor has had enough sun. If I learn anything, I'll call you."

Yeah, right. I figured that the odds of Heather calling me were about up there with the chances that Sam would.

"See you 'round, Heather," I said.

"Yeah, sure. Especially with you being the new neighbor and all."

I got in my car and drove back to my trailer park feeling like a complete weasel.

But I'd learned something. Amber had Emily. The only way I could figure that was if Amber had killed Sam, or the real killers had taken Emily and given her to Amber. Either way, finding Amber was key to solving the case.

I headed home and back to my computer.

With what Pelcovitz had given me, I was able to dig up more information from the Internet.

Amber had married Sam about six months before Emily had been born. They'd moved to McKinney and lived for a year in one of those golf course mansions, and then gotten divorced. During their divorce, Amber had moved back home and someone had tipped off the police to search her. They'd come up with better than a pound of methamphetamine. Enough to stick her in jail for possession with intent and make sure Sam got custody. I didn't like believing that I'd been in love with a guy who would set up his wife that way, but somebody had.

I clicked around a bit more, but I knew I'd reached my limit. I'm a programmer, not a cracker. Although I'd been able to get into the DPD computers, that was just because I knew a couple of cops well enough to learn their pets' names and the names of the girls they had crushes on. Guessing passwords was easy when you know the people. Doing it was called social engineering and it didn't take a technical genius.

When it came to hardcore hacking, I needed to turn to the expert.

Unfortunately, the expert I knew was Patrick Adams.

I called up Angie, got her recipe for peanut butter cookies and went to work.

Two hours later, I had enough burned chunks of coal to host my own barbecue, and eight light brown-lumps that looked vaguely like cookies.

I put the brown lumps on a plate and put the black lumps out for the chickens. Maybe they'd see the offering as a threat and vanish.

I wasn't worried about Patrick being in—he is always in. So I knocked on his door and waited for him to turn the dirty pictures off on his computer.

Men, I decided for maybe the millionth time that day, are impossible to understand mostly because who would want to?

"Yeah?" His muffled voice sounded out of breath. I didn't want to think about what caused that.

"Hi, Patrick. It's Tina."

"What do you want, Tina? I paid my rent."

"I brought you some cookies."

The door popped open.

Patrick had his air conditioner turned up full blast and an arctic wave hit me when I stepped into his trailer. My nipples instantly puckered from the cold and poked out in my t-shirt, giving Patrick a cheap thrill. He ogled way too obviously, perhaps under the impression I'd be flattered. No way.

"Did you see that the courts decided that the law against upskirt shots is unconstitutional?" he asked me.

I could have gone the rest of my life without knowing it.

Instead of answering, I handed over the cookies.

He looked at them suspiciously. "What are these supposed to be?"

"Peanut butter cookies," I assured him.

When he still looked dubious, I added, "Angie gave me the recipe."

That did the trick.

Patrick grabbed one, stuffed it into his mouth, bit down once, and promptly turned purple.

He looked at me in horror, then ran into his bathroom.

"Patrick? Are you all right?" I gave him a minute, then went after him, banging on the bathroom door.

"Fine." His voice sounded weak. "I'll be out in a minute." He paused a beat and I could almost hear his brain grinding. "Uh, why don't you help yourself to one of those delicious cookies while you wait?"

I wasn't born yesterday. And Patrick wasn't the sharing kind. I took one of the cookie-esque lumps and broke it in half.

The insides sort of oozed out. It looked a little slimy, sort of like brown Jello, except it had lumps in it.

Patrick looked even paler than usual when he emerged from his bathroom. "If you ever try to come into my house with cookies again, you'd better show me the bakery label first."

"I'm sorry. Angie said that this was one recipe that even I couldn't mess up."

"You surprise the crap out of me most of the time. No reason you shouldn't surprise her too."

"Next time I'll bring Oreos."

"You always were a big spender, Tina."

"I appreciate your warning about Sam the other day. Did you hear that he was really Sam Goodwin? The accountant behind the Big Cat Telecom collapse."

Patrick sat in his big leather chair, keeping his distance from me as if worried that I might try to force another cookie down his throat. "Maybe."

"The police think Andy might have done it. It turns out that he lost thirty-some million on Big Cat."

Patrick nodded slowly. "I lost a few bucks there too. Pissed the crap out of me."

Uh-oh, I'd forgotten about that. Had I stumbled onto the real killer?

I reached for my purse, trying to look casual.

"I didn't kill him." Patrick shoved his chair away from his computer desk holding his hands in front of his face in a sort of impromptu cross, like an extra in a vampire movie too cheap to provide even working crucifixes. A pair of white cotton briefs clung to one of the chair's wheels.

Yuck.

I found the pepper-spray container and felt around for the top. "Who said anything about you killing Sam?"

Patrick shook his head. "Don't mess with me, Tina. I know you keep pepper spray in that purse. And I also know you'd love nothing better than an excuse to spray me with it."

"What do you know about Sam's ex-wife?" I asked. I didn't let go of the spray, but I didn't pull it out and start spraying either. Holding the threat over him might be the best way to get Patrick's cooperation.

"Nothing." His answer was sullen, but he wheeled himself back to his computer and started clicking.

He looked up several minutes later. "I've got to say that his tastes haven't changed."

"What's that supposed to mean?"

"Talk about white trash."

"Don't you get started ragging on Pleasant Grove. At least I didn't see any chickens wandering around when I was there earlier today."

"You need to do something about those chickens, Tina."

I clenched my fists. "I really don't want to hear about those chickens again, okay? Ever."

Patrick raised an eyebrow. "Sure, Tina. Whatever you say."

I guess he thought I was PMS or something but I'd never seen Patrick back off as fast as that. He was normally just looking for a chance to be annoying—and darn good at it too.

"So what else did you find on Amber?" I decided to follow up while I had momentum.

"Okay, I'm guessing that you have the basics. Credit report, white pages search, stuff like that."

"I wasn't born yesterday."

"Usual credit card debt," he murmured. "Minimum payments for the past year."

So what else was new? Except for Andy, everyone I knew made minimum payments when they could, and was happy to do it.

Patrick clicked away for a few more minutes.

After about a minute, though, I dumped a bunch of paper on the floor, looked under to make sure I wouldn't be sitting on anything nasty, and settled down to wait. Patrick was hooked and the less I said, the more he would find out before he remembered that he was doing me a favor and figured he was wasting his time.

"Now this is interesting," Patrick whispered.

I wanted to get up, shake him by the shoulders and say what is? Instead, I simply smiled. He'd tell me if I pretended that I didn't especially care. Patrick was the kind of guy who had to brag. The more you pretended indifference, the harder he'd try to impress you. Like any guy, I guessed.

He nodded to himself, then suddenly pushed back from his computer. "All right, let's go."

"There is no us," I reminded him. "Give me the info and I'll let you know how it turns out."

Patrick grinned, his teeth a pale green in the fluorescent lighting of his trailer. "That isn't how it works, Tina. If you want what I know, you've got yourself a partner."

"As far as I can tell, you don't know anything. And why would I want a partner? Besides, you never leave this trailer. Why would you want to come now?"

He rolled back to his computer, gave his mouse a single click, and rolled over to his large hot-wax printer. "Here's why I'm coming," he told me, shoving the printout in my direction. "And the reason you'd want a partner is because I'm the one who knows where we're going."

The picture showed an attractive woman with punk-black hair. Raccoon-style makeup circled her incredibly blue eyes, and her shorts rode dangerously up into territory a woman in her twenties should have known to keep covered.

"This is Amber Goodwin?" She didn't look anything like the pictures that Pelcovitz's detective agency had turned up.

"Oh, yeah."

"Don't tell me you've fallen in love, Patrick."

He nodded slowly. "That's exactly what it is. With a model like her, I could make it big on the Internet. No more of this nickel-and-dime stuff."

"No more nagging your landlady," I suggested.

"Well, we could do a spread on what two trailer trash girls do when they're all alone and there are—"

"Enough!" I'd never understand why guys think two girls going at it is so sexy.

He shrugged.

"All right," I finally agreed. "You can come with me to talk to Amber. Once I find out what she knows about Sam and Emily, you can give her your business proposition. But leave me out of that part of it."

He stuck out a hand. "Deal, partner."

I considered his hand and shook my head. I didn't know where that hand had been and I wasn't going to touch it. "Come on, Patrick. Time's wasting."

* * * *

Patrick overflowed the bucket seat on the passenger side of my Storm, one elbow out the open window. His faint odor of sweat and Twinkies filled my nostrils.

I forced myself not to complain. Patrick was giving me directions one step at a time. If I kicked him out, I'd have to head back to Dallas empty-handed. Besides, I'd agreed to this and when I make a deal, I really try to hold up my end of it.

"Sure is pretty out here," he observed. "Ever think about getting yourself some land out in the country, Tina? Maybe a hunting lease?"

It's an enduring fantasy of so many of the people I know that they'll somehow get back to nature. I'd even used that line on Heather. Even so, I was surprised a computer hacker geek like Patrick would fall for it. For people who don't like to leave their trailers, the country is just like the city except the power doesn't work very well and you can't get home delivery.

"I'm a city girl, Patrick. Just because I don't like chickens doesn't mean that I want to come out to the country and blow up animals."

"It's so rustic, though," he continued.

I drove past a graying farmhouse, its back broken by a collapsed hackberry tree. Like most of the places we'd passed, a for sale sign faded on the rusting barbed wire fence that lined the highway.

"I bet I could fix up a place like that," he told me. "I'd raise a few head of cattle, just grow enough to feed myself, put up photocells to generate electricity. I'd be sitting pretty if anything bad ever happened. Self reliance, that's what it's about."

As far as I'd ever been able to determine, Patrick's self-reliance was limited to his love life. The planters outside his trailer held nothing but bare dirt and he'd called me to put his Venetian blinds back in the wall the time he'd yanked on them too roughly.

Still, I didn't argue with his dream. Even a city girl like me sometimes thinks about getting away from it all. From the route we were taking, it seemed likely that Amber had done one better and actually achieved the fantasy.

I'd never spent much time in the Texas panhandle. Although it wasn't far from Dallas geographically, it felt like I'd stepped out of the modern world and into one where the dust bowl and the Great Depression never went away.

My Dallas contemporary-rock radio station faded out. I scanned but picked up only country music. Dairy Queen restaurants seemed to be the center of life in the small towns we drove through, and cattle gave us the evil eye as we cruised past them.

And there were chickens everywhere. I'd never really noticed them before, but my hours spent at the C.R.L. must have sensitized me to the feathered members of our planet's population.

"Think these chickens are involved with cockfighting?" I asked Patrick.

He took a deep breath and I simultaneously realized that he was about to launch into a long lecture and that he didn't have a clue what he'd be talking about. Like me, Patrick was a city person. Even more than me, Patrick's life centered on his computer rather than people.

I held up my hand. "Never mind. We just need to find Amber."

Patrick sulked for the next half hour, which was how long it took to follow increasingly narrow and deteriorating roads to the property that Amber owned—under her mother's maiden name.

It wasn't the best hiding job-sooner or later the police would track her down. That they hadn't done it yet meant that they really thought that either Andy or I had done it and were only going through the motions on the rest of the investigation. I may make fun of the cops from time to time, but they have some really capable computer jocks on staff.

The last mile to Amber's place was a single-lane dirt road. Tires had carved two dirt ruts through the weeds and grasses but whoever drove there regularly had a higher suspension than I. I scraped my way through underbrush until I pulled up to a cute A-frame cabin that would have been at home in an expensive ski resort but looked desperately out of place here in the prairie plains of the Texas panhandle.

"This is it?" I demanded.

Patrick looked as surprised as I was. I guess the pictures he'd looked at didn't show the house anywhere.

"I figured it would be a trailer."

I'd seen Amber's credit report and her apartment. A fancy vacation home didn't fit the woman or her background. So where had the money come from? I knew Sam had lied to me about his background, but if he was still giving money to his wife and making me go dutch when we went out on dates, the guy was lucky he was already dead.

I pulled the car under a tree about fifty feet from her home and turned off the engine.

A sudden quiet reverberated around us. I looked at Patrick, but he seemed frozen.

"Maybe it's all a mistake," he finally admitted. "I thought I was being clever looking up property records under her mother's maiden name, but what if this isn't hers at all?"

"Then we've just taken a long drive for nothing," I told him. I opened my car door. No point in just sitting there. Either we would find Amber or we wouldn't.

I marched up to the door and knocked.

Patrick scrambled after me. "Hey, I'm involved in this too."

"Don't you dare ask her about posing for you until I'm done discussing what went on with Sam."

From inside, I heard the sound of a television. Someone was at home.

I knocked again. And waited. Long enough to get nervous.

Finally footsteps approached the front door. "Who is it?"

"I'm a friend of Sam's," I told the closed door.

The door opened slowly. "I'm not with Sam anymore."

Amber Goodwin exuded an animal sex appeal that would drive a man to distraction. It was no wonder Sam had scooped her into upper-class comfort. Unlike the picture Patrick had shown me, this Amber looked classy. Like someone who would own an expensive vacation cabin in the woods. Someone who could be so demanding of her husband that she could drive him to commit all sorts of crimes to keep her in the clothes and the cars and the houses that she hadn't grown up with and didn't intend to lose.

Amber had given up on the short spiked look and wore her black hair long-almost down to her waist. Like in Patrick's picture, she was wearing shorts, but these highlighted shapely legs and left her ass covered. Her top showed off an impressive figure for a woman as slender as she was. It was intimidating, in a way. It certainly made me wonder why Sam had sought me out if Amber was the kind of woman he was used to dating.

If she was really Russian, you couldn't tell it from the accent. But the dark hair and flawless pale skin didn't look exactly American.

"Sam told me that you had divorced, that he never saw you anymore."

Amber looked at me more closely, then laughed. "Ohmigod. You're the bimbo he's seeing. He told me about you. Tina something, right? That man will never learn."

Sam wouldn't be learning anything ever, but I was. Either Amber was a very good actor, or she didn't know that Sam was dead.

Patrick was sort of edging in on me so I introduced him quickly, not letting him get a word in edgewise. When those formalities were over, I went back to work.

"Is Emily here with you?" I asked.

"She's my daughter," Amber said. She hadn't answered the question, but she glanced quickly around as if to make sure that Emily hadn't sneaked into sight.

"I understand that Sam was awarded custody. So why is it that you have her?"

"Maybe you should ask Sam, don't you think?"

"Maybe. But I'm asking you."

From the look in her eye, I wondered if I'd pushed too hard and she would just slam the door in my face. Then she relented.

"Since you've driven all the way out here, I guess I'll humor you. Yes, I have Emily. Because Sam brought her out here the other day and dropped her off. Even though he has primary custody I spend a lot of time with her. He told me he was going to pick her up yesterday, but he hasn't bothered."

"What time did he drop Emily off?" I asked.

Amber looked at me, then opened her door the rest of the way. "Honey, come on in here and let me tell you something about Sam."

Patrick and I trooped in and Amber poured us glasses of iced tea. The sounds of a Disney cartoon crept through the walls. If Amber and Emily were out here all by themselves, it was no wonder that Amber had invited us in. I know I would have been dying from some adult conversation—for an excuse to get away from another run of whatever cartoon Emily happened to be addicted to at that moment.

I took a sip of the tea and made a face. Iced tea isn't hard. All you had to do is put the sugar in before the ice, otherwise it's impossible to get it sweet enough. Either nobody had told Amber that or she just didn't care.

Amber gave Patrick a suspicious look until I explained that he was just a guy who lived in our trailer park.

"Good, because Sam can be jealous. Real jealous."

Patrick puffed up a bit. As if anyone was going to be jealous about him.

I got my brain working because Amber was talking about Sam as if he was present tense. She was remote out here, but could she really be that remote?

"What did you want to tell me about Sam?" I asked.

Amber glanced at Patrick again, then leaned closer to me. "He's gotten odd. He has these paranoid ideas that someone was out to get him. I've been thinking about getting a lawyer and seeing if I can get back custody of Emily."

I nodded. "I think you'd better do that."

She wrinkled her nose at me. "Having the kid around cramps your style, huh? Believe me, I know how you feel."

I had to tell her. "Sam is dead, Amber. Someone killed him a couple of days ago."

She had just taken a sip of iced tea and froze. Slowly the glass, unnoticed, slipped between her fingers, bounced off the table, and smashed onto the floor. "If this is some kind of a joke-"

"I'm sorry, Amber but it's no joke. I was the one who found his body."

Amber's chin gave a little wiggle and she glanced at the television room.

Until I'd met her, I'd been willing to believe the worst of Amber. Now, I wasn't so sure. But I knew one thing. I didn't want to leave until I'd seen Emily-alive.

"Can we see Emily?"

Amber looked at me like she wasn't sure who I was or what I was doing there. "Why?"

The truth hadn't been working very well so far but I figured I'd give it another go.

"Her father was killed and the police don't know where she is. I'd like to be able to tell them that I saw her and that she was okay."

If she thought that was logical, you couldn't tell it from the look on her face.

"Emily, get in here!"

"I'm busy."

I recognized that tone. It was exactly the tone she always used with me.

Amber shrugged. "You can go in there and check on her if you want to. She never does anything I tell her."

I trooped into the television room. Sure enough, Emily was watching the Disney cartoon about the flying elephant.

"Hey Emily."

"What are you doing here?"

"I was worried about you so I figured I'd check on how you were doing."

"Oh? Well, I'm fine. Did my dad come with you?"

I wasn't the police and I wasn't her parent. There was no way I was going to touch that question. "He can't come here now," I told her.

"Okay." She turned her attention back to the television, tuning me out completely.

I got back to the kitchen just in time to see Amber booting Patrick out the door.

She didn't look especially strong but she must have been hiding some muscles in those skinny arms. Patrick almost flew when she got him to the door.

"Your friend is a disgusting man."

I nodded. "I'm sorry I brought him but he was the one who knew the way."

"Thank you for telling me about Sam," Amber said. "We didn't stay together for that long but he wasn't a bad person. We made a wonderful baby together."

Which was more than anyone had done with me. I'd once thought I lacked maternal instincts but I wasn't so sure any more. Spending time with Sam and Emily had seemed almost like a family, teasing my old dreams back to life.

I looked outside and saw Patrick sitting on a stump examining a scrape on his elbow. He could wait.

"Can I ask you a few more questions, Amber?"

She shrugged. "What difference does it make?"

I took that as a yes. "Did Sam ever talk to you about embezzling money from Big Cat?"

Amber stared at me. "He started working later and later. We were having problems at home so I thought he was just trying to avoid me or maybe getting a little action after work."

"I know this is going to sound strange, but did he ever talk to you about cockfighting?"

Her blue eyes gazed into mine. "You mean birds? Like chickens?"

I nodded.

She laughed, shaking her head. "Sam thought chickens came ready-cooked. One time I was running late making dinner and I asked him to bone some chicken. He couldn't even do that."

She could cook too. I was pretty sure I hated Amber Goodwin.

I decided not to tell her that I didn't think I could bone a chicken either, and that I would just as soon not learn how.

"Did he ever say anything about organized crime? The mob?"

Amber froze. She'd gotten another glass of iced tea and she took a long sip before she met my eyes again. "I think you had better go."

"Listen, Amber. If you know anything, you'll be in danger. You've got to tell someone. Promise me that you'll tell the police if you won't tell me."

"I want you to leave, now." She stood and reached for my arm.

I'd seen what she'd done to Patrick and wasn't about to let her haul me out of her house. Instead I headed for the door under my own power. Once I'd gotten out of her grasp, I kept moving but started talking again.

"I mean it, Amber. If the mob killed Sam, they won't think twice about killing again. If I can find you, they'll be able to find you too. Hiding here is just going to make things easier for them because there are no neighbors around to help."

Amber nodded. "Maybe you're right, Tina. Maybe I should go back to the city. In either case, don't try to see me again. I have nothing more to say to you."

Chapter 7

As we drove back toward Dallas, I tuned out Patrick's whining and tried to think about what I'd learned. Obviously Amber knew more than she was telling. Equally obviously, she was afraid.

I couldn't blame her for that. I was afraid too. But I was more afraid of the police than I was of the mob so I intended to keep on looking.

Except how does one person investigate organized crime?

The more I thought about it, the more I thought about Sam. He must have asked himself the same question and come up with the cockfighting business.

As answers went, this one wasn't very reassuring. Sam's inquiries had gotten him killed. If I wasn't extremely lucky, I would end up joining him. So far, I hadn't shown any signs of being lucky.

I dropped Patrick off at his trailer and called John Halprin.

"Don't tell me you're trying to back out of our date."

I'd barely identified myself.

"I thought we were sort of vague," I answered. "You know, a time to be specified later." The last thing I wanted was to start dating again so soon after I'd lost Sam. Not even a semi-date with my lawyer.

"No way. It's tonight."

Since it was near the beginning of the month and I'd collected most of the rent checks, I actually had a little money. I could afford to pay for my own food for a change so I didn't need to mooch off of John. Still, I had promised Halprin that I'd go out with him. I'm as good a procrastinator as the next chick, but I figured that John would only get more persistent if I blew him off now.

"What time do you want to pick me up?" I asked, conceding the battle.

"How about seven?"

I looked at my watch. It was five o'clock. I consulted my stomach. It could wait. "Seven would be good."

"See you then."

He hung up the phone not letting me have a chance to tell him what I'd found. I stared at my phone trying to decide whether to call him back but decided I could wait until I saw him.

I did call Andy, though. As usual, I got his machine and left a message about finding Amber and that I didn't think she had done it. I mentioned my meeting with Halprin, making it sound like a business deal rather than a date, but telling him I'd see what Halprin could find out about the investigation.

Since I'd sort of made a promise to spend my energies on Amber and let the investigators work the mob angle, I could let myself hope that Pelcovitz and Andy would actually discover something, leaving me off the hook.

Trailers tend to be limited on closet space. I consulted with my closet and discovered about what I'd expected. My date wardrobe was non-existent.

I settled on a pair of jeans that I didn't wear much because they clung to my hips and dug into my waist when I bent. They were clean, at any rate. Then I added a little top with ties at the waist. The mirror warned me I might have gone too far. The message I wanted to send was friendly. Like I wasn't just dating Halprin because he'd blackmailed me into it, but not that I was ready to jump into bed with him. He was my lawyer and he wasn't sending me any bills.

Instead of friendly, I looked a bit slutty. I don't mind low-class-that's where I was born. But slutty crosses a line somewhere. But I wasn't sure I even wanted to get near that line with Halprin.

One thing I learned about men, if you're wearing clothes with obvious ties, they'll spend most of your date thinking about how to untie them.

Halprin knocked on my door before I could switch into something baggy.

For a former nerd, John looked good.

His sunglasses were stylish and lacked any hint of electrical tape. He wore khaki slacks and a golf shirt that didn't advertise anything.

"Looking good, Tina," he told me. "Love that shirt."

"Thanks, John. You clean up pretty good yourself. Uh-"

I almost invited him in, then remembered I had nothing to serve him and had bras hanging from most of my doorknobs. Instead, "Let's go. I'm starving."

We went to one of the new restaurants up on Bishop Arts District. The District was one of the areas that the city had plowed some money into trying to jazz up our part of Dallas. I wasn't sure the city's scheme would work because I sure couldn't afford upscale very often and there were a lot more working people like me than there are rich people, but as long as John was paying, I was happy to do my part for civic improvement.

I tried to ignore John's look of increasing astonishment as I put down my entire plate of pasta and sent back for seconds on the garlic rolls provided with dinner. I was hungry and I was worried. When I worry, I eat.

I didn't talk much for the first twenty minutes but my silence didn't stop John from running through the conversational gamut. He told me about his television habits (he liked the shows on decorating), shopping (he was for it), and the new color lines for Fall (he thought they were just what the style scene needed).

My stomach and my ears both filled up at the same time. Suddenly I couldn't stand it any more. "John, I don't know anything about colors or decorating. And the only shopping I do gets done at the Salvation Army Store on Jefferson."

"Oh, no," he explained earnestly. "I read a detailed article about this in Men's Virility Magazine. It said that ninety-three percent of women like to hear about things like this rather than guy topics like cars and football. It lets them connect to the guy. It's the Venus, Jupiter thing."

"Venus, Jupiter?" I guess I wasn't tracking.

"Men's Virility says that you have to think like women are aliens if you're going to get lai. . .," he sputtered to a stop, then relaunched, "I mean if you're going to have effective communications leading toward a meaningful relationship."

Spare me from Men's Virility I thought. "Maybe we could talk about the case," I suggested. "Pretend like we were both humans instead of ninety-three percent of women or space aliens."

He shook his head disapprovingly. "That would be work, Tina. This is supposed to be a date. Women get bored when men bring their work home from the office."

"More from Men's Virility?"

He nodded happily. "I just got my first issue. It's got fashion advice too. It's opened a whole new window for me."

He was trying, which was a lot more than most of the men I knew. I wasn't looking for a man, but I figured the least I could do was give him a little advice.

"I think you have to take the magazine's information in context," I said. "Generally it's true that women don't care about cars and football. But it's hard to want to talk about decorating shows if you live in a trailer and you're worrying about whether the cops are going to arrest you soon.

My guess is that giving advice for dating murder suspects could be a little specialized for a general-interest magazine like Men's Virility. So you're going to have to trust me on this. I haven't had time to give much consideration to the new fall colors since I've been worrying that the only colors I'm going to be wearing are black and white stripes."

He chuckled. "You know that nobody wears black and white prison uniforms any more."

"Yeah, John. I do know that."

He sighed. The magazine had probably promised him he'd be in like Flint. Instead, he was still batting zero.

"I joined a health club," he told me.

"That's great, John. Because I'm about to leave and you'll have to run to catch up with me."

"All right, Tina. You aren't getting into the spirit of this dating thing but I'm willing to give you more time. I understand that you've just been through a loss and want you to know that I'll be there for you when you feel like—"

"You didn't forget to look into my case did you, John?" I'd had more of the new-man talk than I could stomach-even with the ravioli holding things down.

"Hey, no way did I forget," John protested. "I was in court today and afterwards I chatted up a couple of detectives I know."

They were probably still laughing about the chat but I nodded gratefully. "Learn anything?"

"They've been looking at the sister to see if she might have some involvement. It turns out that Sam had a will. He left everything to his daughter but the wife and sister are joint executors."

"Which means?"

He shrugged. "I don't know? I mean, legally it means that they get to decide how the money gets spent. But in terms of giving them a motive to kill, I don't see it. Doesn't sound like there's more than a couple of hundred thousand in Sam's estate. Not that they've been able to find, anyway."

Sam had scammed tens of millions of dollars out of Big Cat Telecom. He'd lost a lot in the stock market disaster, but he'd stolen millions more than he'd lost. The mob/chicken/gambling connection was making more and more sense.

"You're telling me the cops think Katherine did it so she could get access to a couple hundred thousand she'll just get to watch for the kid?"

"She'd get it all if it turned out that the kid had been killed at the same time. They're thinking that Emily's body will turn up sometime. Maybe Amber's too."

I shook my head. "They aren't dead. Not yet, anyway."

John's eyes got round. "You know something, Tina. Don't hold out on your lawyer."

I was learning something about John. He'd be Mr. Sensitive Man when he thought that would get him something and hard-assed lawyer when he that might help. Maybe John had layers to him after all. I wasn't ready to think about another guy so soon after losing Sam, but I could think about who I might think about later. John had possibilities.

"When I saw Amber and Emily earlier today, Amber told me that Sam brought Emily to her. She was alive and thought Sam was too."

"You shouldn't go off detecting on your own, Tina. You could get hurt."

"Give me a break. From what you just told me, the cops don't have a clue. So sooner or later they're going to come looking for a fall-gal. If I try to be careful and not get hurt, I'm going to prison. I've spent enough time in the holding tanks to know I don't want to graduate to the big leagues."

"Uh-"

"But what I want to know is, how come Sam only has a couple hundred thousand. He ripped off Big Cat to the tune of mega-millions.

"Everyone knows there's a lot more money hidden somewhere," John reminded me.

Unless the mob had taken it.

"John, I think the police have this all wrong. I think that there's a mob angle and that they're the ones who killed Sam."

He looked at me like I'd started speaking in tongues or something. "Tina, we're in Texas. There is no Mafia down here."

I didn't really think it was relevant-or true, but I trotted out Amber's Russian birth. The Russian mob is active these days and that it doesn't have any respect for the old Mafia boundaries.

He shook his head. "I don't see what this buys you, Tina. The jury wants to believe the police, not some crazy story about the Mafia and Russians and chicken fighting."

I got mad and I stood up. "You know, John, I think you should spend a little more time reading that magazine of yours. The funny thing about us women is that some of us like fashion and some of us like decorating. But none of us like being treated like complete idiots. I've been working my butt off on this case and I think I've learned more than anyone else."

"But Tina-"

"And don't you dare tell me that the police know what they're doing. They've plugged this case into their formula book and come up with some profile of a girlfriend or jealous lover."

I was pissed and John knew it. He reached back into the deep resources of Men's Virility magazine and came up with the one answer that could save him.

"How about dessert, Tina?"

* * * *

Andy was waiting outside my trailer when John dropped me off.

John took one look at my pacing ex-husband and punched too hard on the break pedal jerking his car to a stop that sent the wheels skidding across the gravel of my parking lot.

"I guess I should just leave you here," he grumbled.

So much dating. With my ex-husband suspected of murdering my most recent lover, I guess I shouldn't have counted on men lining up to be next.

"Thanks for helping me out," I told John. I leaned over and gave him a quick kiss on the cheek and tried to ignore the way he kept his eyes on Andy.

"I'll really dig into the case now," he promised. "I've got some ideas about the mob angle. Maybe I could run them by you tomorrow." He glanced at my ex-husband. "Or maybe I'd better not."

"Andy didn't kill anyone and he isn't jealous," I told John.

"According to Men's Virility-"

"Stuff Men's Virility Magazine," I told him. I made myself take a deep breath. "Let me know what you learn."

Maybe I should have told Andy to bug off and invited John in for the night. At the time, though, I was glad the date was over. I've kissed plenty of frogs in my time, but John's skin had felt cool, damp, and not at all prince-like when I'd kissed him. I didn't want to wake up next to that. I was afraid I might break out in warts.

"Hey Halprin," Andy said as I got out of the car. "Hi, Tina. Good to see you, babe."

John shuddered but managed "Uh, Anderson."

"I appreciate you working with Tina on this case." Andy gave John a big smile.

"Case? Oh, yeah. The case. Well, that's what we've been talking about all right. The case."

Andy looked puzzled and John jammed his car into gear and fishtailed out of the lot.

"Are you sure you don't want me to hire you a real lawyer?" Andy offered.

"He's just nervous," I told him. "He took me out to dinner and when he saw you, he thought you might kill him too. Like you did Sam."

Andy grinned. "I can see how this whole thing could cramp your love life."

"You think? Maybe you're right. Maybe having your boyfriend murdered and being a leading suspect might put a damper on things for a while.

"Hey. Tone down the sarcasm. I'm sorry."

"Whatever."

He stood there with his arms crossed across his chest until I finally gave in.

"Do you want to come in?"

Andy nodded slowly. "Yeah. We need to talk. Your message got me thinking, Tina. And worrying."

With any other guy, I would have worried about the mess in my trailer. But Andy had seen me at my worst. He ignored the bras hanging from every doorknob in the place and sat in the only comfortable chair I had.

I pulled up my computer chair and straddled it. "You mean my message about finding Amber? What about it?"

"The whole thing seems funny to me. Why was Amber hiding if she didn't know Sam was dead? Why did Sam take Emily to her in the first place? He hadn't said anything about it to you earlier that day and we know they weren't exactly on friendly terms."

I'd been worried about that too, although letting a little girl see her mother once in a while didn't seem that much of a stretch.

"Basically I think he learned something between when you left in the morning and when he took Emily to Amber," Andy said. Whatever he learned is what got him killed."

"And then there's the big question," I added. "What happened to the money?"

Andy stood, tried to pace across my floor, then punched a fist into his palm. "This place is ridiculous," he told me, taking his frustration out on my trailer. "Why don't you let me buy you a real house? Someplace at least big enough that you could take two full steps before you hit a wall."

I just sat there looking at him. Of all the people in the world, Andy should have understood why I couldn't let him buy me a house. From the time I'd been two years old, my mother had told me that I needed a man to take care of me, that I couldn't ever make it on my own. And I'd believed her. I'd latched onto Andy in High School and draped over him like white on rice. If I was ever going to get over my feelings of inadequacy, I needed to prove that I could make a life on my own. If I couldn't, what possible use would I be for anyone else? Even if my biological clock was telling me that I needed to drop everything and start having babies.

Of everyone I'd known, only one person had believed in me-Andy. And now I was getting it from him, too.

The silence continued until I hit my discomfort limit.

"I'm tired and I'm going to bed now," I told him. "Go home."

* * * *

I got up early the next morning feeling great. After two cups of coffee, I sat down at the computer and finished knocking out the cell-phone game I'd been working on.

If you're a programmer, you live for days like that. Days when the code just flows as fast as you can type it and it seemed more like you were remembering it from a dream than actually working at it. Modules compiled correctly the first time thorough, game graphics looked better than I had ever seen on a cellphone screen, and the answer to every stumbling block I ran into just sort of popped into my mind.

I was just putting in the final touch-a little audio tag I'd created-when I heard a knock at my door.

"Just a second," I shouted. I was in the flow and I needed to finish before getting distracted.

"Ms. Anderson?"

The high-pitched female voice sounded familiar. For a few seconds, I grasped for context. Then I wished I hadn't.

The police were back.

I clicked the save button and headed for my door.

"Halprin told you I'd found Emily," I guessed.

Detective Dikens was back, along with the way cute Mike Heath.

Dikens didn't meet my smile. "Have you been here all night?" she demanded.

I shrugged but had no reason to lie. "Since about nine. Are you going to tell me what's going on?"

At least they were asking about last night. I hadn't been out rescuing chickens that night. I didn't think this was about chickens, though. Dikens seemed focused on homicide.

"I understand that Mr. John Halprin was your attorney."

It wasn't a question so I just nodded. "Okay."

"Is this correct?" She sounded exasperated.

"He was and he still is." Unless Andy had done something crazy like firing him. In that case, I'd just hire him back.

"I see." Dikens paused dramatically. "And when was the last time you saw Mr. Halprin?"

My heart dropped. This wasn't about Andy trying to fire him. "Something happened to John?"

"Please answer the question."

Detective Dikens might look like a sweet little girl, but she was coming down on me now like a locomotive. "He dropped me off here around nine last night," I admitted. "We had a date but it didn't last long."

"And why was that, Ms. Anderson?" This was Heath jumping in. He probably thought he could distract me with his turquoise eyes and great butt.

Well, he wasn't completely wrong because I was distracted, although not by his body. Fortunately for me, I hadn't done anything wrong the previous night. Unfortunately, being innocent had never kept me from saying something stupid before.

"I wanted to talk about the case. He wanted to talk about home decorating."

"Whose home?" Dikens demanded. He sounded puzzled.

It was a good question. With all of John's talk about Men's Virility, I hadn't even thought to question whether he might be probing my interest in a more permanent housing situation. One involving the two of us.

I figured it was just as well that I hadn't picked up on that interpretation at the time. The date would have ended even sooner and even John's timely desert suggestion wouldn't have been able to save it.

"Generic houses and generic decoration," I answered. "He recently subscribed to a magazine on how to talk to women. It made for a complicated evening."

Dikens laughed and Heath grimaced. But the detective's laughter didn't last long. "Did you invite him in after he brought you home?"

I shook my head.

"Why not, Ms. Anderson?"

All right, my mind wasn't making all the connections it should, but all of a sudden things clicked into place. This wasn't about me. The police were still after Andy. When I told them that my ex-husband had run my new boyfriend off, they would come down on Andy like gangbusters.

For a startled second, I let myself consider the possibility that they were right. I'd never thought of Andy as the jealous type, but what were the odds that I would have two boyfriends murdered in a row? My neighborhood might be rough, but it wasn't that rough. There had to be a connection and Andy seemed like the most obvious one.

I was tempted to ask for a lawyer then, but I didn't think that would go over well. They hadn't come right out and told me that Halprin was dead, but they hadn't left much doubt in my mind either.

I decided to temporize about Andy while I tried to get my thoughts in order.

"Even though I live in a trailer park, that doesn't mean I invite every guy who takes me out into my bed." I turned up the anger meter a bit. "I just lost my boyfriend, you know."

"You just lost another one," Heath interjected.

The cat was out of the bag now.

"He's dead?" I'd seen this coming but it still hit me like a baseball bat in the ribs.

Dikens glared daggers at Heath but it was too late for that. "Ms. Anderson, we are investigating John Halprin's apparent murder. Withholding information in a homicide investigation is a crime."

I swallowed hard, forced myself to nod. "Murdered?" John might have tried to hard, but he'd been a friend and he'd done everything he could to help me.

Dikens sighed again. "Let's start with a timeline. What time did Halprin pick you up?"

I realized I was standing in front of my trailer in the middle of the morning. Probably everyone in the park was watching out their windows by now, keeping track of their adventurous manager.

"Why don't you come in? I'll make coffee," I suggested.

Heath's turquoise eyes didn't look so sexy when he gave my trailer a look filled with contempt. "Perhaps we should go down to the police station."

I shook my head. I'd been through this before and I wasn't about to change. "Am I under arrest?"

"This is just an informative interview," Dikens said.

"In that case, I'd prefer to stay on my own turf."

* * * *

I only had about five minutes worth of information but I had to repeat it so many times that it took more than an hour before the detectives finally left. I'd admitted to them that Andy had been there because I figured that Andy would tell them and they'd be suspicious of me if I forgot to mention it. But I knew they were on the wrong track. Andy wouldn't have killed Halprin.

Still, it couldn't be a coincidence that the two men I'd dated recently had both been killed. If the police couldn't figure out that link then I'd have to do it. But to do that, I needed to think. And to think, I needed to eat.

My refrigerator was empty so I did the next best thing-called Angie.

My girlfriend and I headed for Oak Lawn. We settled in with our biscotti and caramel lattes and I told her about Halprin.

"It's got to be the mob," she told me when I'd asked her thoughts on the mystery connection.

That had been my first reaction too, but I didn't see the connection to Halprin. My confusion must have registered because Angie shook her head.

"You've got to understand men. Halprin wanted in your pants, but he thought he wasn't worthy. So he read his Men's Virility Magazine and really worked the lines he learned there. When that didn't work, he decided to find another way to impress you. Like bringing you the solution to the case on a platter."

That made some sense and I told Angie so.

She looked at me like I was finally catching onto the totally obvious. "I know you and you couldn't have spent a couple of hours with him without telling him about the possible mob connection. Since you didn't invite him in afterwards, he had an entire evening alone to dig into the case. He probably figured he'd show you that he could be better for you than Andy was. Next time, he would have been in like Flint."

"Except there isn't going to be a next time," I said feeling sorry for myself.

Angie gave me the smile she usually reserved to reward clients who came through with an especially big tip. "So now we have another reason to find out the truth. Dallas doesn't have enough single men as it is. We can't have the mob going around killing everyone who takes a look at you."

Angie's heart was in the right place but sometimes her priorities were a little out of whack.

"So what do you suggest?"

She took another sip of her coffee and looked into the room behind us. I could tell she was clueless and hoping for inspiration. I knew that feeling.

"If only we knew what Halprin found," I said, breaking the silence and letting Angie off the hook. "Because they wouldn't have killed him if he hadn't found something or at least looked in the wrong place."

She nodded, then lit up with an idea. "What do you say we break into Halprin's house? I'll bet he's the kind of guy who kept everything on an electronic organizer. We'll probably find his exact plan."

She actually stood and headed for the café's door before I grabbed her. "Are you trying to get us arrested? That's a dumb idea even for us."

"What?"

"Halprin was a lawyer, not a trailer dweller. The police will be all over his apartment like cheese on macaroni. If we set foot anywhere near his complex, we'll be cooling our heels in jail trying to come up with a rational explanation for our stupidity."

Angie sat back down. "Oh, yeah."

I took a deep breath. "Besides, Halprin probably used his lawyer connections. We wouldn't know how to follow those and the police do, if they bother to look. What we need is another angle into the mob."

She looked at me suspiciously. "Like what?"

"I know you're an independent," I told her, "but aren't a lot of hookers connected somehow?"

She shook her head. "You don't want to go there, hon. For most prostitutes, the mob connection is just drugs. Here in Dallas, pimps are independents. It'll take forever to work up the chain if we started on the drug angle. Not only that, too many of my sisters of the street would sell their mother, let alone the competition, for a dime rock." She took a sip of her coffee. "After what happened to Halprin, we've got to believe that the killers are suspicious and ready to react."

"But Halprin's murder also means they have something to hide. Something that isn't too well hidden."

Angie took a small bite of biscotti and pushed the pastry across the table to me. "I've never liked these things."

"That makes one of us." I grabbed the almost complete biscotti and stuffed it in my mouth.

I was still hungry so I looked at the menu-and came up short.

"There is one other possibility."

Angie raised an eyebrow. "Yeah?"

"Your friends in the Chicken Rescue League. We know Sam was working with them. We know they have it in for the mob. Why don't we see if they'll help us?"

Angie grabbed the menu out of my hands and stood. "Let's go, girl."

Chapter 8

I'd started feeling guilty almost as soon as I'd thought of the Chicken Rescue League people. I was already responsible for getting Halprin killed. I didn't want anyone else on my conscience.

Angie reminded me that the chicken people were already involved, that Sam had involved him. It was the chicken people who had gotten us involved, not the reverse. Besides, they didn't have to help us if they didn't want to take the risk. Finally, Halprin's death wasn't my fault. I hadn't killed him, the mob had.

Her words weren't much help, but they didn't hurt.

Angie had the names and phone numbers of most of the guys in the CRL. The woman has an incredible knack when it comes to men.

I blew off her suggestion that we start with the guys in the action group. Of course Angie could get them to go along, they would be thinking with their gonads instead of their brains. I wanted someone smart.

It took a couple of hours to track down the speaker. Mona Lewis lived just outside of Tulsa, Oklahoma, and traveled the chicken rescue circuit. Fortunately for us, she'd returned to Tulsa for a few days after her meeting with the Dallas group. If we wanted to drive up, she was willing to meet with us.

For once I was flush. A rumor had gone around the park that I'd offed Sam for being late on his rent. People I hadn't seen in months showed up with their overdue rent money.

I poured two quarts of oil into the Storm's maw, filled the tank, and threw a couple more quarts of oil into the trunk.

For most people, Tulsa is only a few hours of driving. For the Storm, it would be a major outing.

The police had told me not to leave the metroplex while they'd been harassing me about Halprin, but I figured that a day trip didn't count.

First thing the next morning, Angie and I hit the road.

Angie was still nodding after a big night, her yawns badly contagious, but I sucked down some caffeine and managed to keep the car on the road.

Lots of people think Texas is boring because it's flat and mostly desert. There are plenty of parts of Texas that make a lie out of that cliché-mountains in the far west near El Paso, beautiful hills around Austin, and pine forests in East Texas. Unfortunately, the drive north pretty much fit the stereotype.

Oklahoma, when we finally got there, was a bit more hilly, but had the look of neglect that came from a state that still hadn't recovered from the great out-migration of the dust-bowl years.

Still, we weren't there to sightsee. Thanks to the mob my ex-husband was a police suspect and my boyfriend and my lawyer were dead. It was time for Tina Anderson to strike back.

Even without an address, I would have recognized Mona's place. Everywhere I looked, chickens ran freely, hunting for bugs or seeds or whatever chickens eat, squabbling among themselves, and terrorizing the grackles that are the basic scavenger in most of the southwest.

After the five hour drive, I was hungry. Angie got my saliva flowing when she started talking about grabbing a couple of birds, wringing their necks, and frying up some lunch.

That wasn't going to be happening.

Mona met us at the doorway to what had once been a mansion but had fallen on tough times. Or rather, had fallen in with rough company. The chickens didn't have the run of just the property. Hundreds of them roamed through the house, pooping on the furniture, and generally were being disgusting. Lord knows I'm a bit of a slob, but even I have my standards. If Mona had ever met a standard, she'd ignored it.

She yanked a plastic ground cover off of a couch and offered us a seat.

I looked closely before I took it, especially when a chicken beat me to the cushion I'd been heading for. Sure enough, an egg rested between the cushion and the back.

"Come on, Suzie," Mona said. "We have company." She scooped up the egg and put it on the coffee table like a trophy or something. Weird.

The chicken gave me an evil eye and hopped off.

"You name your chickens?" Angie wasn't sure whether to be shocked or delighted.

"Not all of them, of course. Just my pets."

Mona held up a hand to forestall a comment that hadn't been coming. "I know what you are going to say. That keeping pets demeans the animal. And most of the chickens on the property are living in their natural state. But a few of them spent too long with people. So I keep them inside and take care of them." She shifted her voice into a high-pitched cooing. "Isn't that right, Suzie?"

I wasn't sure that chickens even had a natural state but for sure there was nothing natural about Suzie. She hopped up into Mona's lap and pushed herself against her as if begging to be stroked.

"I tried to pet one of the chickens we were rescuing. A big red critter named Hector," I told her looking for a bond. "He clawed the heck out of me."

Mona nodded seriously. "That's part of the crime of cockfighting. Chickens are naturally peaceful animals who get along well with humans and others. But their keepers train them to attack. It's like taking a nice poodle and turning it into a vicious killer. Absolutely criminal."

I ignored Angie's obvious hints that she would like something to eat. I wasn't going to touch anything in this house and didn't think Angie would either if she thought about it. Although, come to think of it, she touched, and ate, plenty of things that I wouldn't.

"Ms. Lewis, I was wondering if you'd ever met Sam Katz. He was active in the chicken rescue movement."

Mona nodded. "I understand he was murdered. A terrible loss to the organization."

"Did you know that Sam Katz was actually Sam Goodwin? An accountant accused of fraud and embezzlement."

Mona laughed. "Sam? You've got to be kidding. If the man found a ten-dollar bill on the ground he'd probably take it to the police in case someone had reported it missing."

That hadn't quite been my impression of Sam, but at least it indicated that Mona had known him.

Angie chose that moment to break into the conversation. "We suspect that Sam was killed by the same mob that organizes the chicken fights."

Mona nodded slowly, then poured herself a cup of tea.

I was glad I hadn't asked for anything when I saw what was floating on the top of her cup. Suzie had been a bad chicken.

Mona sort of fished the worst of it out with her sugar spoon and took a deep sip.

I swallowed hard and made myself complete Angie's thought. "We want to get to the bottom of this, Ms. Lewis. I mentioned the mob connection to my lawyer and he claimed he was going to research it. He ended up dead as well."

Mona put Suzie on my lap and stood. "You're quite right to come to me, honey. Wait here for a minute." I think the last sentence was aimed at the bird rather than me, but with Mona it was hard to tell.

Suzie gave me a suspicious look. For a moment I thought she was going to join the crowd and bite me too. But then she settled down into my arms and went to sleep.

"Isn't that cute?" I suggested to Angie.

"Be cuter fried," she replied.

I shushed Angie and stroked the bird's soft feathers.

I'm pretty sure that chickens don't purr, but if Suzie wasn't purring, she was doing its close cousin.

Mona took more than a minute, but when she came back, she was filled with energy and plans.

She handed over a fat file. "Here are the reports that Sam did for us." Another sheet of paper was a printout map of all of the places where Sam had undertaken direct action. Finally, she gave us a list of the CRL workers who had taken part in any of Sam's capers.

I wouldn't have guessed that the mob would bother to infiltrate the Chicken Rescue League, but Mona's energy and suspicion were both contagious. I found myself wanting to tie up Sam's fellow operatives and beat the truth out of them until I discovered which one had betrayed him. Because how could the mob have learned about Sam if not through another CRL worker?

* * * *

It took me almost two hours to go through Sam's reports. From what I could tell, he had involved himself in CRL activities almost as soon as he'd vanished from Big Cat Telecommunications. The timing had to mean something, although I had no idea what. If he had started with CRL first and they'd showed a sudden increase in wealth, I might have believed that he had embezzled all that money for a good cause. But his first meeting had taken place two weeks after the embezzlement had been discovered. Admittedly, he could have been gambling to try to recover some of the money he'd lost.

Other than that, the big surprise in Sam's reports was how many fighting cock breeders resided within five miles of my trailer park.

Mona wouldn't make copies and wouldn't let us take the file from her house so, between pushing off pet chickens, I read each page and then handed it over to Angie in case I'd missed anything.

Sam's voice came through in his notes notes so much I was choking up as I was reading. That's my only excuse for missing the obvious.

"Holy crap, Tina. Didn't you see this?" Angie jabbed her finger at the page I'd just handed her.

"What?" Even looking at it, my mind drew a blank.

"When was this?" She searched for a date and came up with one about a month before. "Someone must have recognized him during this raid. Come on, Tina. Stop sniffling about your lost boyfriend and start thinking like Nancy Drew."

I snatched the page back from her and read it over, twice. The first time through, I got a feeling. The second, it jumped out at me. "Ivan Vorobev? Isn't Vorobev Amber's maiden name?"

"Right. So Sam raids his brother-in-law's ring, somebody recognizes him, and bingo." She clicked her fingers. "The mob makes a hit."

"It could be coincidence," I argued weakly.

"Maybe. But it could be the break we've been looking for."

Mona had caught up another chicken wandering around her living room and made calming noises to it. "It's okay, Deena. The loud people are going to be leaving any minute now."

I jotted down the addresses, then Angie and I took a hint and left.

"I'm so hungry I could eat one of those chickens with the feathers still on it," Angie told me once we were back on the highway. "Let's stop."

Eating chicken didn't appeal to me. We stopped for a burger and I tried not to think about warm brown cow-eyes.

Sometimes maternal instincts can be a bitch.

* * * *

Back in Dallas we drove by the address Sam's report had listed for Vorobev's establishment.

It looked like one of a thousand run-down bars in the Fair Park region of Dallas. Beer posters featuring bikini-clad nymphs who had obviously never subjected their body to the calories of alcohol were plastered to the outside walls providing a tacky finish that barely hid the lack of paint. Not coincidentally, I thought, they would also cover what windows might have existed and prevent the curious, or legally minded, from looking in.

At eight in the evening, the bar was dead. Not even the neon Corona Beer sign was lit.

"Ever hear of this place before?" I asked Angie.

She shrugged. "Huh-uh. Looks scary."

I drove around the block and then headed down the alley, stopping outside the back of Vorobev's bar.

Once there, I shut off the engine and listened.

Twenty-four hours a day, Dallas was alive with noise. Airplanes roared overhead, destined for nearby Love Field. Traffic swished along the highways, Trucks ground through on their way to Chicago, or Houston, or one of the innumerable suburbs that strangle the city. And ubiquitous ice cream vendors in hand carts, bicycle rickshaws, and broken-down vans, sent chimes and hooting music through every neighborhood.

I was about to give up when the sound of a rooster crowing broke through the white noise of the city.

I couldn't help it, I screamed.

"I guess we're at the right place," Angie said when I'd calmed down enough to listen.

"Yeah. Whatever Sam pulled, they're back in business. So, what do you say? Want to come back later tonight?"

I was hoping Angie would remind me that we weren't likely to be welcome, that they'd already killed Sam and John, and that we weren't going to find out much hanging around a chicken fight.

Naturally she disappointed me.

"I'll bet I make a fortune," she told me.

I shook my head firmly. It was one thing to sneak out of the CRL meeting and leave me with the chicken lovers. Abandoning me with bloodthirsty chicken killers was something else. "You stay with me or we don't go," I explained.

She laughed and told me she'd been kidding, but I wasn't so sure. Angie loves money and Angie loves sex. The two together can even trump friendship.

I drove home and took a nap.

At midnight, my alarm went off and I slammed the clock, knocked over my lamp, and tripped on my shoes when I got out of bed.

I wanted to wear black jeans and sneakers so I could sneak and run. A rare bit of sanity told me that I would stand out like a virgin in a frat-house dressed like that. Instead I pulled on a short red dress and high-heeled sandals and taped up my boobs so I wouldn't have to wear a bra and I still looked like I had cleavage. Five minutes in front of the mirror and I was as much of a sexpot as was going to happen.

Angie looked wide-awake when I swung by her trailer. She wore a little blue number that zipped up the front and had a big ring on the zipper. She'd left it halfway unzipped to display her assets which, needless to say, put mine to shame.

If I'd had that much cleavage, I'd want to show it off too. Still, Angie always made me feel like getting dolled up was a complete waste of my time.

"You look good," she told me.

She was so obviously sincere that I felt like a jerk having jealous thoughts about her. "You too, Angie."

"So, are we ready to go?"

I wanted to tell her I wasn't, and didn't think I would be, ever. Instead I nodded. The longer I waited, the less ready I was going to get.

My Storm wheezed into back into action and we headed back to Vorobev's place.

If his neighborhood was dead at eight, it was hopping at one in the morning. Three huge motorcycles stood blocking the door. Pickup trucks sporting reflective naked women hanging from mudguards filled the parking lot. Wisps of smoke, some scented quite differently than tobacco, escaped from the barely open door to the bar.

"Looks like we've found a party," Angie told me.

"Yeah. Now let's see if we can find a place to park."

The lot was full and we ended up a couple of blocks away.

Most of the streetlights were out-shot our or burned out, I wasn't sure which. The streets were lit, however, by lurid neon from the neighborhood tattoo parlors, late-night coffee shops, and bars.

As we approached Vorobev's place, the throbbing beat of music shook the sidewalk. Motorcyclists chatted near the door, creating an obstacle course for our approach.

Angie and I stepped through the motorcyclists and I tried to push open the door.

"Where do you think you're going?"

I don't know how I'd missed him because he was huge. Rolls of fat cascaded down from his chin to the top of his low-hanging shorts. Across his naked chest, tattoos snaked through the flab making an abstract design that would probably thrill a modern art student.

The man hadn't bathed recently and I couldn't help taking a step back from where he blocked the doorway.

"Uh, we thought we'd have a beer." I gestured to the posters of the bikini-clad women.

"Full-up. Fire code."

Two guys stepped around us, gave Angie a once-over, and entered the bar without a question being asked.

"What about them?" I demanded.

"They were already in. Counted in the number."

"We hear this is a great place to meet people." Angie gave a little hip roll and let her zipper creep down an inch or so. If she let it go any lower, I was afraid we might have an escape-breast on our hands.

"Come on, girls. I wasn't born yesterday. Just get out of here and don't go making trouble."

He crossed his muscled arms across his massive chest. They sort of sank into the rolls of fat. Gross.

If you live in a trailer park, you learn that there are a lot of times when twenty dollars works miracles. I thought this could be one of those times and reached into my purse.

The bouncer's hand caught mine before it could come out. He might have been fat, but he was quick-and strong. His grip on my wrist felt like it might just squeeze until my bones turned into toothpaste.

"Take it out nice and easy," he warned me.

I came out with my wallet. "I thought maybe you were looking for a cover charge," I explained. My voice was quavering and I felt like my knees were knocking together. I didn't intend for some overweight bouncer to intimidate me, but I'd be lying if I said I wasn't scared. "What do you say to twenty bucks?"

"What do you say to taking a hike?"

He gave me a shove, holding on to my wrist just long enough to spin me around as I rocketed away from him. My purse flew from my numbed hands.

Money, my phone, makeup, and my pepper spray went flying everywhere.

I scrambled after them and had the pleasure of seeing the bouncer look concerned-for a fraction of a second until Angie used the diversion to dart past him.

If he'd been distracted at all, it didn't show. He caught the back of her dress with one massive paw and yanked her back.

I'd wondered what kept the zipper up. Everyone around learned the answer to that question. Not much.

Angie's zipper popped and her boobs slung out of that blue dress like bowling balls coming down the return.

"Take your hands off of me." Angie doesn't get mad often, but when she does, watch out.

The bouncer's answer was cut off by a roar from inside the club-the human voices almost overwhelming the screech of a dying bird.

"Okay, I guess you can go in now," the bouncer told us. "It's twenty bucks each. He stared at Angie's breasts for a moment, then snickered. "Let's call it a cover charge. Get it?"

"Yeah? Well cover this." Angie thrust a fist into the bouncer's Michelin Tire Man stomach.

And bounced.

He looked soft, but those layers of flab might as well have been concrete for the size of the dent Angie put into them.

The bouncer's eyes darkened. "That was a mistake, girlie." He caught her fist before she could retract it and squeezed.

From Angie's expression, she agreed that she'd made a mistake but didn't know what to do about it. Her primary weapon, sex appeal, was on full display and the bouncer didn't even seem to notice.

I scrambled for the pepper spray, but one of the motorcyclists kicked it away from me.

Uh-oh. Time to think fast. "Let her go," I demanded. "We're friends of the owner. Ivan Vorobev."

He must have loosened up a little because Angie's look of anguish faded to one of extreme discomfort. "Oh, really?"

Decision time. If I lie and he finds out, does he kill Angie? If I tell the truth, does he kill her?

"Uh, not really. But I know his sister Amber."

"I can believe that. She always did like to hang around with low-lives."

He let go of Angie's fist.

Angie yanked her hand back, shook it out a little, then stuffed her boobs into what remained of her dress.

Keeping her breasts hidden, earned Angie a chorus of boos from the circle of voyeurs we'd been collecting ever since we'd arrived. I guess it was turning out to be a major treat night at Vorobev's bar with cockfighting inside and topless cat-fighting outside. A pervert's delight.

"Just how do you know Amber?" the bouncer asked. He looked like he was trying to be friendly, but he wasn't very good at it. His black eyes were still beady and mean and his smile got as lost in fat as his arms had.

Telling him that I used to date her ex-husband-a man Vorobev might have had killed—didn't seem like a good idea.

"I sort of met her last week."

"Yeah? Where?"

Uh-oh. Amber was hiding from someone. If it was her brother and I blurted out the location, I'd have another body on my conscience. I could sort of convince myself that I wasn't responsible for Sam or John. I didn't think I'd be so lucky with Amber.

"I, uh, can't tell you that. I think she's hiding from someone."

"Someone like me, you mean." He took a deep breath.

With a guy that size, a deep breath is a big deal. Flesh flowed into wrinkles, he seemed to grow two inches, and I found myself backing away to give him room.

"I'm not going hurt my sister. If she's hiding, it isn't from me."

I gaped. Obviously I'd blown it bigger than usual even for me. He wasn't just the bouncer, he was the man I was investigating.

So what would Nancy Drew do now?

My brain was firing blanks and I looked to Angie for inspiration.

She looked miserable. She held her dress closed with one hand because Vorobev had broken her zipper, one of her heels was hanging from the shoe, and her free hand was still trying to work out the knots that Vorobev had squeezed it into.

No help there.

"Come inside. I'll buy you a drink," Vorobev invited. "A friend of my sister's is a friend to me."

Considering what had happened to Sam, I doubted that. Although maybe Vorobev thought Sam had betrayed his sister, giving him more motivation to kill.

"What do you think?" I asked Angie, wondering what would happen if we tried to run.

She shook her head just a little. She was a true friend, but she'd had a scare. Worse, Angie knew more really dangerous people than I did. She dealt with them on a nightly basis. If she thought it was too dangerous, I wasn't going to argue.

"You're coming," Vorobev said, putting a massive hand to each of our backs and propelling us into the bar. "I'll get you a safety pin for that dress."

* * * *

From the outside, Vorobev's bar was a disgusting mess. The inside was ten times worse.

Deafening music blasted from speakers, sub-woofers shaking the floors to the point I thought I might get seasick. Neon beer and whiskey ads provided most of the lighting although there was florescent lighting over the twin pool tables.

A Lucite cage about ten feet in diameter stood in the middle of the main room, dominating the entire establishment. Other than a layer of sand a couple of inches deep at the bottom, the cage was empty.

"We have mud wrestling here sometimes," Vorobev explained. He didn't try to be convincing and I wasn't convinced. We'd found a cock-fighting ring, but Vorobev had kept us outside until the fight was over so we couldn't prove anything.

What the man didn't know, though, was that we hadn't come to shut down his cockfighting operation-although I would have loved to do that. We were there to investigate murder. And Vorobev looked more suspicious every moment.

Vorobev pulled a couple of longnecks from his cooler, popped the caps, and pushed them across the bar. "On the house," he reminded us.

I thought about turning him down flat, but all of a sudden, I needed a beer.

I noticed that my hand was shaking when I grabbed the bottle. Well, I wasn't going to beat myself up about that, I was scared. I must have held the beer's neck in a death-choke as I brought it to my lips chugged about a third of it down.

I set the bottle on the bar and looked at Vobobev before I could stop and think.

"Wanna tell me what you're really doing here?" he demanded after giving me a chance to take a deep breath.

"Looking for a good time?" It was a feeble answer and we both knew it.

He shook his head. "I don't think so. You could scare up a good time in a lot safer neighborhoods than this."

"Slumming?" Angie suggested

Vorobev laughed. "I said you were pretty, not classy. If you were an SMU sorority type, I might buy the slumming thing."

This was getting a little personal. "Like you should talk. I mean, look at you."

He leaned closer. I caught a massive wave of unwashed body scent and almost gagged.

"I'm going to give you a little warning, Tina Anderson," he breathed. "Don't go messing with things you don't understand. Nobody wants to hurt you, but if you aren't careful, you're going to get hurt. You hear what I'm saying?"

When he used my name, my blood felt like it had run through an air conditioner. Until then, I'd felt safely anonymous. But if he knew who we were, running away wouldn't provide us any safety at all.

Angie knew that as well as I did, but panic doesn't heed logic.

"Let's get out of here." Angie grabbed my arm and tugged.

I was afraid that Vorobev wouldn't let us go but he laughed again as we skittered out of his bar like two cockroaches caught in the light.

"That wasn't one of our better investigations," Angie admitted as we both yanked off our shoes and sprinted the couple of blocks to my car. "I think Nancy Drew would have acted smarter than we did."

"No shit," I agreed.

"How do you figure he knew your name?"

I'd been asking myself the same question. The most likely answer I could come up with was John Halprin.

Vorobev had to be the killer.

* * * *

It was three in the morning when we got back to the trailer park, but when we got there I realized that if Vorobev knew my name, he knew my address too.

"Want to stay with me?" Angie asked.

"If he knows who I am, he'll be able to figure out who you are," I reminded her.

"Yeah? At least it would be two to one."

I didn't think that the two of us would stand a chance against him. Heck, even if we both got to take whacks at him with a baseball bat first, I figured he could still take us. Besides, Vorobev looked like he had plenty of friends who wouldn't think twice about casual violence.

"I'm going to call Andy," I told her. "Maybe we can stay with him."

"You think that's smart with the police thinking he's the killer? It'll make it look like killing your boyfriends brought you back to him."

She was right but I was desperate. Vorobev had hit me where I lived and I was running, like always, to the Andy. "Like we've done anything smart so far?"

"Good point."

Andy didn't seem especially happy to hear from me at three in the morning. When I told him what we'd done, he sounded even less happy.

"Get your butt over here where I can watch you," he ordered.

That was what I wanted anyway, but his attitude bothered me. "We can take care of ourselves."

Angie shook her head desperately. No way we could take care of ourselves with Vorobev after us.

Fortunately, Andy didn't see Angie's anguish and didn't know how strong his bargaining position was. "Sorry, Tina. You know I worry about you."

"Yeah, and I worry about you too. That's why I'm investigating. I don't want the police to decide to go after the rich guy because he's convenient and everybody loves the idea of the rich guy taking the fall."

Being poor made me painfully aware of how much enjoyment could be gained watching the rich and famous get into trouble. I didn't mind so much when it happened to complete strangers. I'd mind even less if it happened to some of the rich jerks I'd known back when I'd been married to Andy. But I didn't want it to happen to any of my friends. And Andy, ex-husband or not, was still more than a friend.

Andy changed his tack. "I'd feel a lot better if you were here," he told me.

"Is your mother still there?"

"Uh-huh. She's having her place remodeled. Again."

I almost told him no. But Angie's distressed expression persuaded me to swallow my pride. "All right. We'll come for tonight. No promises on what happens next."

"Fair enough," he said. "I'll be looking for you."

So we ended up spending the night in Andy's Strait Lane mansion.

Chapter 9

I slept in late the next morning, my adrenaline stocks being completely exhausted. It was closer to lunchtime than breakfast when I finally headed downstairs to Andy's kitchen, my body craving caffeine and fat grams.

By sleeping late, I'd managed to miss Karen Anderson, Andy's mother and my biggest anti-fan. Karen always has a fad and this year it was Tai Chi. From what I'd read in Cosmo, Tai Chi is supposed to open your charkas or something like that. It looks to me more like women trying to be grasshoppers but the good news was, it got her out of the house.

I managed to snag a couple of Danish that had been intended for an in-home business meeting that Andy was holding and an oversized Anderson Software mug full of some of the best coffee I'd ever tasted.

Life was good.

When the kitchen door opened, I thought that Angie might emerge. Instead, Andy and Kevin Franklin came in for refills on coffee.

Andy must have told Franklin about the tough time I'd been having lately because he came right over and looked me in the eye. "You've got to be careful, Tina. There are some bad people out there."

"Tell me about it." My run-in with Vorobev had made me more conscious of this than ever.

"I hear you've found a connection between Sam Goodwin and the mob. That sounds like good news from an investigative sense but bad news personally," he said. "I told Andy that he should hire you a bodyguard if you're going to keep on working this."

Just what I needed, I thought. Some muscle-bound jerk to follow me around and get in the way. Although I wouldn't have complained if one had just happened to be at Vorobev's bar the previous evening. Especially if he happened to be one of the hunky types of muscle-bound jerks.

"I'll manage."

I think Kevin had to resist the urge to pat me on the shoulder like I was a cocker spaniel or something. "I'm sure you will," he lied. "But the mob connection explains a lot about what's been going on."

Franklin's words gave me a jolt like my first hit of coffee. "Explains what?"

"What happened to the missing money. You know Goodwin managed to steal hundreds of millions of dollars. So where'd it go? His entire estate seems to consist of a trailer, some worthless stock in my company, and a few hundred thousand in the bank. Peanuts."

I wouldn't have called hundreds of thousands of dollars in ready cash peanuts, but I also wasn't a high-tech multimillionaire like Franklin or Andy.

"So you think-"

"Based on what you've found so far, I think the evidence is starting to point at the likelihood that he wasn't embezzling for personal gain. The whole thing could have been a mob scam. Maybe Sam got tried to get cute and keep some of the money himself, or maybe they cut him short on what they promised him." He sat down next to me and took a deep drink from his coffee mug. "He's probably a mob connection that Big Cat's employee screening didn't pick up."

"Something like his wife being the sister of a Russian mobster?"

Kevin opened his eyes wider. "Is that what it is? Andy didn't mention that angle. I knew Amber was Russian, but I just assumed that meant she was one of those, you know, mail order brides. It isn't as if Sam had much in the way of social skills." He started to take another sip of his coffee and stopped suddenly when he realized what he'd said. "I mean, no offense, Tina. I'm sure you saw something in him that most other women, uh. . ."

I let him trail off. There wasn't any way he could work himself out of that mess and I didn't especially feel like rescuing him.

"Kevin was just going," the ever over-protective Andy interjected. "I'll see you around, Kevin."

"Squash tomorrow?" Kevin asked.

"Got a meeting with Pelcovitz. Until I learn how long that'll take, I won't know my own schedule."

For Andy, not knowing his schedule would be like me not knowing what was in my refrigerator. The idea had to be unusual and frightening. Then again, being a suspect in a murder investigation was unusual and frightening. So the meeting with his lawyer was probably the best idea going.

"I'll see you around, Tina," Franklin offered as he took the hint and headed toward the kitchen door. "I can find my way out, Andy."

Andy waited until Franklin closed the front door behind him and then sat down next to me at the kitchen table.

"Sorry you had to hear that. Franklin is pretty much the pot calling the kettle black when it comes to discussing social skills."

"I guess. But I'm not offended," I told him honestly. "I liked it that Sam was a good and loving father and that he. . ." this time I was the one who trailed off. Andy and I might be over, but I wasn't about to go into a blow-by-blow of my love life.

"Want to tell me some more about Vorobev?" Andy asked when he'd picked up that I was finished with that part of the conversation. "I gather that Sam's brother-in-law is mob-connected."

I nodded. "Looks that way. I got a chance to look at Sam's reports for the Chicken Rescue League and he was pretty convinced that the mob controls most of what's going on in Texas cockfighting. He laid out a lot of the connections and believe me, they're scary. From what Angie and I saw last night, we know that Vorobev's bar is a cockfighting venue. Plus it was one of the places that Sam investigated for CRL-shortly before he was killed."

"So you think his own brother-in-law might have killed him?" For Andy, family was sacred.

"If you met him, you wouldn't be as surprised," I said. "Vorobev is the kind of guy Steven King would write a novel about."

"No kidding," Angie broke in. I hadn't noticed her walking in, but she plopped down at the table next to us and grabbed a peach from the fruit basket. "Vorobev is major-league scary."

We'd been too tired to give him the entire scoop the previous night, so we gave him the rest while we ate.

"You guys have got to pull back," Andy said. "We had an agreement that Pelcovitz investigate the mob angle but you've been running all over the country stirring up trouble.

"Tina already found the ex-wife," Angie reminded him. "That was her part."

"Once Halprin got killed, all the rules changed," I added.

"Leave the dangerous stuff to Pelcovitz," Andy rubbed his hands into his face. "Please."

He stood up and headed for the door. "I'll station some rent-a-cops at the trailer park, but I'd still like you two to stay here for the next week or two. There've already been two murders. I wouldn't want to have you on my conscience too."

With that ambiguous statement, he vanished out his front door.

"Those Danish any good?" Angie asked.

"The blueberry-cheese ones are the best." I hoped she didn't make me admit that I'd sampled one of each before deciding which were my favorite.

She looked over the tray. "Any of those left?"

I checked, my cheeks getting more and more heated as I looked down to the second layer. "Uh, no. I must have gotten the last one. The chocolate chip ones are pretty excellent too, though."

She took one of those and savored a bite. "You ever notice something?"

"What?"

"I don't turn Andy on. I wonder how come?"

I was used to her so I hadn't really noticed, but the oversized t-shirt Angie wore as a nightshirt barely covered her butt-and left nothing to the imagination where here chest was concerned.

"He's probably just faking it," I told her.

She shook her head. "Don't think so. I think he's the kind of guy that just prefers slender brunettes to curvy blondes."

I put down the last bite of the raspberry Danish I'd been eating. If I stayed at Andy's house for two weeks, slender would become a distant memory. "Anyway, what are we going to do about Vorobev?"

"What can we do? We'd have to rent a tank to find something bigger and stronger than him."

"I think we need to get the CRL action committee into the plan." I knew Andy was right and that I should back off, but I have a hard time running away from people who threaten me. "Unless I missed my reading, CRL never got around to raiding the place. Sam was killed too close to when he'd investigated it."

"Don't be crazy. If anything happens, Vorobev will know we were behind it," Angie insisted. "He knows your name, Tina. If we'd stayed home last night, the police would probably be finding us about now. And they'd probably just write it down to another couple of low class chicks getting themselves killed by partying with the wrong lowlife." She paused just a beat. "I don't want to go that way."

Angie doesn't get scared much. Usually she is the one who pushes me into crazy things while I'm holding back. This had to mean I'd really whacked out this time.

I felt terrible for dragging Angie into this mess. Sam hadn't been her problem. John hadn't been her problem. And Andy wasn't her problem. She'd never even have met Vorobev if it hadn't been for me. What was worse, I hadn't really thought about the risks when I'd dragged her in. I'd just thought about myself and needing some company.

"Oh, Angie, I really got us into a mess this time, didn't I."

Her eyes glistened for a second, but she swiped them with a napkin. "Hell, girl, we'll get through, somehow."

I was used to Angie being the brave one and felt lost without her pushing me on. Not that I planned to end up like Sam or John Halprin. But we were already in too deep. Even if we backed off now, I didn't think that Vorobev or his bosses would just let us walk away.

I told Angie that. I could tell she wanted to disagree. Hell, I wanted her to disagree and tell me how I was wrong. But she finally nodded. "I see that. But what good would it do to annoy Vorobev even more?"

Now that was a good question. I had gotten myself so caught up in fight-or-flight that I hadn't even figured out what I could be fighting for. Or how I could possibly win.

"Maybe we can find something out. If we can connect him to Sam's murder, the police will keep him too busy to come after us."

Angie wasn't impressed. "That's your plan? We're going to poke a stick in the fire-ant hill just in case there might be a goldmine underneath? Nancy Drew would never do that."

"Do you have any better ideas?" Please. Please.

"I'm not sure how to find a worse one."

"Suppose we just meet with the action committee guys. Maybe they'll have some ideas. Worst thing that can happen is you'll make a few bucks."

Angie brightened at the thought of sex and money. Still, her answer didn't fill me with confidence. "I didn't think you could come up with a worse idea, but asking those guys for advice just might be it. I'd be surprised if those losers couldn't figure something even dumber than raiding Vorobev."

* * * *

"Are you crazy? They'll kill us." Tom's face turned an attractive shade of lavender.

James and Tom had agreed to meet us at the Cosmic Tea Cup on Lemmon Avenue. Fancy tea and yoga are a little out of my usual circles, but James and Tom seemed to fit right in. Until I told them that Vorobev was mob-connected and that we wanted to do a chicken rescue raid on his bar. Then they looked like they wished Vorobev had finished the job so they wouldn't have to deal with us.

"Every night we do nothing, more chickens will die," I reminded them.

"I only got involved in the whole Chicken Rescue program to meet women," Tom told me. "Once I came to a meeting, Sam told me that the really hot chicks go for the action committee guys. That's why I'm here. I didn't do it because I want to get killed."

"You have any complaints about the woman you met?" Angie demanded, her back up.

Tom looked at the faded Oriental rug. "No complaints. Except, Sam never said anything about having to pay for it."

"I supposed you'd rather take a girl out on at least three dates, spend a bunch of money wining and dining her, and waste hours on end pretending to be interested in her cats. And then she decides maybe she just likes you as a friend."

Tom looked like he'd had a major revelation. "Hey, dating is like that isn't it? I mean, you just want to get lucky and you have to go through all of this-"

"We don't need to hear it," I told him. I happened to like men at least pretending that they wanted me for something besides pure sex.

"Right," Tom said. But he sort of chuckled, as if we were sharing a big joke.

Time to change the subject. "Since they killed Sam, we've got to figure that they're on to CRL," I reminded them. "If we just wait, one of us may be next." It wasn't a lie, exactly. But it did exaggerate the truth.

James had remained silent until then. Now he shook his head slowly. "What you're asking isn't realistic," he told me. "With Sam dead, there are only two of us left in the Action Committee. You already told us that Vorobev recognized you so he's got to have some inside information. If we raided him, we'd just be giving him an excuse to come after us. Besides, he knows you're interested. They'll certainly be guarding the bar or setting booby-traps of some kind. There's no chance in the world that we can get in and accomplish anything."

He turned to Tom, his tone angry. "And if you don't care about cruelty to animals, maybe you should find another organization to belong to."

Tom nodded slowly, looking at Angie out of the corner of his eye. "Guess you're right. You can just call me gone." He stood and walked out before any of us had a chance to argue with him.

James shrugged in my direction. "That didn't work. I was trying to buck him up, not make him run."

"We're wide open to suggestions," Angie told him. She lowered her voice a little and introduced the slightest tremble. "Tina and I are scared."

"It sounds like you were real brave when you confronted Vorobev," he said, patting her on the hand. When Angie decides to play for a man's sympathies, he's pretty much a goner.

"Huh-un," Angie told him. "We were scared silly. Look at this." She held out her arm on which bruises matching Vorobev's fat fingers lingered.

James stroked her arm. I could tell he wished I would just disappear so he could have magic moments with Angie. I would have obliged him, but we needed to do something and that wasn't it.

"We could, you know, escalate this to national CRL headquarters,"

James suggested, finally letting go of Angie's bruised appendage.

I told James that bringing in the bureaucrats never seemed to help much to me and got a scowl in response. "They keep a database of all the cockfighting venues we find. And who owns them."

"We already know who owns this one."

James gave me a look that said he really wanted to stop talking and start making time with Angie, but he was a gentleman and didn't blow me off. "It's the only suggestion I have. And get real, here. I'm thinking that Tom was right about how stupid it would be to break in on a guarded mob hangout. It isn't as if Vorobov didn't warn you."

"Why don't you check out that CRL database and let James and me discuss next steps?" Angie stood and tugged James out of his seat. "And don't go anywhere until I get back."

"I don't think this is a good idea," I said.

Naturally, they didn't listen.

* * * *

While Angie and James were off doing the nasty, I dug out my cell and started making calls.

National CRL headquarters started off by denying ever having heard of an action committee, let alone supporting illegal activities.

But once I persuaded them that I was for real, they did admit to having a database of known and suspected cockfighting venues. "Strictly for informational purposes," the Assistant Vice President I'd gotten bumped up to assured me. "We don't condone illegal behavior, even against scum like cockfighters."

As a compromise between ancient yoga and modern reality, the Cosmic Tea Cup Café had installed some computers with high-speed Internet connections. I was able to log onto CRL site, follow the hidden links the officious V.P. pointed me to, and get quick responses to my searches.

The CRL database was stunning. In North Texas alone, it listed hundreds of suspected and confirmed breeding and fighting locations. Most of the sites were accompanied by photos that looked like they'd been taken by low-quality spy cameras, or carefully palmed cell-phone cameras. I thought about the risk that those photographers would have been taking. Anyone caught taking pictures of illegal cockfighting would be lucky to have their camera broken and their nose bloodied.

With the number of sites listed it was no wonder the Dallas branch of CRL had been able to keep its action committee busy. They could raid a different breeder every night and never have to drive more than twenty miles.

With this many chickens being bred for fighting, it was amazing that there weren't mass escapes and traffic blockages the way it happens when cattle trucks break down and the cows escape—a frequent occurrence in Texas.

By the time Angie and James got back, looking a little frazzled and with big smiles on their faces, I had a list of locations and an idea.

"I've got it," I told them. "We stay away from Vorobov's, at least at first. Suppose we pull an all night-raid? Hit a dozen of these places-maybe even more."

James looked willing. After the good time Angie had just shared with him, he'd probably have looked willing if I'd told him we were going to jump off the Southwestern Bell building.

Angie, on the other hand, might be happy but she hadn't lost her sense.

"Once we raided the first couple, they would know something was up. They'd have plenty of time to send warnings to each other," she reminded me. "They'd catch us for sure. And even if they didn't, what possible good could it do? I mean, it isn't like chickens are scarce. They'd just buy some more. Besides, this isn't really getting at Sam's murder, is it."

"I think it's a good idea," James said, coming to my defense. "We could release hundreds of birds and make a real dent in the problem. Most of what the Action Committee has done up until now has been too small of a scale. We disrupt one night's entertainment, but like Angie said, there are always more roosters. If we targeted the entire supply chain, it might take weeks for them to recover. It's a natural step up Sam's economic model. He would have loved us."

"But how would it help track down the killer?" Angie demanded. "And that's what we've got to do if we want to get Tina out of trouble."

"Uh, that's important, of course," admitted James. "But it's really about rescuing the chickens, isn't it?"

James was a sweetheart. I was a selfish bitch and I knew it. I'd spent my time thinking about how I might cause problems for the mob. James, on the other hand, was still focused on purely altruistic goals. Saving the poor little chickens before they got the chance to slice each other to bits.

"The chicken raid is only part of it," I admitted to James. "We've got to find a way to push the mob's hand. Make them react and maybe make mistakes."

He wrinkled his forehead. "Won't work. First, they'll come after you. Second, Angie is right—raiding a bunch of breeders isn't going to help catch a killer. If the mob is involved, they aren't going to have hidden

106

murder evidence in their chicken cages."

I knew they were right, but doing nothing couldn't be the answer. We needed to go out and stir things up, make them react. "Okay, here's a question for you. Why did they kill Sam?"

James grabbed that one. "Because they found out he was messing with the cockfighting business. They never went against CRL's more traditional moves."

"Probably because CRL is practically advertising for them," Angie suggested. "Any publicity is good publicity."

"Maybe," I said. "But killing someone is risky. Until I saw that database, I had no idea there was so much cockfighting here in Dallas. Setting a few chickens free wouldn't really put that big a dent in the system."

"Which is probably why Sam never considered anything crazy like a mass release," Angie said. "He realized they'd have to react to a crazy stunt like that."

"Maybe. But they reacted anyway." I knew I was leaping to a conclusion but I did it anyway. "They must have thought he knew something dangerous. They killed him and then they searched his trailer looking for it. That's why they left such a mess."

"Like what?" James was interested even if Angie was shaking her head.

I thought fast. What could the mob be afraid of? What would make them want to kill somebody like Sam? "It couldn't just be that he knew about Vorobev's involvement. They wouldn't have needed to search his place if that had been all."

"So we know what it wasn't," Angie said. "But what was it?"

Okay, I meant to think fast. I could feel the gears spinning but nothing was coming out.

"Maybe we could let them tell us," James suggested.

That sounded encouraging, if unlikely. "You have an idea?"

"Just your idea. Suppose we did your raid, but even bigger? Suppose we really mobilized and rescued every fighting chicken in Dallas? And then we announced that we used some of Sam's materials to help us identify targets. They'd guess we had the rest." He swallowed hard. "Uh, then they'd come and kill us. Forget I said anything. Why would we want to piss off a bunch of guys who've already killed twice?"

"It's brilliant," I said. Brilliant might have been an overstatement, but it was a plan. Which was more than I'd had.

James glanced at my laptop. "Are all of those really cock-breeding locations?"

"And fight venues."

"Incredible. Even I didn't know it was that big a problem and I've been involved with CRL for a couple of years. We even got a spot on National Public Radio. But who listens?"

"It's how you send your message." I'd learned that lesson when I'd posted my first program on the Internet. I'd spent months building a Doom-style first-person shooter which I still thought was one of the best games out there. In the first week I had it posted, I'd gotten exactly zero downloads. You've got to get the message out to the world-whether you're dealing with software or rescuing chickens. And the chicken message would be an easy one to deliver.

"Maximum impact," I continued. "We'll release all the chickens in Dealey Plaza first thing in the morning. Traffic will be backed up, all the bankers and commuters will see it."

"Oh, yeah. KERA will pick that up for sure," James said, getting with the program. "They're on Harry Hines, only a few blocks away."

"KERA?" Angie ready to send the men in white coats after them.

"You know, public television for North Texas," James reminded her.

"Everybody who watches public television is probably already at the CRL meetings," Angie told him. "You're going to have to reach beyond that. Like maybe Fox."

Angie had a point, but she was missing the big picture. Hundreds, thousands of liberated chickens running through Dealey Plaza was going to attract a lot of attention. This was the kind of weird news that Fox would eat with a spoon. KERA would focus on the issues of cockfighting in the community. Fox would hit the emotional chords with chicken suffering.

"We'll just have to make sure a CRL spokesman explains that this was all possible thanks to Sam's work, which I'd found after his death." This was really coming together.

"Then they kill us to and we've proved what?" Angie was still being difficult.

"Andy's lawyer will arrange a bunch of bodyguards," I said. "When the mob comes after us, we'll capture the killers and find out what they were looking for."

Angie buried her face in her hands. "I knew we could come up with a dumber plan than just raiding Vorobov's place, but I didn't think either of us could come up with one this bad. This is the single dumbest idea you've ever had."

If she was right, I had a doozy on my hands. Because I've had some truly stupid ideas in the past. Unfortunately, I'd also acted on most of the worst.

"We've got to do something," I argued. I knew it was weak, but this was the only idea I'd come up with. Other than raiding Vorobev's bar directly. And that was sure suicide.

"Even if your plan worked and Pelcovitz's guys caught whoever came gunning for us, all we could prove was that they were pissed because we'd freed all those chickens," Angie said. "How could we prove a link to Sam's murder?"

I'd been so caught up in the mental picture of thousands of chickens roaming around Dealey Plaza that I had forgotten basic logic.

"You guys are just into negative thinking," James said. As soon as he'd got the idea of being on television, he'd been sold. "A mass raid is a good plan and we're going to do it. We've got to do what we can to catch Sam's killer, even if it's a long shot. Besides, this is the first idea I've heard that can actually put a real crimp in this evil industry."

His voice started rolling when he got going and he went on like that for a while, making short punching gestures with his hand and occasionally rolling his eyes toward the Cosmic Tea Cup Café's painted ceiling.

"You aren't a preacher in real life are you?" I asked when he finally slowed to regroup.

He looked properly abashed. "Uh, well. Yeah."

"How do you fit your business with Angie into that?" I hadn't gone to church much since my father had walked out on my mother had found salvation through alcohol rather than religion, but that didn't mean I wasn't interested.

"I admit I'm not perfect," James told me. "And I feel pretty bad about involving Angie in a relationship that certainly smacks of exploitative and patriarchal values. On the other hand, she seems to enjoy it and I certainly do." He trailed off. "I can be a bit hypocritical at times, I guess."

"I'm an entrepreneur," Angie told him.

"With the patriarchal society we-"

"Sorry I asked."

He had the grace to look Angie in the eye. "Sorry. And I would like to take you out, if you'd like to go."

"A date?" she demanded.

"Only if you wanted to."

"I'll think about it."

I almost dropped my teeth. Not dating was a point of pride for Angie. No free samples had been her motto since high school. This was so cool.

"Anyway, we've got to do this thing," James effused. "I can get action committee members from all over Texas and Oklahoma so it won't just be us running around in the pickup. Even the members who don't normally involve themselves in action committee activities would be willing to come down and set the chickens free, all at the same time. It will be great."

"But-" Angie might as well have held her breath. James was on a roll.

"We'll be helping the chickens, of course, but the human victims are even more important. Cockfighting is plain evil. Men who should be spending their money on their families are wasting it drinking and gambling. You have no idea how many fights start at the cockfights-with stabbings and robbery and even murder the result. If we can shut it down, we'll be doing something good and important."

It sounded a little like the arguments for prohibition or the war on drugs, but I didn't feel like arguing the point. Besides, I'd seen enough at the CRL meeting to know that chicken fighting is about as disgusting as a so-called sport can get. "Tell you what, James. If we can get twenty other CRL members to help out, I'm with you. I've got the list of locations. We can make it happen."

"What about you?" he asked Angie.

"I'm going to find Tom. It turns out that he was the only one of us who had any sense in the first place."

James's face turned a bit purple, but he nodded abruptly. "I understand that this isn't really your issue, Angie."

She shook her head. "No it isn't. I think people should be left alone to make their own mistakes. And I also think that people shouldn't go out of their way to get themselves hurt. There are enough ways to get killed without searching out new ones."

I was surprised when she actually walked out-since I had driven. But Angie is her own person.

"I think she likes me," James told me once Angie had slammed the Cosmic Tea Cup Café door behind her.

I wasn't sure door-slamming counted as flirtatious behavior.

"We need at least twenty volunteers," I reminded him.

"Help me with the plan," he urged me. "I'm good at talking, but I'm not so good at, you know, the details."

If there's one thing a programmer has to be, it's a detail person. I spent the next half-hour outlining a plan of attack. Using Mapquest, a spreadsheet, a free web-based project management program and the CRL database, I mapped out a plan of attack. Each of the ten two-man teams would make four hits. We'd also need a group of about five teams with rental trucks to collect the birds since the action teams' pickups wouldn't be large enough to hold all the chickens we rescued. Depending on timing, it looked like we could pull the entire thing off in two hours. Say between two and four in the morning, giving us time to have the birds at Dealey Plaza by daybreak.

"You're incredible," James told me when I handed him the PERT diagrams scheduling each team's hits. "I never could have done this."

Considering what was going to happen when the mob figured out that one Tina Anderson was behind the great chicken raid, James's words didn't comfort me much. They just meant that I was digging my grave. Still, we'd be doing something, stirring up something. And when the mob came looking for whatever Sam had left behind, we'd at least have proof that they were involved with him, that Sam's death was nothing to do with me or Andy. I wanted to find Sam's killers and make them pay but I'd settle for reasonable doubt about me and Andy.

After James drove off, I discovered that Angie had stolen my car. It took me two hours, three bus transfers, and a mile walk to get back to Andy's house. All that time, I worried about my car. Angie had lost her driver's license when she was eighteen and hadn't driven since.

* * * *

Angie and I, and my Storm, with only one more small dent, spent the next week living with Andy, eating fancy pastries and drinking wine that cost more a bottle than we paid in rent every month. Angie hadn't changed her mind about helping James and me with the plan, but at least she hadn't told Andy what we were doing.

Which was just as well because Andy had plenty to worry about.

If I'd known how the police would react when I moved into his house, I would have found somewhere else to live. I'd known they'd think my moving in was more evidence that Andy had killed my boyfriends to keep me for himself, but I didn't imagine they would take it so seriously. I must have had twenty heart-to-hearts with different police detectives.

Detective Dikens showed up with Anna Standoff, a police counselor who, Dikens claimed, could teach me about abusive relationships and how to recover from them.

I had grown up watching my parents fight so I figured I knew more about surviving abusive relationships than Standoff ever dreamed of. I quickly learned that Standoff didn't want to hear about reality. Anything I said that didn't fit into her neat categories was put down as denial.

The cops must have thought that I could tell them something, give them the evidence they needed to go from motive to conviction against Andy. Their theory seemed to be that they would eventually wear me down, get me to open up through repetitive questioning. The only problem was, whenever I talked about the mob and chicken-fighting, they just rolled their eyes. They weren't interested in going there.

The cops kept me so busy I didn't know how to react when James called and said he had his twenty volunteers-plus another ten to man the collection trucks and another thirty to stage the mass release. Because over-success was a problem. Sixty people couldn't keep a secret if their lives depended on it.

Unfortunately, it was my life depending on it, not just theirs. Which made it even less likely that we could move before the mob heard about our plans.

We needed organization-and the police were keeping me too busy to think.

When all else failed, I went to my best friend.

"I've already told you I don't want to have anything to do with it," she insisted.

"There'll be lots of men."

She shook her head. "You've used that line one time too many. What there'll be is lots of chickens. Can you believe James was a preacher?"

"You've done ministers before, Angie." She used to brag to me about some of the big-name holy-rollers who'd paid her for a little sin. The list read like a TV Guide ad for the Church Channel.

"I thought James liked me." She was sulking. "He hasn't called."

"Of course he likes you. But he's a true believer about these chickens and making a difference. He thinks he can help people this way. There's more to him than just his hormones."

"I suppose you think that's good."

I shrugged. "Good if you want a nice guy. But it's a problem for us. Because he's already told at least seventy people about the plan. If nobody stops him, he'll probably put out a press release in the Morning News before we rescue a single bird. And the police have got me so caught up in interviews that I can't head him off and I can't really help him. I need your organizational skill, Angie."

"Are you sure James likes me?"

I told her I was sure.

"And you You really need my help?"

"Oh, yeah."

"I guess I'll have to pitch in, then. What's the plan?"

She perked up when I told her that James had the only printout of the plan that I'd created. At least I hoped he did. My idea was to use cell-phones to give everyone their assignments in real-time when they needed them. That way if anyone got stopped, they wouldn't be able to give away the plan and we could route around the holes. For all I knew, though James had posted the plans on the bulletin board at the CRL meeting.

The man meant well.

Chapter 10

When Angie learned what a mess James had made of the plan, she accelerated the schedule, letting the volunteers believe they were coming to a training session rather than the real raid. So, less than two weeks after I'd had the brainstorm, I found myself in a rented cargo van with Tom.

It was the middle of the night, and we were deep in enemy territory.

"I still think this is a crazy idea," he told me.

"Yeah? Well, why are you here then?"

"Because James said he would kick my ass if I didn't participate."

"You're afraid of a preacher?" I downshifted and turned onto an alley behind a run-down strip mall. From the outside, the mall looked like it was all boarded up, just waiting for the wrecker's ball. According to the database, it had been converted into a holding center for birds on their way to or from the region. Striking here could make the Dallas cockfighters very unpopular with their colleagues in other parts of the country. Which could mean they'd have a harder time getting birds, selling birds, or arranging an audience. All of those were good news for us CRL folks.

"I'm not afraid of anybody," Tom insisted. It was a lie, obviously. But I decided not to call him on it. I wanted him to do the heavy lifting. After Hector had bitten me, I was prepared to be cautious.

Although the front of the strip mall had been all graying plywood, the back was steel bars and hefty padlocks.

Fortunately, I'd learned a lot in our first raid out in Greenville. I wore gloves and had swiped a huge bolt cutter from Andy's oversized tool shed.

The cutter slipped off the lock a couple of times, so I simply cut through the steel latch it held shut.

"Go for it," I told Tom.

"But-"

"You carry them out and I stack them. We discussed this already, Tom."

I think Angie stuck me with Tom to get me back for entangling her with the plan. One thing I knew for certain. If everyone else out there was as incompetent and indecisive as Tom was, we weren't going to rescue many chickens tonight.

"If they have a silent alarm, we're going to have company," I reminded Tom when he meandered back with a single crated chicken.

That got him running.

We loaded up the back of the rental van and took off.

Sure enough, a couple of muscle cars with dark-tinted windows passed us within blocks of the strip mall. I couldn't guarantee that they were responding to an alarm, but I wouldn't have been surprised.

"Team H, reporting," I said into my cell. "Target H-A clear. Possible intercept warning, however."

"How full are you?" Angie asked.

"Stuffed to the gills. Any more and H-2 is going to have rooster on his lap."

"How come you get to be H-1 and I'm H-2?" Tom demanded.

"I'm busy," I told him.

"I've got a mother-ship at Ledbetter and Twelfth. Head there for discharge." No question, Angie had gone into full spy mode. Forget about Nancy Drew. Angie was Mata Hari.

"Roger," I told her, getting into the spy stuff despite the fact that I was just talking on my cellphone. "We'll drop and go. Please designate target H-B."

And so it went.

Despite Tom's continued carping, we made seven raids that night. The next best team only made five. It was a dubious record, but I was proud of it and proud of Tom.

"You know that is hundreds of chickens we found and liberated before they could be used for foul purposes," I told Tom as we headed for our last drop-off.

He looked at me like I'd gone crazy. I guess four in the morning was a little too early for bad puns. In fact, my mother generally told me it was always too early for bad puns.

Two of the locations came up empty. One looked like it hadn't seen a chicken in a year-a simple example of a database that needed more regular updates. The last location, though, looked as if it had been cleaned out only minutes before we'd gotten there. That scared me. We skedaddled out of there like a house afire and I called in a warning.

We'd taken too many risks as it was. Now that the mobsters had been warned, there was too high a risk of walking in on armed and awake bad guys. I told Angie to abort everything. We'd done enough.

After the last drop-off, I swung by Andy's house, hosed out the rental van, and then got into the Storm and headed downtown.

* * * *

At six-thirty in the morning, the C.R.L. volunteers released twelve thousand chickens.

It was a thing of beauty.

Big fluffy white chickens, pretty golden-red chickens, and Darth Vader-looking black chickens wandered around the Dealey Plaza park, chased off the curious squirrels that had been sniffing around the mounds of seed the volunteers had laid down for the released birds, and generated enough crowing to register on the Richter scale.

Two of the roosters got into a fight but separated after yanking out a few of each other's few feathers. Abundant space, plenty of food, and more females that you could shake a stick at eliminated any reason for testosterone illogic that morning. Amongst the chickens, anyway.

Right off, most of the chickens got down to serious eating business. Only a few of them started right off exploring beyond the famous J. F. Kennedy assassination site. I still swear I don't know how a pair of roosters got into the museum on the 6th floor of the old school book depository.

Three minutes later, the volunteers released the second batch of five thousand chickens, then, mostly headed for home. They had children to get ready for school, jobs to go to, or simply wanted to keep their names out of the newspapers.

By then, the first batch of chickens had eaten. The hungry second flock pressed them away from the food and the first bunch spread out through downtown Dallas.

I sat in my car and giggled. This was going to be even better than I'd imagined.

Angie was still on her phone offering directions to those suburbanites who had gotten lost in the to-them mysterious streets of Dallas and in one case, I later learned, arranging bail for a pair who had mistaken a bank for a chicken holding area and been caught trying to break in.

A few C.R.L. hard-cores and media-hounds hung around to get whatever publicity or glory they could manage.

I thought better of joining them and continued driving circles around Dealey Plaza.

I was on Elm Street near the corner of Houston when it happened. A chicken hopped in front of me and then stopped to investigate something in the street.

Naturally I jammed on the breaks. Even if it hadn't been part of the plan, I wasn't going to run over a cute white bundle of feathers.

Behind me, a few cars honked, but enough people could see the chickens wandering around that no one went crazy. Besides, it wasn't as if we'd pulled this stunt in the evening when people were trying to get home. When you think about it, who was really in a hurry to get to work in the morning?

Three minutes later, with the help of a bunch of curious chickens and a few more C.R.L. plants in the streets near Dealey Plaza, we had a complete traffic snarl-up.

Drivers started laying into their horns, which startled the chickens, made cars in adjacent streets slow down, and gave the whole thing a more festive air, sort of like we were having a party. What it didn't do was make anybody move. We had gridlock.

Traffic helicopters arrived a minute or two before the police helicopters did.

The roar of helicopter turbine engines and the hard wind from helicopter rotors did a wonderful job scaring the chickens into spreading further, slowing commuter traffic on streets the chickens hadn't gotten to yet, and generally making a mess of the situation.

A few bicycle-mounted cops weaved in through the traffic, trying to get to the center of the action, their car-bound colleagues stuck with the rest of us.

The news crews came close behind. I don't know how they got through the traffic snarls, but we went from nothing to about ten crews in less than a minute.

I get most of my news from the Internet, but I knew enough to know that things don't really happen if they don't make it to television. Despite my joking about James sending out a press release, getting the attention of the news crews was vitally important to the CRL and to my plan. The mob could simply write off the loss of a bunch of chickens. What they couldn't stand was being embarrassed-or thinking that whatever information Sam had tracked down could still be in dangerous hands.

Our chicken raid was big news.

James was in heaven. KERA, the Dallas affiliate of National Public Television, homed on him like he had a sign on. He gave an impassioned speech about animal rights, the degradation that cockfighting does to both humans and birds, and his hope that the police will take a stronger stand against this crime. Right before the reporters got bored, he got to the critical part of the talk. "It's thanks to the late Sam Goodwin, and the information he left with his girlfriend, Tina Anderson, that we were able to pull this off. He'd been researching the mob when he was suddenly murdered. So, this is for Sam.

The police couldn't have timed it better-just as James had completed his sound bite, they stepped in and grabbed him.

James must have been staying up watching old news clips from the civil rights movement because he went limp when the police grabbed him, making them drag him toward the paddy wagon that was parked almost half a mile from where he'd been apprehended. The traffic jam and wandering chickens gave him a long and uninterrupted camera shot.

Fellow CRL members cheered him as he went by. I didn't think that he would be in jail for long and I was sure they'd never actually bring charges against him. For what-illegal discharge of barnyard fowl?

To my surprise, the next CRL member up was Karen Anderson's friend Mrs. Heath.

I'd always seen Mrs. Heath as a golf and cocktails do-gooder. Someone who would do the right thing as long as it didn't risk messing up her big hair or sculpted nails.

Obviously I'd let my reverse snobbery blind me. In her early fifties now, Heath might just have been a campus radical during the Viet Nam era. It was hard to remember, but Texas had a few radicals back in the old days.

Heath let the police have it, blaming them for letting mobsters run illegal cockfighting and gambling and murder CRL members, then wasting resources arresting citizens when they gathered to peacefully protest the corruption that made the mob activities possible.

It was another sound bite that couldn't help making the morning news. Especially when the police dragged Heath off, her skirt hiking up to expose some better looking legs than I'd guessed. Mrs. Heath was full of surprises. Maybe I needed to take up tennis or golf or something if I wanted to look halfway decent when I got to her age.

A couple more CRL members lined up to be arrested, but most suddenly remembered that they had left the iron on or something and started to disappear.

Angie was in a state, cell still at her ear as she reminded the teams that they weren't finished. We were chicken fans, after all. We'd decided to herd the birds down to the Trinity River floodway where they could munch on bugs and, like the Roman mob, subsidized grain.

A few of the retreating CRL members turned, shamefaced, and grabbed the bags of chicken scratch we'd left on the park lawn, laying a trail of feed down to the riverside where the chickens could lead more fulfilled and independent lives.

Angie was dressed in her working uniform-supershort skirt and a tube top that barely contained her impressive chest. It didn't take The Fox Network people long to spot her and determine that she'd make a better network exclusive than another video of a middle-aged chicken-lover.

The Fox camera crew was pushing through the crowd from one

direction when I noticed Vorobev and a couple of almost equally unpleasant looking men pushing through from the other direction.

I cut into Angie's cell and let her know that our time was up.

She looked around, spotted Vorobev, and took off, her fuck-me red shoes flying.

I restarted my engine and took off down the mercifully unblocked North Record Street when she hopped in.

The two of us pretended to be just a pair of pink-collar workers on our way to boring jobs as bank secretaries or something as we weaved through chicken stragglers, police cruisers, and a few more of those scary black cars with fully tinted windows.

"That was pretty fun," I told her.

"You owe me," she answered. She was still breathing hard and her right ear looked like she'd mashed it with her phone a few two many times.

"I'll pay you back."

"You'd better believe you will."

* * * *

We turned on the news as soon as we got back to Andy's. The amazing chicken raid had made it onto CNN and Fox as well as the local channels. Typically, CNN covered James while Fox led with shots of Mrs. Heath's legs and sexy black panties. I hadn't noticed at the time, but Mrs. Heath had been prepared. She'd worn thigh-high stockings and a thong to get maximum news coverage and minimum physical coverage. My respect for that woman went up another notch.

"What are you two up to?" The angry tone let me know that Karen Anderson had finally tracked us down.

I'd managed to stay away from my mother-in-law for the two weeks we'd been living in Andy's house but apparently that was over. She stormed into the media room like the Bismarck in search of defenseless cargo ships. Although I knew that Tai Chi is really just a sort of dance routine rather than a practical martial art, she came off as pretty scary in her oriental-looking outfit. The woman also had put on some muscles since the last time I'd seen her. If it came down to a fight, I would have bet on her rather than me, despite the twenty-five years she has on me.

"Have you seen this story about cockfighting, Mrs. Anderson?" Angie asked with a butter-wouldn't-melt expression. "The police have arrested your friend Mrs. Heath."

"Impossible." Despite her denial, though, Karen sat and turned her attention to the television.

"It turns out that the Chicken Rescue League broke into dozens of cockfighting and breeding places last night. They freed thousands of innocent chickens," Angie went on.

"Sounds like the type of idiot thing Carole would get involved in," Karen agreed. She paused for a minute. "That minister fellow is a bit of a hunk, though."

Angie shot me a glance, but kept her mouth shut.

"What?" Karen demanded.

"He's sort of a friend of Tina's," Angie told her.

"Really?" Karen made a little moue, then smiled. "Does he know how dangerous that can be?"

"Mrs. Anderson!"

"You've got to admit that a minister would be a bit of a stretch. Not that you don't need saving more than most."

"He isn't that kind of a friend."

Karen glared at me. "Of course not. Not when you've still got your sights set on Andy."

I didn't know how to answer that. The truth was, I still found Andy fun and sexy. If there had been some way we could separate lifestyles from romance, the two of us might have found a way to be together.

Not that I was going to tell Karen that.

It turned out that it didn't matter what I said. Karen wasn't in listen mode. "The police seem awfully curious about Andy in connection with your late boyfriends. As if he'd waste his time chasing after white trash like you, Tina. Even I know enough about crime to know that it's always the girlfriend or spouse who does the killing. Not some distant ex-connection."

"I didn't kill anyone," I told her patiently. "And Andy didn't either."

That didn't go over well. Her face turned a mottled purple. "Of course Andy didn't kill anyone. He can have any woman he wants. At least he could until he had a couple of trailer-park-trash females horning in on his home, eating his food, and scaring away anyone decent."

Karen Anderson has never been my favorite person and this conversation wasn't making me want to change my mind. "How lucky for Andy that we're moving out this afternoon," I told her.

That stopped her in mid-bitch and gave her the first smile I'd seen on her in years. "You're really moving out?"

As if I'd waste my energies lying to her. "We have a plan that will clear your son of all of this nasty speculation. Now we're going to execute. But we have to do it from our place." I almost put my hand to my mouth. I didn't think Karen was the killer, but I also didn't think much about her ability to keep quiet.

"Oh. Well, whatever anyone says about you, you always were a clever little thing," Karen told me.

Well, I guess that was as close to a compliment as Karen Anderson could come.

"Do you think all of the publicity about the chicken rescue operation will make the city crack down on organized gambling?" I asked. As a woman-who-lunches, Karen knew a lot more about what was going on in the political world of Dallas than I did.

She shrugged. "For a few months. Then there will be another cause and the cock-fighters will be back."

Women who lunch aren't supposed to be cynical. That was my job. Still, a few months would be plenty. It was enough time for the mob to feel the squeeze, to lose some serious money, and to decide to take their revenge on the women who had made it all possible.

"I think it's time to talk to Andy," I told Angie.

* * * *

"You did what?" Andy didn't know whether to shout at us or to laugh at us. Pelcovitz, on the other hand, ostentatiously covered his ears so he wouldn't have to hear about the illegal activities that we had undertaken.

"We know that the mob is behind the killings," I reminded him. "And we also know that the police aren't investigating that angle at all. So we decided to push. We didn't hurt anyone who wasn't already a criminal."

Pelcovitz shook his head sadly. "My investigators are still working on the organized crime angle, Tina. You should leave these things to professionals. Setting a flock of chickens free in downtown Dallas is not the way to operate."

Professionals who hadn't gotten anywhere in weeks. "Your so-called professionals didn't even turn up Vorobev," I reminded him. "Do you really think they could put pressure on anybody?"

Pelcovitz stared at the table but didn't answer. From my standpoint, that was as good as an admission that he had let Andy down.

"Don't even think about moving out," Andy told us. "If the mob is gunning for you, you've got to stay. I'll bring in extra security."

"We're going back to the trailer park," I said. "Rents are about due. You don't think anybody is going to pay if I'm not all over their butts, do you?"

"Do you think I give a flip about their rents?" Andy demanded, reminding me who owned the Shady Rest Trailer Park. "You're taking too big of a chance this time, Tina."

I shook my head. "The only reason I'm living in a trailer park you own is because I think I do a decent job managing. If I thought it was charity, I'd be out of there. So we'd all better care about the rent. Besides, I'll have to go back home sooner or later."

"You don't have to go back," Andy said. "Why don't you move back in with me on a permanent basis. My mother can move into a suite at the Mansion on Turtle Creek if she gets in your hair."

"Hey. What about me?" Angie demanded.

"You want to move in with my mother?" He quirked an eyebrow at her.

Andy was my buddy, but we'd had a go at marriage and it hadn't worked. So, why did my stomach feel like it had been turned inside out?

I faked a laugh. "Very funny. Now do you want us to explain the plan so you can help, or should we just count you out?"

He thought about that longer than I'd hoped he would. "We could really use your help," I added.

Finally Andy sighed. "Explain the plan. Maybe we can figure some way to keep your cute little asses out of the wringer."

"They were looking for something in Sam's trailer," Angie started.

"So we had James let them know we'd found it. We figure, if it was worth killing Sam for, it'd be worth coming after us."

"Not to mention we gave them a big reason to be seriously pissed at us."

Andy looked at me, then at Pelcovitz. "Is any of this making sense to you?"

The lawyer shook his head. "Why would you want the mob mad at you? It's suicide."

"Not suicide," I insisted. "They'll send someone, your bodyguards will catch them, and we'll have instant reasonable doubt. After all, what jury is going to believe Andy killed Sam when we have captured gangsters who were going after whatever treasures Sam had?"

Pelcovitz nodded slowly. "It isn't a sure thing, but a viable alternative, especially supported by hitmen in custody, could help. I suppose it would be too much to expect them to send the same killers after Tina that they used for Sam. But if they did, we'd probably be able to pick up some physical evidence."

"If they don't respond quick enough, we can go back to Vorobev's bar and try to order chicken from his menu." Angie smirked at Pelcovitz. "But only if we took bodyguards."

Andy blinked when I stopped, then stared at me. "That's the plan?"

"Hey, you know they're going to be mad."

"Honey, I'm mad, but you're crazy. This is going to get you killed."

"That's where you come in. Or rather, where Pelcovitz comes in."

"I can give you bodyguards," the lawyer said.

"You can use Sam's trailer," I said. "The police finally freed it up and it's not being used while I wait to see what Katherine and Amber decide what to do with it. It'll be a good place to hide."

He nodded slowly. "I can do that."

"We need enough bodyguards for both of us," Angie added.

"Maybe the two of you should stick together," Pelcovitz suggested. "It would be harder to cover both of you separately."

"I've got to work," Angie said.

"Really? What do you do?" Pelcovitz asked.

"You don't want to go there," Andy broke in. "Angie, how about taking a vacation for the next couple of weeks."

She shook her head. "I've already taken too long off."

I put my face in my hands. The mental picture of Angie doing her hooker business while a couple of beefy guards looked on was too much to bear. Andy was right. Angie would be terribly exposed if she insisted on continuing her operation.

"Maybe you could limit your enterprise to known good-guys for a while," I suggested as a compromise. "You know, guys like James and Tom."

She considered. Angie likes sex, but she isn't particularly interested in sudden death. "I guess I could do that."

Pelcovitz huffed a little. I think he was getting the idea about Angie's entrepreneurship. I wasn't sure if that huff expressed disapproval or interest. Probably both. In my experience, the normal male reaction is a bit conflicted.

"Then we're in business," I announced without letting Pelcovitz have a chance to clarify his feelings. "We'll make your mom happy and be out of here in an hour. The bodyguards can move into Sam's trailer and keep watch from there. If Angie needs to go to work, maybe one of the guards can drive her."

Andy wanted to argue, but he could tell it wasn't going to do him any good.

"If your guys let anything happen to Tina or Angie, you can kiss your business with Anderson Software goodbye," he growled at Pelcovitz.

"I'll take care of it."

Andy nodded abruptly. "I've got to get back to work if I'm going to pay for this mess."

He stomped out.

I felt a little queasy. Once in a while, I get the feeling that Andy isn't really over our marriage.

When I get that feeling, I wonder if I'm missing something and whether the cops could be right about their simple explanation for my string of dead dates.

Chapter 11

Nothing happened that night except that one of the bodyguards ran over a chicken during a shift change.

They joked about eating it but I told myself that they were probably just doing the male thing, covering up their emotions. I was pretty upset by the accident and Angie told me to chill out, that it was only a chicken.

So I turned around and told Pelcovitz's goons that that they were out of there if they didn't behave. Still, the accident made me more aware of the ticking clock. It wasn't in their nature for the bodyguards to stay inconspicuous very long and the odds were that someone in my park was in the mob's pay.

We needed to speed things up. I think Angie had been kidding when she'd told Pelcovitz we'd go to Vorobev's bar, but it was the best idea we could come up with.

We waited until midnight, notified the bodyguards, and headed out, my yellow Storm followed, oh-so-discretely by two black SUV's full of Pelcovitz goons.

Vorobev wasn't happy to see us.

"What the hell do you think you're doing, hanging around here?" he demanded.

"We just wanted to see if there was any good cockfighting tonight, Ivan," I told him.

"Cockfighting is illegal." He almost snarled the words. I got the feeling that our raid had worked and he'd lost business because he couldn't bring in any birds. I couldn't imagine anyone who deserved it more.

I laughed at him, then planted the lie. "Illegal? According to what Sam left me, little things like that don't really bother you."

He was wearing a shirt and sunglasses that night but, even in a pair of overalls that would make a Nebraska farmer proud, he looked scary rather than laughable.

He grabbed at my arm and yanked me close to his foul-smelling mouth. "You girls are in trouble. You know that? Everybody knows you're responsible for that do-gooder thing downtown. You and blondie here."

I ignored his poisonous breath and giggled. "Have you ever thought that downtown might be just the beginning. Sam would have wanted it that way."

"Don't get me started about that traitor."

One of the bodyguard SUVs angled closer. I could imagine a gun barrel sticking out the window pointing in Vorobev's general direction. It didn't fill me with a lot of confidence. What I'd seen of Pelcovitz's goons had been pretty pathetic. They'd probably shoot someone if they had a chance, but I wouldn't give any odds on them hitting Vorobev instead of me.

Angie took the cue from me. "Who could have guessed that there would be so much crime here with all the people we already have in jail?"

"There's crime here all right," Vorobev told her. "And the two of you have gotten in way over your heads."

I tried to yank away from him, but his grip didn't move. Then he shoved me away like he was flicking a bothersome insect.

"I'd say I warned you, but it's too late for warnings now. If I were you, I wouldn't even lay low, I'd start running. And keep running until I was so far away from here it wasn't even a memory.

He blocked the door to his bar when Angie and I tried to go in, and just stood there like an oversized lump until we finally got back in my car and headed for home.

Walking the half-mile back to my car while the bodyguard SUV trailed along gave me time to think about how stupid the entire plan was, and how likely it was that I was going to end up hurt.

It had only taken Vorobev an instant to grab me. Even if the bodyguards had been ready, with itchy trigger fingers, I guessed Vorobev could have snapped my neck as easily as he'd wring a chicken's, and get it done a long time before the guys could react.

The bodyguards might arrest him, or even shoot him afterwards, but that would be a bit late for me.

Saving Andy was important. Staying alive while I saved him had to count for something too, though.

After what had happened, I wasn't sure I'd be able to do either.

* * * *

The next morning, Angie called me to tell me she was wrung out, ready to throw the whole thing over and head back for the streets.

It took me an hour to persuade her that she was being an idiot, but I felt antsy too. I switched on the computer and messed around with a program I'd been working on, but I made such a muddle out of my code that I shut the computer off without saving anything.

In Andy's house, the plan had seemed brilliant. Back in the trailer park, it seemed brain-dead. Sitting around waiting for something to happen wasn't working and it wasn't me.

I had to get out and do something. But whatever I did, I'd be setting myself up as a target. So I was caught in a bind.

The Chicken Rescue League

When Angie stomped into my trailer with a plate of cookies I knew we were in trouble. She only bakes when she's desperate.

I ate four of the chocolate chip and pecan monsters she'd made and then downed two strong cups of coffee while I waited for the sugar, fat, caffeine, and chocolate to restart my system and get some ideas flowing.

As I reached for the fifth cookie, my brain clicked on for what felt like the first time in days.

"Let's go see Amber again," I said. "We know her brother is connected, which makes her the most likely link between Sam and the mob. There's got to be something she can tell us. Something she might not have said with Patrick breathing down her neck. Who knows, she might even have whatever the mob was looking for. Remember, Sam went to see her the day he died."

Angie shrugged. "Beats sitting here in the heat."

I called the goons and told them not to bother following us. The mob wasn't going to be hanging out in the Panhandle, unless they followed us there.

The leader, a no-neck named Phil, argued with me, but I drew the line. I suspected that Amber was hiding from the mob more than from the police and I wasn't going to lead them to her. Even if she had I.D.'ed me to her brother.

I made Angie keep an eye on the makeup mirror under the sun visor to spot anyone behind me and then used everything I'd learned about evasive driving from a Discovery Channel special I'd watched while we'd been staying at Andy's. It's funny, but while you're watching those shows, you really think you're tracking. Then when you try to use what you learned, you find out that they just sort of talked past a lot of the critical details. That one where you spin around and end up going the opposite direction is a real killer-as another dent in the Storm proved.

"I don't see anybody following us," Angie insisted after I'd almost killed her for the eighth time. Her voice sounded a little shaky.

"They're probably switching off, using radio to reconnect," I told her with the confidence of someone who doesn't have a clue how little she knows. "Just look for any car that seems familiar. They'll have to recycle sooner or later."

"I guess— Oh my gosh, watch out for that tree."

I swerved just in time. What were they doing planting trees in center strips anyway?

It seemed like every car we passed was either a sandalwood colored SUV or a red pickup truck. After a few minutes of intense staring at everyone, everything started to look familiar. And a little blurred around the edges.

Still, I gave the evasive driving everything I had. I tore through a police station parking lot at a million miles an hour, went the wrong way down a one-way street, drove through two car-washes (partly to confuse any pursuers and partly because I'd heard that the high-pressure water can dislodge or disable many commercial tracking devices), and did the old wait for a yellow light and then tear through it trick.

I thought I'd caught one then because someone followed me through one of the red lights. But then I looked and saw it was just some teenaged punk who thought he was a hot driver.

By the time I was satisfied, Angie was ready to kill me and I figured that anyone smart enough to follow us was either insane or clever enough to track Amber Vorobev-Goodwin down on his own.

The rest of the drive, I kept Angie alert by asking her to check out cars. Twice I made her call tag numbers in to Pelcovitz, who had his secretary look them up on the computer and see if they were registered.

They were all false alarms. No recently stolen or counterfeit tags showed up. And the pickup trucks I was so sure were following quickly turned off the road into one of the miniranches that dotted the panhandle countryside.

By the time we got to Amber's place, I was ready for a nap.

Amber's television was on and, from the sound of it, Emily was watching the same cartoon she'd been watching when Patrick and I had been there a couple of weeks earlier. I didn't know much about kids, but I did know that they could watch the same show again and again, especially if it has really annoying music in it.

Amber looked like she was ready to go crazy. Her hair needed a cut and her eyes practically bugged out when Angie and I pulled up.

"Let's get out of here. I've got to get a beer," she told me the second she opened the door.

I nodded. "Right. Let's all go get something."

"Bars won't let Emily in."

"There have to be places we can get a beer that also have food for kids. Come on."

The back seat in a Geo Storm isn't much to write home about. Emily seemed to think climbing in back was an adventure. Her mom didn't look quite so enthusiastic but I figured she wasn't going anywhere once I got her wedged in.

We went to a Bennigans, got Emily a tiny box of crayons, and ordered a round of beers for me and Amber, a milk for Emily, and a martini for Angie who had stayed up all night the previous night watching Thin Man movies and had decided she was going to turn into Nora Charles instead of Nancy Drew.

I didn't remind her that Nora Charles had been a society rich-girl. People are always going out of their way to bust up my fantasies and so I try letting others hang onto theirs. Channeling Nora Charles wouldn't hurt me or Angie and so I let Angie wallow in the character.

"So," I said to Amber once we got our drinks and the waitress wandered off. "Tell me about your brother."

"Ivan? Or Vlad?"

Uh-oh. Ivan was scary enough. I didn't want to hear about another one. Except I figured I needed to.

"Let's start with Ivan?"

"Uncle Ivan," Emily shouted, happy to be able to join the conversation and seize the center of attention for herself. "He's so funny."

That hadn't been my reading of the man so I just looked at Amber.

"Oh, yeah. Ivan is a cut-up," she explained. "Vlad is the serious one. He went into business and did accounting. In fact, he introduced me to Sam. Vlad tried to get Ivan to do something with his life, but Ivan only wanted to hang out with his buddies. So, running a bar was a perfect solution."

"Did you know Ivan holds cockfights in his bar?"

Amber shook her head. "Impossible. Ivan couldn't hurt anything, he's so gentle."

If Ivan was the gentle one, I was really in trouble.

"Has he always been with the mob?"

Amber shrugged again. "It wasn't like that."

I figured if I was going to pay for her beer, she could at least answer my questions. "Why don't you tell me what it was like?"

"When you come to a strange country, nobody knows what to do. So you look for someone to show you the ropes. It wasn't bad for me because I was barely more than a baby. But my brothers had it tough.

"Us immigrants tend to stick together," she continued. "We help each other out. When Ivan wanted to buy his bar, he went to some old friends. They lent him the money and he helps them sometimes."

Helps them by breaking kneecaps, I guessed.

"What about Vlad? Is he still doing accounting?"

She shook her head but looked serious. "Vlad disappeared around the same time Sam lost his job and divorced me. My life had been so perfect and then, all of a sudden it turned into shit."

"Mom, you said a bad word."

Amber looked like she wanted to strangle her kid but I couldn't blame her. If I'd spent a month trapped in a cabin with a bratty kid and a couple of Disney movies, I would have been going crazy too.

"How do you mean, disappeared?" I asked.

"You know, puff. Not there any more."

I thought hard, but Angie beat me to the next question. "Do you think he's hiding?"

"I think he's dead," Amber said.

Talk about a conversation stopper. Fortunately Emily was distracted by a cartoon show on one of the monitors, but Angie and I looked at each other like one of us had stepped into a big pile of dog shit and each of us suspected that we still had the evidence on our shoes.

"You think-"

Amber cut me off before I could ask for details. "Why else would Sam leave me? I mean, look at me." She thrust out her chest and stretched a too-long leg out of the booth, almost tripping our waitress.

"I'm pretty. I'm good in bed. We had a great child. I think he was protecting me, trying to make whoever killed Vlad think that I didn't have anything to do with it. And now they killed Sam too. Maybe Ivan next."

I couldn't help wondering if Sam had thought I was boring in the sack after living with Amber?

"Did Vlad and Sam work together at Big Cat Telecom?" I asked.

Amber wiped her eyes, blew her nose, and finished off her beer. "I need another one."

"Go for it," I encouraged. Maybe she'd tell me something if I got her drunk.

The waitress was hiding, probably trying to stay away from Amber's extra-long legs, but I flagged her down. After an upgrade to chocolate milk for Emily, another beer for Amber and a second Martini for Angie, we were ready to get back to work.

"It's an acquired taste," Angie told me when I asked her how she liked the Martini. I wasn't sure if she meant that she didn't like it, or that she was being considerate. I try not to acquire tastes for things that cost money.

Amber finished most of her second beer before she got around to answering my question.

"Vlad and Sam worked together for years. Before Big Cat, at Big Cat. I even think Vlad tried to persuade Sam to move with him when he changed jobs a couple of years ago. But Sam was a big shot important guy at Big Cat. He wasn't about to leave that."

"But Vlad left?"

She nodded but I saw the glint of a tear in her eyes. If she was acting, she was a talent.

"Where did he go?"

Amber finished the second beer. "You know, that's sort of funny. He never told me."

Amber got three more beers, but I didn't get much more information out of her and so we finally trooped back to the car, me about sixty dollars closer to my credit card limit and Emily, Amber and Angie sloshing with all they'd drunk.

"I am so sick of hiding here," Amber told me.

I could identify. For a lot of people, living out in the woods a million miles from anybody is a dream. For me, it was right up there with sticking bamboo shoots under my fingernails. "Want us to take you back to Pleasant Grove? You've got to have a lot of mail piling up." Unless I wasn't the only one to clean her out.

Amber considered, then shook her head. "Sam thought I would be safer here so I'd better stay here." She paused a beat. "Uh, there is one thing, though."

Uh-oh. I had a feeling my credit card was going to get some more action.

"What's that?"

"Can we stop at Target? If I don't get a couple more videos, I'm going to die."

About two hundred of my dollars later, we hit my credit limit and made the rest of the drive to Amber's retreat.

As Amber wiggled her way out of the car, I thought of one more question. "Did you tell your brother that I'd visited you?"

She was drunk enough to giggle when her jeans got stuck on a door panel and then yanked.

I'd thought she might rip her jeans. No such luck. Instead, she bent back the rusty sheet metal in my car. Just what I needed-another dent.

She straightened, then shrugged. "I don't remember. Maybe. I call him every week. Don't worry, though. I use my cell. There's no way he can track me."

It wasn't Amber I was worried about but I didn't tell her that.

"Try to think, Amber. This is important. When I met him for the first time, Ivan knew my name. Did you tell him?"

"Hang on a minute." She ran to her house, opened the unlocked door, and vanished.

"What do you think that was about?" I asked Angie.

"I think she needed to go to the bathroom," Angie told me. "Did you see that she had six beers? In about forty-five minutes. That's some serious chug-a-lug."

"Maybe you're right. I guess I'm just lucky she didn't throw up in my car."

There I went tempting fate again.

"I don't feel so good."

I hadn't forgotten about Emily, exactly, but I hadn't thought about her being in the back seat with five glasses of chocolate milk inside of her.

I got out in a hurry, pulled up my seat, reached in to undo Emily's seatbelt-just in time to get blasted by about a gallon of slightly used chocolate milk.

"Eeyou," Amber told me when she emerged from her house a couple of minutes later. She was buttoning up her jeans looking a lot more comfortable. "You look like you lost a mud wrestling tournament."

Amber struck me as the kind of woman who would know about that, although I wouldn't have put her on the losing end.

"I need to wash up," I told her.

"Don't drip on my floor."

Amber's bathroom mirror gave me the bad news. Emily's projectile vomiting had ended up everywhere. I had to take a shower, shampoo my hair, and borrow a t-shirt from Amber before I could get out of there.

As Angie and I finally headed out the door, Amber grabbed me. "I'm pretty sure I didn't mention you to Ivan. He must have heard about you from someone else."

* * * *

Angie was drunk.

During the entire three hour drive home, she sang dirty songs, gave me a recruiting talk in the joys of being a hooker in Dallas, and reminded me that it would be my fault if I got her killed.

I thought the dirty songs were pretty funny. The rest of her remarks though, I didn't have a lot of use for. The worst part was, they didn't even distract me from what Amber had said. Where was her brother Vlad? If he'd been killed, who had done it?

Two accountants who had worked together had both ended up dead, at least if Amber was right about what had happened to Vlad. It was barely possible that this could be a coincidence. But even coincidence would be stretched for two mob-connected accountants to be killed, especially when one of them had been involved in one of the largest scams in corporate history. So, the real question was, why had the mob decided to kill their own guys?

"You'd better call your bodyguards and tell them you're coming home," Angie sang to me. "Cause they're probably pawing through your underwear right now and you don't want to catch them doing it."

I didn't want to think about that, but what I'd seen of the bodyguards that Pelcovitz had supplied us made me wonder if she wasn't onto something.

I went ahead and told the goons we were coming home.

Chapter 12

The next morning I woke up feeling great. I was on my second cup of coffee before I figured out why—I was happy I was still alive. I'd been certain that Vorobev and his mob buddies would have reacted by now. It's times like this when you realize how little it takes to make you happy.

I spent a few minutes on the computer listing everything I could think of having to do with the case and decided that I needed to talk to Kevin Franklin about what had happened at Big Cat Telecom. Franklin knew Sam had ripped him off. But I didn't know if he realized Sam was not the only mob-connected accountant in the organization. Where there were two, there might be more. Maybe including some who were still alive.

A call to Andy led to an early afternoon appointment with Franklin.

I decided to see if Angie wanted to come with me. I reached her door just in time to see one of the bodyguards heading out. My brilliant and mercenary friend had figured out the perfect way to combine safety with income potential. Pelcovitz was paying them to watch Angie and me, but I guessed they were losing money on watching Angie.

I told her about my appointment with Franklin, but she shook her head. "He's a goodie-two-shoes Christian with a capital 'B' for boring," she told me.

"You know him?"

She shrugged. "I met him at one of Andy's parties. I spent half an hour chatting him up. I know he wanted it-I mean, guys can't disguise the bump in their pants. But he laid on some story about it not being right."

She paused, reflecting. "Maybe he was just too cheap to pay for it."

"He did go bankrupt," I reminded her.

Angie laughed. "Come on, Tina. In a corporate bankruptcy it's the workers who get the shaft. Executive mucky-mucks always manage to protect themselves."

My friend the socialist-philosopher-hooker. Who would have thought it?

What I did think was that if Kevin Franklin knew that Angie was a hooker, he might be a bit distracted if I brought her with me when I went to talk to him. Which didn't sound like a good thing.

"I'll leave half the guards here," I told her. "You're going to stay in, aren't you?"

"Depends on which half the guards you take."

I was halfway back to my trailer when I realized she might be serious. Could she really have done half that crew already?

Why was it that I could go for months without a guy even noticing me while Angie only had to walk into a room to be surrounded? Not to mention the fact that guys who got interested in me seemed to be ending up dead a lot lately.

Right outside my trailer door, a chicken stopped me. One of its wings dragging on the ground and it gave me a pathetic cheep.

I tried to shoo it away, but it just sat there looking at me like it had finally found its mommy.

"Go see Angie," I urged it.

The chicken clucked a couple of times but didn't move.

"What?"

Unfortunately, chickens don't talk so this bird couldn't tell me what it was thinking.

"I'm going inside now," I told it.

I opened my door and stepped in, but the chicken was faster than I'd guessed. Bum wing or not, it hopped in ahead of me.

"If you're not careful, you're going to be dinner," I threatened.

The bird turned around a couple of times, like a cat, then settled down on a stack of old Dallas Observers I had left in the corner with the idea that I'd eventually get around to recycling them.

"You're starting to piss me off," I said.

Except she really wasn't. Maybe it was that battered wing hanging down, but I felt sorry for the pathetic animal.

I bent over to check out the wing. Maybe it was broken. Maybe it needed a splint. I could see the headlines. Tina Anderson, nurse to the chickens.

The second I got close, that miserable bird pecked me on the nose.

I stumbled to the bathroom, pressed some Kleenex against my nose to stop the bleeding, and used the mirror to check out the damage.

All right, maybe it wasn't luck that Angie was getting all the guys. Right then, I looked like something the dog dragged home. Except any self-respecting dog would leave me in the street where he found me.

* * * *

The Storm wouldn't start.

I wasn't too surprised. I'd been putting a lot of miles on that car lately and it probably needed a vacation.

I thought about hitching a ride from the bodyguards, but how conspicuous would that be? So I took the train. A couple of bodyguards trailed along with me while a few others sat in their comfortable air conditioned SUV and got to feel superior.

Fortunately, Kevin's office appeared to be only a five-minute walk from the train stop. Unfortunately, I had to take two busses to get from my place to the closest light-rail station. I was going to be late.

I'm normally a slob. Comes from hanging around with software geeks during my formative years. While the rest of the trailer-trash set had been learning to apply thick coats of makeup, I was hacking up an improved double-buffering video algorithm. In the winter, I wear jeans. In the summer, I wear shorts as often as I can.

I'll blame it on my mirror-shock, but I'd actually dolled up a bit to meet with Franklin.

Franklin's office wasn't quite as close to the Plano train station as MapQuest had indicated.

By the time I got to his office, Dallas's summer heat had turned me into a wreck. My dry-clean-only silk top clung to me like I'd let some fraternity brother pour water over me. My black pants kept crawling up my rear. And those cute little sandals with what had looked like a minimal heel back in the Payless Shoe Store were killing my feet.

"Mr. Franklin has another meeting," his admin told me when I stumbled into his reception area. "When you stood him up at two, he rescheduled around you. Perhaps you could come back tomorrow?"

I stared at her.

Naturally, she was perfectly made up, her stockings showing sexy black seams, her summer dress just barely discrete enough for office wear and her hair poofed and big the way only a native-born Texan can manage.

I, on the other hand, was a dripping and disgusting mess. It had taken me two and a half hours to travel across all of Dallas and its northern suburbs and not a single air conditioner had been working.

I was a wreck and I was mad.

"I'll wait," I told her.

"Mr. Franklin has quite a full schedule," she warned me, her nose going up slightly. "We've got our end-of-quarter operations review meetings going on this week. You were lucky that he was able to schedule you in at all."

I tried to remember if I'd ever been that perky. Maybe I had been when Andy and I had founded Anderson Software and thought we'd conquer the world. One thing for sure, I'd never thought that my boss's importance reflected on me. It was pretty obvious that little Miss Priss here hadn't gotten that e-mail.

"I'll tell you what, Missy," I offered. "You just pass Mr. Franklin a note and tell him that I want to talk to him about the mob's infiltration of his accounting department. If he says he's too busy to talk to me today, then that'll be his decision."

The admin's dainty nostrils flared at the Missy comment but I was past caring.

"There is no mob infiltration of our accounting department," she assured me. "If you don't leave, I'll have to call security."

I pride myself for my patience but I think it had gotten baked out of me in the hundred-plus degree heat. "Look, sweetheart. Franklin wants to talk to me. He's not going to thank you for protecting him. He's probably going to fire your ass for keeping me away. So why don't you go check with him? If I'm lying, your security guys can throw me out then. If I'm not, maybe you'll be able to keep your job for a while." Until she screwed up again, at least. But that wasn't my problem.

She opened her mouth to argue with me but backed down in the face of logic and fear. After all, even if I'd missed the appointment, Franklin had wanted to see me.

"I'll see what Mr. Franklin says," she told me. "Wait here."

As if I'd run away after browbeating her into getting off her rear.

Twenty seconds later, she emerged from the door behind her desk. Franklin followed her, his arms already wide for the obligatory hug, took one look at me, and stopped short.

"How's the other guy look?"

"Very funny. My car broke down."

"Looks like it got in a few good swings first."

He was looking at my nose. I'd managed to stop the bleeding but it still had a dent in the end where that chicken had hacked it.

"That wasn't my car. I lost a fight with a chicken," I explained.

His expressions reflected his thoughts as he processed that answer, obviously trying to figure out if I was joking or pulling his leg somehow. It probably never occurred to him that I was simply telling the truth.

When it looked like my explanation was only going to drive more questions, I told him it was a long story.

"Right." He ushered me into a conference room filled with guys in suits. I guess casual days had gone out when Big Cat Telecom had filed for bankruptcy, because these guys (not a woman in sight now that the perky admin had escaped back to her Solitaire game) could have been escapees from a 1950s movie in their gray and navy.

"We'll pick it up in an hour," he told them. "Take a break."

The young flunky who'd been standing at the projector wanted to argue, but Franklin's glare cut him off short.

Almost miraculously the other men evaporated, leaving Franklin and me alone. The bodyguards had stayed out in their SUV.

"You look like you could use a drink," he told me.

I wasn't interested in Kevin Franklin. If I wanted a rich nothing-but-business type, I would have stayed with Andy, who at least had a good sense of humor. But I still didn't need Franklin telling me that I looked like a sack of shit.

I almost told him that, but bit back the words at the last minute. I wanted Franklin's help. Of all of us, he was the one who could best figure out what Sam had been up to, how things were connected. Besides, Andy still owned a big chunk of Big Cat. If Franklin's accounting was still dirty, I needed to give him a heads-up.

I settled for a Diet Coke.

"Diet Vanilla Coke all right?"

I nodded, accepted the icy can he yanked from a dorm-style refrigerator under the conference table, and took a deep hit.

He waited patiently until I'd swallowed, then looked at his watch. "What's this about problems with my accounting?"

I took a deep breath. Even after everything Big Cat Telecom had been through, this wasn't going to be good news for him.

"You know I've been looking into Sam's murder, of course," I reminded him. "I think you were there the other day when I told Andy that I'd found a mob connection to Sam."

He nodded. "Which might explain what happened to the missing money."

"Right. But it turns out that Sam wasn't the only mob-connected accountant in your group."

He nodded slowly. "I gathered that from the rather cryptic message you gave Bambi."

"Your admin's name is really Bambi?"

He snorted. "I can't help it. That was her parents' choice."

I wondered if they'd been prescient or whether Bambi had spent her life trying to live up to the name. Either way, she'd succeeded. It was an ambiguous accomplishment.

"I saw Amber Vorobev yesterday," I told him. "She said that her husband Sam and her brother Vlad were often a team."

Franklin nodded, then went to work on his Palm, clicking the stylus against the small screen.

"I never had a Vlad Vorobev on the payroll," he finally concluded.

"Amber was positive Vlad worked with Sam."

"Really?" He scratched his head. "Maybe he was a contractor, or with the auditors."

"Maybe." Amber hadn't sounded like she knew exactly what her brother, or her husband, had been up to.

"It would make sense if he was with the auditing team," Franklin mused, more to himself I thought, than to me. "The two groups are supposed to check each other. That could help explain how Sam was able to get away with the embezzlement thing as long as he did. If we can just find this Vorobev guy, we can get some answers."

"Amber thinks that Vlad is dead," I told him.

Franklin slammed a fist into the heavy wood of his conference table. "Damn it. Every time we start to get somewhere, this happens. Is she sure?"

I shook my head. "She told me she thought he was dead because she hasn't heard from him in weeks. If she has any reasons, she sure didn't share them with me."

He rubbed his hand. I think he'd hit the table a little harder than he intended. "Next step has got to be putting Amber in touch with Big Cat's lawyers."

I shrugged. "Maybe. But she's afraid and she's hiding. If you want to give me a number, I'll ask her to call your legal team." I paused a second. "I'm not sure I understand—what difference could it make? You're already in bankruptcy, aren't you?"

Franklin's smile wasn't especially pleasant. "Yes we are. Thanks to Sam and now this Vlad. But if we could prove that the auditors were involved, we could sue them. Admittedly they might not have much left to be sued for after all they paid out during their last auditing disaster, but it could help pay back some of my creditors."

I guess that made sense. I opened my mouth to say so, but Franklin beat me to the punch.

"I'm something of a laughing stock with most of the business leaders in town these days, you know. Your ex, Andy, is about the only one who'll have anything to do with me. And he only tolerates me because I let him beat me in squash and because he has some major software invested in one of our hardware products. If I could prove that there was a conspiracy, that would make me look a lot less stupid for the way the bean counters pulled the wool over my eyes."

For just an instant, Franklin's eyes gleamed. So many guys have their whole ego caught up in their jobs and it looked like Franklin was one of those. Having his fellow millionaires think highly of him was a big deal.

"I've got two questions for you, then," I told him.

He clicked his stylus on the palmtop again. "Shoot."

"First, could the two of them have done it alone or would they have to have other people on the accounting team involved?"

He clicked for a few seconds. "Good question and I'll find out. What's the second one?"

"Is there any way of finding out without tipping off anyone who's still here, still connected, and waiting for you to make a mistake?"

Franklin laughed and didn't bother typing that one in. "I'm not a genius on these things, but I think that if I ripped a company for a few billion, I'd be moving on, not sitting around waiting to get caught. I'm pretty sure that if anyone else was involved, they're off somewhere working for a new sucker. Big Cat certainly isn't worth pillaging after what we've been through. Not with the bankruptcy judge breathing down our backs all the time."

I couldn't argue with that logic so I didn't. "Maybe you're right, but someone is sensitive. My lawyer, John Halprin was investigating the mob connection when he got killed," I reminded Franklin. "So be careful."

His smile faded. "Good thinking." He paused a bit. "Hey, you too. I mean, you've really been going to town about this. Are you sure you're going to be okay?"

I shrugged. If our plan worked, I would be okay. If it backfired, I'd end up in a landfill somewhere. The worst thing was, besides Andy and Angie, I wasn't sure anyone would even notice.

Franklin didn't think much of my non-answer. "I've got a couple of sharp guys in corporate security. Maybe one of them could give you a little run-through on safety. You know, staying out of dark alleys and stuff like that."

I'd reached my limit. "I'm a woman, Franklin. Know what that means? That means that I get to spend my life watching out for dark alleys and for guys who get a little drunk and think that makes them entitled to catch a little trailer park ass. So don't you go telling me that some muscle-headed no-neck can give me advice about keeping my ass safe."

He held up a hand. "Hey, Tina. I was just trying to help. You don't have to bite my head off."

"Tell you what. You do your job and I'll do mine," I said. Belatedly I remembered that I'd brought up the issue of safety first. Maybe I had overreacted.

All right, I had definitely overreacted. But I figured if I apologized now, it would just make things worse. Besides, I'm not good at apologizing.

"Look into the accounting angle," I told him. "And call me if you find anything."

He knuckled a mock salute. "Will do, Tina. Uh, have you told Andy about this yet?"

"Not yet."

He grinned. "Good. Because I'm going to call him now. And then I'm going to whip his butt on the squash court."

He stood up, his smile widening even more. "You don't get it, do you, Tina. This is what I've been praying for. A chance to clear my name. If you ever want anything from me, just give me a call. I owe you big."

Before I could turn, he grabbed me and planted a fat kiss directly on my lips.

If he'd stuck his tongue in, I would have given him the old knee in the groin move. But he seemed to be celebrating rather than getting nasty. Or maybe little Bambi outside used up all of his sexual energy.

"All right, Kevin," I warned him. "Enough."

"Oops. Sorry, Tina. Guess I got carried away."

"Yeah. I'd say so."

"I'll look into this and call you," he told me.

"Great."

I backed out of his office as quickly as I could.

Bambi gave me a dirty look like I was invading her territory, then sniffed as I left the office.

* * * *

Andy was sitting in my trailer when I got back.

"Where the hell have you been?"

"You know where I was. You set up the meeting."

"You were supposed to meet with Franklin at two. It's," he glanced at his watch, "half past seven."

"My car wouldn't start."

"Get one of the goons to drive you."

"Oh, yeah. That would be inconspicuous. No one would guess we'd set a trap if I just started driving around with a bodyguard. Maybe I could get another tattoo. Protected by Texas Bounty Hunters and Detectives, Inc."

"This isn't funny, Tina. You and Angie set off by yourself yesterday and riding public transportation, even with a guard, isn't safe."

I looked for a snappy comeback but came up empty. "Okay, you got your nag in. Anything else?"

He shrugged.

Then I remembered the chicken. It was still sitting on the stack of old newspapers. I'm not an expert at reading chicken expressions, but it looked hungry to me.

The CRL volunteers had put out cracked corn for the chickens we'd rescued and thought that they ate bugs too. Well, if my chicken was going to eat bugs, she was going to have to catch them herself. The closest thing I could think of to cracked corn was popcorn. I plugged in my electric popper.

"Don't tell me that's going to be your dinner." Like most guys, Andy doesn't think it's a meal if it isn't meat.

"It isn't for me."

"I don't really feel like popcorn."

"It isn't for you, either. It's for her." I gestured toward the pathetic bird.

"My God, is it alive?"

"You've been sitting inside for how long and you didn't even notice?"

"It didn't say anything."

Andy could be such a guy.

"Well she's hurt and she looks hungry to me."

"Speaking of which, have you eaten?"

I put out the chicken's popcorn, snagged a couple of kernels for myself, and tried to remember the last time I'd stopped to eat. "Breakfast."

"Want to go to Gloria's?"

When we'd started Anderson Software, we were dead broke most of the time. When we got a contract, we'd sometimes splurge and go to Gloria's Restaurant, a place that serves wonderful El Salvadorian food and incredible Margaritas.

Eating there would be like old times.

"Last two guys who took me out ended up dead," I reminded him.

"I'm glad you remember that, babe," he told me.

"I'm not your babe."

"Just because we're not married doesn't mean I don't care."

I felt like a heel. "Give me half an hour to get showered and changed. This shirt can stand up by itself."

"I could scrub your back."

I couldn't help it. I was tempted. Andy was about as sexy as a guy can get. But I didn't feel like being sexy right then. I felt like Typhoid Mary. Even thought I knew it was illogical, a part of me believed that if I got romantically involved with anyone, they'd end up dead too.

"I'm hungry," I told him. "I can get ready quicker without your help."

"All right. I'll take a rain check."

I didn't need hot water after that.

Instead of my normal trade-show t-shirt, I wore a little tank that Angie had given me for my birthday. It's cut low in front and high at the waist. Andy hadn't seen my belly-button stud and I was in the mood to be noticed.

Andy noticed.

"I, ah, I called and had your car towed," he told me. "Starkey will get to it tomorrow."

I wanted to hit him. "I can't afford to get my car repaired this month."

"It'll be safer for you," he reminded me. "You can owe me if you insist."

Just what I wanted. Owing my ex-husband.

"Did I mention how nice you look?" I asked him. All right, I was fishing for a compliment. Shoot me.

He stumbled but caught himself. "You too, Tina. I don't think I've seen the belly-button thing before."

If I'd known I was going to have to keep my stomach sucked in all the time maybe I would have worn something else.

"Yeah, and after I fill up at Gloria's, neither you nor anyone else is likely to see it again for a while." A horrible thought crossed my mind. "You are paying, aren't you?"

"My treat," he agreed.

* * * *

"I can't believe you've found all this when Pelcovitz didn't find anything."

I'd gotten the Super Special, which is a sort of sampler of Gloria's specialties. Andy had the Churrasco Tipico. The way he looked at me, I really started to worry that he wanted something more than food. We'd been there, gone through that. Even if I wasn't death to dates, I knew better than start up again with Andy.

The case was the prefect distraction. "We got a few lucky breaks," I said. "I think Amber trusts Angie and me somewhat just because we're women."

Andy took another bite of his steak and chewed thoughtfully. "Kevin Franklin called me. Said you've got evidence that the mob was behind his business problems. He also told me he wasn't going to be a weenie on the squash court any more."

I couldn't help laughing. "He'll still be a weenie."

Andy smiled too. "Maybe. But you're going to do a lot for his reputation." He paused a beat. "I hope you're around long enough to enjoy that."

I briefed Andy on what I'd learned and mentioned that I was concerned about Franklin's safety. And that Franklin hadn't taken my warning very seriously.

Andy got a laugh out of that too. "I got a call from Pelcovitz. He told me that his detective agency got an offer to double normal pay if they'd bodyguard Kevin starting this afternoon. Kevin may talk tough, but you definitely scared him."

"Good. I wouldn't want to be the only one scared around here."

Chapter 13

I woke up with my body tingling and ready for sex.

We'd gotten a Texas thunderstorm during the night, dropping the temperature from the steamy nineties down into the comfortable seventies. At some point, I'd even pulled a small blanket over myself.

I let myself luxuriate, wallowing in the comfort of my bed and savoring the warmth of my bed companion.

Companion? After a couple huge margaritas, I'd been a bit susceptible to Andy's charms and spent half an hour making out in his car. But I'd sent him home after that.

So who was with me?

I jerked to full awareness and spun in my bed.

My companion squawked and fluttered to the floor.

A warm egg almost followed but I caught it before it crashed. My friend the chicken had decided I was the perfect bed-warmer.

And I was faced with a dilemma.

Could I eat my chicken's progeny? I didn't think so.

But was the egg a potential chick or was it simply unfertilized protoplasm?

One thing for sure, I didn't want a bunch of chicks running around adding to the chicken overpopulation in the trailer park. I had enough problems keeping the complex fully occupied without having to explain the joys of three o'clock in the morning rooster crowing.

The chicken, my chicken, gave me a trusting look and I knew I couldn't eat that egg even if I'd been starving. Fortunately, her wing didn't look like it was bothering her any more.

The only solution was to unite my chicken and her possible offspring with the gang the CRL had rescued and that was now making its residence along the Trinity River.

I swooped up the bird and headed for my car.

For a painful moment, I thought it had been stolen, until I remembered Andy saying he'd had it towed to the garage.

It's about three miles from the trailer park to the river. Not a bad walk, but it isn't exactly the nicest neighborhood in Dallas and I'd be doing it with a chicken in one hand and an egg in the other. Oh, well. Sooner started, sooner finished.

The bodyguards trailed along discreetly, driving a couple of their black SUVs in around me.

Patrick caught me before I'd even gone a quarter of a mile and pulled over, lowering the passenger-side window.

"I noticed you heading off," he said. "Want a ride?"

Under normal circumstances, I would rather walk on broken glass than owe Patrick a favor, but carrying a chicken wasn't exactly a normal circumstance. The bird pecked me in the arm just then and I decided, what the hell. I made sure one of the bodyguard vans was in range, then nodded. "I'm going down to the river," I told him.

"Hop in."

Patrick had a brand new set of wheels-a shiny Cadillac Escalade with leather seating and an air conditioner that cranked out the cold air. It was a sort of charcoal gray, with neon purple lighting along its running boards, and it had those fancy wheel covers that spin the opposite direction that the wheels are turning.

A bumper sticker on the back read ask me about the girl next door.

I got in.

The frosty air really hit me when I closed the door and I thought of that poor egg. I rolled down the window and told Patrick to get rid of the A.C. Assuming that the egg really was a chicken-in-the-making, I didn't want to be responsible for any problems.

Patrick gave me a sour look, but did as I asked.

"Where are you off to?" I asked him. I've got manners enough to try to make conversation when someone does me a favor.

"Just thought I'd go for a ride in my new vehicle." He pronounced the 'h' in vehicle like a Texan, although I knew he was a Yankee.

"Cool car, Patrick. Must have been expensive."

"I had a bit of a windfall. Decided to reward myself."

I hadn't thought Patrick had rich old relatives but who knew?

"You weren't following me, were you?" Call me suspicious but Patrick wasn't usually the helpful sort.

He looked hurt. "How could I possibly have followed you? I didn't know you were here."

"Right. Well, anyway, I appreciate the ride. I know that all those chickens around the park are a little annoying sometimes and I wanted to set this one free where it could have a better life."

"Okay." He paused a beat. "You going to do anything with that egg?"

"That's disgusting," I told him.

At least he didn't say anything to me about taking off my clothes and letting him see me naked. Instead he told me a story about how he'd met a guy who had found a box full of Rolex watches that had fallen off a truck and sold him one for only ten dollars.

It wasn't a great story and it wasn't a great watch, either. The thing was such an obvious fake that even Patrick should have recognized it, except that he really wanted to believe. And maybe he wanted it to impress whatever female was handy. Sadly, Patrick was just as fake as the watch. Even a horny and indiscriminate woman needs to imagine that a guy wants her for something more than just sex. Patrick's desperation, lack of basic hygiene, and disinterest in anything that didn't lead to sex within five minutes of an introduction would continue to doom him to a life where sex existed only on the computer, new wheels and new watch notwithstanding.

I didn't tell him that because I knew he wouldn't hear me. I did warn him about things falling off of trucks, then got out of his SUV to free my chicken.

"Thanks for the ride, Patrick," I told him as I started down to the wide floodway that makes up the Trinity River park. About once every five years, there's a big enough flood that the river spills its banks. It had been a good decade since it had actually reached the levies. I figured that Charlaine would be safe enough.

I'd resisted naming my chicken until I nestled her egg down into a little impression in the earth and then set the chicken on it. Now that I was letting her go, I couldn't fight the temptation any longer. It's pathetic that a twenty-seven year-old woman has to take out her maternal instinct on a chicken, but that's how things had worked out for me.

I had to wipe a little moisture out of my eyes when I set Charlaine down. Not tears, I assured myself. Crying over a chicken would be disgraceful. But there was just a little catch in my throat.

Patrick was waiting for me when I clambered back up the levy, the bodyguards discreetly parked a distance away. I caught the glint of binoculars so I felt slightly safe-not that Patrick was a threat.

"Want a ride back?"

I froze. Maybe he was more dangerous than I'd thought. Patrick had been in my park for years, but that only meant that the mob couldn't have planted him for me. It certainly didn't mean that he didn't have a mob connection. Now that I thought about it, the mob is active in the pornography business.

"I thought you were on your way somewhere."

"I'm just cruising my new wheels," he told me. "One direction is as good as another."

He'd said he'd had a windfall and I'd assumed inheritance. But suppose it was mob-money? The temptation to flag down the bodyguards and have them haul Patrick off was almost more than I could stand. I resisted, though. Patrick paid his rent and even the mob surely wouldn't want him on their payroll.

"Now that I don't have Charlaine, I'm looking forward to the walk," I lied. "Some exercise would be good for me." That part wasn't a lie. And the temperatures hadn't really begun their morning climb yet so I wouldn't sweat all over myself.

He revved his engine. "Your funeral," he told me.

Which was exactly what I was afraid of.

* * * *

When I finally got home, I saw six goons were wandering around the trailer park looking exactly like the chickens. This is after I'd walked three miles so as not to call attention to them.

I put a finger in the squad leader's chest. "You'd better get your guys out of sight. Somebody is going to call the cops if you're not careful."

"You going out again today?" he demanded, ignoring my request.

I thought about it, but not for long. I'd spent most of the month at Andy's house or running around town and I didn't have a car. It was definitely time to stay home and catch up on some of my programming projects.

The goons had big sacks of donuts and sausage/biscuit sandwiches. I took a couple of eggs out of the refrigerator, then stuck them back in. They made me think of Charlaine and I felt that unwelcome moisture pushing its way through my eye sockets again.

Finally I settled for a bowl of grits. They aren't my favorite, but if you put enough butter in them, you can get them to taste just like-uh, butter. Yum. My milk was about a month past its expiration date-which is a little much, even for me, so oatmeal was out of the question.

I logged onto my computer and ate grits while I looked through my e-mail.

Incredibly, someone had responded to my website and wanted a proposal for a software project. This only happens about once a month, so I'm pretty stoked when it works. It was a Dallas company looking for a restaurant management system. There was a public-domain database program that I had played with before that had most of what the company wanted so I could knock out the custom part of the project in no time.

I fired back a quick proposal and they liked it. The company deposited a thousand dollars into my PayPal account almost before I finished deleting all of the e-mails from people wanting to improve my sex life. If they knew how dangerous my sex life could be, they wouldn't have bothered.

I managed to put together a quick-and-dirty prototype of the restaurant management program in a few hours. It was fun, really, and made me remember why I'd fallen in love with the computer back when I'd been in high school. You have to think about how everything is connected, then figure out ways to model that through database logic.

I guess you have to be a real nerd to love it, but hey. If the shoe fits, you wear it.

Angie brought over some lunch. Fast food supplied by the goons. Mooching food off people was getting to be a habit.

Angie wanted to talk but it didn't take her long to figure out that my brain was still somewhere in the middle of database normalization. She finished her cheeseburger, wiped a smudge of grease off my nose, and left.

I got back to programming, taking the code to where I would have to understand their workflow in order to complete it, then dropped my customer an e-mail telling them that I'd be happy to come to their place to show them status and talk through the remaining customization details.

Because it was after normal quitting time, I didn't really expect an answer right away, but the restaurant business works funny hours. Two minutes later, I had my answer. They suggested that they come to me since the restaurant was swamped and they didn't want any of their customers to think that they were having an inspection or anything.

I guessed that meant that they were the type of high-class restaurant that doesn't cater to freelance programmers-who are known as lousy dressers. If they were expensive, that would explain why I'd never heard of them. Sam wasn't exactly a big spender on our dates and a lot of nice places had opened in Dallas without sending me engraved invitations.

I wrote back and said I'd be happy to meet with them, giving them directions to my trailer.

They said they'd swing by at ten, after the big dinner rush.

Which gave me a chance to eat the second hamburger Angie had brought by. After eating, I put on my professional attire, which consisted of a pair of khaki slacks and a short-sleeved blue denim shirt (way too hot for summer in Dallas, especially if your air conditioner is broken).

I called the bodyguards to let them know I'd be having a late evening visitor and not to shoot anyone, then I got back to my computer. I buried myself in tinkering with the program.

Any program like this has two basic components. One is the database and its linkages. The second is the user interface. On the database side, you need to make sure you can track the orders and prices, payroll and schedules. Ideally you link orders back to an inventory control system, letting the restaurant know when certain items are getting low. To be a little fancier, you track which items are ordered, which make the most money, and even which are returned by the customer, linking returns to specific cooks if necessary. A restaurant that consistently serves something that gets sent back doesn't stay in business for long. The right kind of program can save big bucks.

The database work is hard, but intellectually satisfying.

I'd spent most of the day on the data side, putting together enough database linkages to show how the whole system would work once I populated it with actual data. I spent the couple of hours before the restaurant managers were scheduled to arrive fine-tuning the user interface.

I was pretty excited when I heard a knock at the door and realized that it was already ten o'clock. With any luck, I'd blow their socks off. Since there are about twenty million restaurants in the country and they all seem to talk to each other, I was mentally calculating how I could resell this base program at five thousand a pop to maybe a million restaurants. It would be a definite kick to tell Andy I was richer than him but that I still wanted to live in my trailer.

I threw opened the door with a stupid grin on my face, stuck out my hand—and froze.

Vorobev and one of the bouncers from his bar grinned back in recognition.

* * * *

I should have been scared. Instead, I was pissed. This wasn't fair. I'd gone to a lot of trouble on this program. I'd low-balled the bid because I knew I could use my success as a model, reselling the same basic design to a bunch of restaurants. And it turned out that the whole thing was a fraud, an excuse to get Vorobev invited to my house and, not coincidentally, my all-clear to the bodyguards. The mob probably knew exactly how my bodyguard situation was set up.

Being pissed off probably slowed my reaction. Still, although I knew it was hopeless I tried slamming the door and going for my pocket mace.

Sure enough, Vorobev blocked the door on a beefy forearm, and caught me with one hand, picking me up by the waistband of my slacks.

I had a little wiggle-room in my pants, which meant, I suspected, that I hadn't been eating enough lately. Normally that would be good news but when an overmuscled, testosterone-laden male picked me up like I was a cat, I wished I weighed a couple of hundred pounds and could give him a hernia.

"What are you doing here?" I demanded.

Vorobev set me down on my couch, pressing on my chest until I was all the way seated.

With most guys, a hand on my chest would have meant something. Whether they were copping a feel or participating in a mutual thing, there would be a sexual overtone. Not with Vorobev. He didn't care about me as a woman. For him, this was strictly business.

All of which meant that my feminine wiles wouldn't be working tonight.

Since my feminine wiles work about as often as a Democrat is elected in Texas, that wasn't a surprise. Still, it was a disappointment. I could use an edge.

"You've been stirring up a lot of trouble," Vorobev told me.

Behind him, the bouncer took out a roll of duct tape and yanked off a strip.

"You don't have to do that," I said. "I'm not going anywhere."

They both ignored me and the bouncer taped each of my legs to a leg of the couch.

"Now she really isn't going anywhere," he told Vorobev.

"I'm not going to gag you because I want you to talk," Vorobev said. "Except if you make more noise than you have to, the conversation is going to end in a hurry. Understand?"

I understood all right. I had a feeling that when the conversation ended, so would I, so I was willing to prolong it as long as possible.

"I'm all ears," I told him.

"That chicken thing got a whole lot of laughs on the radio," Vorobev told me. "I was listening to one of those shock jock morning shows today. They're still talking about it. Guess you got a pretty good joke in, huh?"

I nodded. He hadn't asked a question and I didn't want to risk having duct tape applied to my mouth.

"Guess you think it was pretty funny too?"

I shook my head. "What you do to those poor birds is disgusting and definitely not a joke. I'm glad we were able to slow things down, even if it is only temporary."

He brushed a hand across my face in a sort of slow motion slap. It didn't hurt, but it was as if he didn't even notice my attempt to resist.

"Chickens are stupid animals," he told me. "We let people go and punch each other around and give each other brain damage. We call that boxing and it's a sport worth billions. With chickens, nobody gets hurt, some poor farmers make some extra bucks, and a few roosters get to have the time of their lives. So what's your problem?"

Considering my alternatives, I was happy to have a philosophy debate with Vorobev. So I let him know that I thought boxing was disgusting too, and that cockfighting brings out the worst of both people and chickens.

He shook his head. "We're not going to have any more of those stupid stunts, Tina Anderson."

"Right. No more stunts." Could this mean he wasn't going to kill me?

He leaned closer. He was in range now, and my hands were free. Still, his bouncer was right behind him and I wasn't going to try something adventurous unless it had at least a chance of doing me some good.

"Tina Anderson, why are you messing with us? You never cared about chickens until a few weeks ago. Then, all of a sudden you're a bigwig in the CRL. How come?"

If I hadn't been taped to my couch with a three hundred pound gorilla of a man threatening to turn me into a corpse, I would have laughed. As it was, I found my sense of humor pretty well squelched.

"I found out Sam had been looking into cockfighting before he got murdered. So I figured I'd look too."

"You've been talking about Sam on the radio and stuff. What's he got to do with anything?"

I shook my head. "Your bosses didn't do much of a job at preparing you for this visit, did they?"

When he didn't say anything, I went ahead.

"Sam was investigating the chickens and he got killed. Sam was my boyfriend and I decided to find out why he got killed before the police decided to pin it on me, just so they could close a high-profile case and grab some headlines.

"That's when I looked at the papers Sam had left with me. They provided a pretty good motive for Sam's death-and with you here, I think my case just got better. The chicken-fighting mob is behind Sam's death. Which means you killed your own brother-in-law. I think that's pretty low."

Vorobev's lips turned down in a major scowl and his fists clenched so his arms ballooned up like Popeye's.

"Bullshit."

All of a sudden, I was pretty sure that Vorobev hadn't killed his brother-in-law-and hadn't known that his own mob had done the dirty work. Which meant that I might not be dead after all.

Time to talk fast.

"I met with your sister the other day, Ivan. Know what she said?"

"Amber?"

"You have any other sisters?"

He wouldn't meet my eyes. "None of your business."

That was interesting. "Well, Amber was the one I met. She told me she thought the mob killed Sam. And she thinks they killed Vlad too. They didn't tell you that they were going after your family like that, did they, Ivan?"

All right, that wasn't exactly what Amber had said, but I was a little panicked and needed an edge.

"Just slice her like you're supposed to and let's get out of here," the bouncer urged. "We don't have time to listen to this shit."

"I decide what I listen to," Vorobev told him. "And I decide what I'm going to do. So you keep your mouth shut and do what you're told."

The bouncer was too afraid of Vorobev to argue with him, but he wasn't afraid of me at all. The look he gave me said that if by some miracle Vorobev decided to leave me alive, that didn't mean I was out of it. I'd have to watch myself in the future because my new friend the bouncer just might be coming for me.

"Nobody messed with my family," Vorobev told me. "That isn't the way things work."

I still didn't have any sense of humor going but I made myself laugh anyway. "Is that what they told you, Ivan? Well guess what? They lied. They'll do whatever it takes to make money, and to keep it safe. Sam stole billions for them and they took it and then shafted him."

He was shaking his head but I didn't think he could reject what I was telling him that easily. "Watch her," he told the bouncer. "But don't touch her unless she tries something. I've got to make a call."

He stepped back and yanked a tiny cell from his pocket.

The bouncer moved closer.

He wasn't as fat as Vorobev, but he looked like he went to the same minimalist tailor. "Guess you're the kind of girl who likes to stir up trouble," he told me. "Guess you think you're real smart getting Vorobev worked up about his family."

I wasn't sure how smart I was being. It was quite possible that I was just ensuring that they would hurt me real bad before they killed me. Right then, though, I didn't have a lot of options and I'm not the kind of girl who would just stop fighting because the odds didn't look good.

"Family's important," I reminded him. "Bet you wouldn't like it if they came for one of your sisters. Especially if they had to drag her out of your bed."

"Bitch."

"Keep it down," Vorobev commanded.

I wanted the bouncer to shut up entirely so I could hear whatever

Vorobev was saying, but that didn't seem to be the game plan.

"I'm going to ask Vorobev to take a quick walk outside after he's done with the phone. Give me a chance to have a little fun before we stick you," the bouncer told me.

* * * *

Vorobev's face is always a plum color, so it took me a minute to realize that he was even redder than usual.

"You've been shitting me," he grunted. "Whoever killed Sam, it wasn't a sanctioned hit. And nobody knows nothing about Vlad, neither."

Generally I would have corrected grammar that bad but this didn't seem like the time.

"You don't really think they'd tell you the truth about something like that, do you, Ivan?"

He shook his head. "I think you're saying what you believe, Tina Anderson, but you're wrong. There's something going on here that you don't know."

"Yeah? So why don't you tell me."

He scratched his crotch absently. "That's the worst part. The big guys don't seem to know either. It's a bitch."

Well, that hadn't gone very far. I decided to go back to the line that had almost worked before. "Do you really think they'd tell you they'd offed your brother-in-law and your brother? Now that you've started asking questions, they're going to think you're a risk too. Cut me loose and let's figure out what we need to do next. Maybe we can both come out of this alive."

Sitting and planning next steps with Vorobev was right there on my list of least favorite things to do, but it sure beat out getting killed.

"That isn't the way they do business," he assured me. His tone seemed intended to convince himself as much as me, but it seemed to be working. I wasn't going to win this argument.

Unfortunately, if I couldn't persuade him, I thought I'd be out of the persuasion business permanently.

Vorobev pulled a long knife from one of his motorcycle boots and stepped closer. "You've been causing too much trouble, Tina Anderson. This won't hurt," he assured me. "Much."

I threw a cushion at him, but he just batted it away.

"Better hold her arms," he told the bouncer.

"Right."

The bouncer's hands gripped my arms from behind, yanking them above my head until they felt like they were being ripped from the sockets.

"I'm real sorry about this," Vorobev told me. He nestled the tip of his knife against my chest, probing for a gap between my ribs.

He lied. He hadn't even broken the skin and already it hurt like the devil.

We don't have earthquakes in Texas so, when my entire trailer started shaking, my first thought was that we'd been hit by a tornado.

The bouncer dropped my arms and Vorobev stepped back. "Shit."

"What the hell?" The bouncer looked around wildly, then went flying when the trailer shook a second time.

This time, a huge section of my front wall bulged in.

"Better get out of here," Vorobev said.

"What about the chick?"

"We'll worry about her later." Vorobev and the bouncer exited just as Patrick's SUV smacked into my house for the third time, this time actually smashing through the wall, its oversized wheels churning up my living room carpet, the purple neon lighting glaring against the darkness outside.

Patrick gave a huge blast with his horn-the first eleven notes of Dixie-and Vorobev and the bouncer hightailed out the front door.

* * * *

Patrick waited until he heard their truck peel off before emerging from his Cadillac, a box-cutter in his hands. "Don't worry, Tina, I'll get you out of there."

But that's as far as he got because the goons appeared.

They threw Patrick on the ground, cuffed his hands behind his back, and one of them held a gun to his kidneys while another planted a big booted foot on his head.

"Let him go," I demanded. "He just saved my life."

"He was coming after you with that box cutter," the head goon reported. "Good thing we were here to protect you."

"You guys are wonderful, all right. You let a couple of mob types come in and duct tape me to my own furniture and threaten to kill me, but when one of my neighbors manages to save me, you really nail his ass."

"But-"

"Let him up, you idiots." I knew I wasn't being very fair. After all, I had told them that I was expecting visitors and to back off. But after what I'd just been through, being fair was low on my priority list.

"Thanks, Tina." Patrick's voice was muffled because one of the goons still had his foot pressing Patrick's head into the floor. At least they hadn't hurt him too badly.

"He has a weapon," the bodyguard argued.

"Maybe one of you supposed bodyguards could take that weapon and cut my body free," I suggested. I was still taped to my couch and didn't want to be stuck there if my trailer collapsed, which looked increasingly likely.

One of the bodyguards liberated me while another tried to find the keys to Patrick's handcuffs.

It took a while, but they finally managed to free Patrick.

We all stepped outside, to the picnic table near my trailer. I collapsed, rubbed the circulation back into my legs, then took a deep breath. "So, Patrick. Want to tell me about it?"

* * * *

Patrick gave me his best shot at an innocent look-boyish smile, eyes slightly downcast but not enough so he didn't meet my gaze, and a little foot-shuffle action. I knew I was on to something.

"Come on, big guy. How did you know that I was in trouble?"

Patrick is the kind of guy who can't read without moving his lips, look at pictures without unzipping his pants, or think without steam rising from his brain. I saw his eyes roll as he got ready to answer my question and I knew he was going to send a lie my way. I wasn't wrong.

"Well, Tina, it's like this. I just happened to be walking by and I heard something. Everyone in the park knew about your bodyguards, so I figured that maybe one of them had gotten carried away."

Which was why he had driven his brand-new SUV through my living room wall rather than just knocking and asking if everything was fine.

I considered his story, then shook my head. "Nope, Patrick. I just can't make myself believe that one. Care to try another?"

He looked at the ground. "All right, I'll be straight with you. It's a little embarrassing for me to say this, but it was just pure luck. My car went out of control. Must have had a couple too many glasses of wine with dinner. I'm not a big hero type. Just clumsy and lucky."

I was willing to believe the clumsy part. What I couldn't believe was that Patrick had been clumsy enough to bash into my trailer three times in a row. And that he'd accidentally had his four wheel drive engaged at the same time.

Besides, when Patrick's lips were moving, you had a pretty good idea you were getting another lie.

A lot of the neighbors had emerged when they'd heard the crash, but most of them had gone back to their trailers now that they knew it was just Patrick. Angie, though had stuck around, along with at least ten of the goons. I turned to her now.

"Angie, do me a favor," I said.

"Sure."

"Grab Patrick's key from his ignition and run over to his place. I want to know what's showing on his computer."

Patrick held up a fat hand. "Hey. I've got a right to a little privacy, you know. Besides, I did just save your life."

"And I appreciate it," I told him. "But that doesn't mean I'm not interested in how you knew I needed saving. Of course, if you'd rather wait for the police to arrive, you can tell them your story. I'm sure that they'd be as interested as I am in how you just happened to plow into my house."

"All we need is the cops. That would really make my week."

I took that as an okay and sent Angie off.

A couple of the goons went with her. It looked to me like most of them wanted to. But their leader made the rest of them stay where they could keep an eye on me.

While Angie was gone, they got on their cells with Pelcovitz.

Angie came back about the same time Pelcovitz and Andy pulled up. Pelcovitz and Andy looked worried. Angie looked mad as hell. "You guessed right."

I glared at Patrick. "You were bugging me, weren't you? After all we talked about, you were still going to put my pictures on the Internet?"

Then I remembered the fancy new car. With an emphasis on new. "Ohmigod, you've already put them up, haven't you? What a creep."

He shook his head. "I was going to let you know, Tina. Honest. Besides, the spread is incredibly tasteful. I set it up as, you know, sort of an artistic site. Just an ordinary girl from the poor side of town. There's a lot of interest in that kind of thing. It wouldn't be right to just let that demand sit there unserved."

I didn't want to know about the demand for trailer trash babes and I definitely didn't want to hear Patrick's moral justification for sneaking a hidden camera into my trailer. And Patrick had the nerve to talk about his own right to privacy.

He could see that his argument was going nowhere so he changed tack. "If I hadn't bugged your place, you'd be dead now, Tina. You should be thanking me, not yelling at me."

I looked at my house. Patrick's big S.U.V. had driven a huge hole through my living room wall. Worse, he'd smashed it directly over my computer. Everything I'd worked on for the past month, since my last backup, was almost certainly destroyed beneath the knobby wheels of his oversized and overcompensating toy.

Including that restaurant management program I'd worked so hard on. Not that Vorobev had really wanted a program. He'd just been looking for a way to get past my guards. I guess everybody knew about the goons.

Patrick had a point, though. He had saved my life. I didn't owe him enough to let him keep my pictures out there, but I couldn't justify sending him off to jail, either.

"Right. Get the hell out of here and take those pictures off the Internet."

"Just one minute, if you please," Pelcovitz objected. You could tell he was a lawyer. The way he put his words together put my teeth on edge.

"What?" Patrick had been up from the picnic table bench and heading back to his trailer.

"If I understand correctly, Ms. Anderson was assaulted and you captured that assault on video."

"Maybe." Even caught red-handed, Patrick wasn't going to admit anything before he knew where this was going.

"Did you store that video?"

"Wouldn't be much point in taking it if I didn't save it," he answered.

"What you have on your computer is evidence of a crime in progress. I'm obliged to insist that the computer be seized and turned over to the police."

Seeing Patrick's face fall when he thought about his beautiful computer being turned over to the police, almost made me laugh. He'd invested most of his adult life in collecting pictures of naked women, including, it turned out, naked pictures of me, and now he was going to lose the whole thing.

I almost laughed, that is, until I processed what Pelcovitz's suggestion really meant.

"No way." Patrick and I both exploded at the same moment.

Pelcovitz ignored Patrick. "What's the problem, Ms. Anderson?"

"If the police get Patrick's computer, there'll be naked pictures of me all over the police station." I may not know a lot about Patrick's porn business but I know plenty about the police."

Pelcovitz looked nonplussed. "Without the evidence, how do you expect to make charges stick against your assailants?"

I didn't really care about an assault charge. Even if I got Vorobev and his bouncer locked up, how would that help? The mob had plenty of gunmen and knifemen to send after me if that's what they wanted to do.

What I wanted was to get some closure on the two murders that had taken place. I'm not the world's best judge of character, but Vorobev had seemed distinctly shocked when I'd told him about Sam's murder. I didn't think he'd done it.

Which didn't have to mean anything. For sure the mob's leaders were smart enough that they wouldn't have sent Vorobev to knock off his own brother-in-law. Still, it could mean that there was something going on that I hadn't even thought about.

"I think we'll investigate some more," I told Pelcovitz. "We can use the video as a threat but I'm not turning it over to the police."

"I'll keep it safe," Patrick promised me. "Trust me."

Which was a big joke. I was supposed to trust Patrick after he'd bugged my home?

"Do you think my truck is okay?" he asked plaintively when I didn't respond to his request to trust him.

I looked at it. The front end was smashed in and the half the neon lighting was out. Since he'd gone with the fade option on his paint, the price notched up a level.

One summer during college I hadn't been able to find a computer-related job so I'd worked in a paint shop so I had a pretty fair idea what this meant. "You're looking at about five thousand bucks," I told him. "Minimum."

"Crap."

He looked at me like he was getting ready to ask if I'd mind just a few more pictures, but I shook my head before he got up the nerve to ask me. "Don't think about it, Patrick. I swear I'll have Vorobev come back and use his knife to change your voice."

"Right." He shook his head. "Five thousand, huh?"

Pelcovitz had been grinding his teeth through my little exchange with Patrick. "You're making a big mistake, Tina."

"Giving the computer to the cops would be a bigger mistake."

Pelcovitz nodded, but I could tell he was pissed. Even before he turned away and started whispering with Andy.

Well, it wasn't my job to keep Pelcovitz happy. My job was to figure out who had killed Sam.

And it dawned on me that if the mob wasn't involved, then maybe Andy was back in the picture. After all, there's nothing like a good red herring to throw the police off the scent. And if Andy was guilty, then everything I'd been doing was just helping him cover it up.

Chapter 14

After everyone but Angie left, I'd given my house a quick lookover. Repairing Patrick's car might cost five thousand, but the trailer was totaled. I was homeless.

I tried to remember if I had insurance, but all I could think about was the stack of bills I'd ignored. Homeowners insurance had probably been in that pile.

Angie dragged me back to her place, sat me down on her couch, and brought me a glass of some of that expensive wine she drinks. She and I both know that it was wasted on me, but she just can't bring herself to keep cheep stuff in her trailer.

I was mooching again. I swore I was going to stop doing that. But not right away.

The moment she handed me the glass, I started to shake.

"It's okay," she told me. "They're gone. Our plan worked."

I looked at her like she was crazy. If this was success, I'd hate to see failure.

"We wanted to scare them up, right?" she continued, obviously trying to talk me past a rough spot. "We wanted to make them move. That's why we went by Vorobev's place last night. That's why we have the goons hanging around."

"Vorobev had his knife between my ribs." Sobs were coming up from somewhere and I was having a hard time getting the words out. "If Patrick had come in half a second later, I would be dead."

Angie looked a little pale around the gills. She took a slug of her wine—unusual for her since she normally sips and savors. "But Patrick did come."

"Yeah." A giggle forced itself up from some subterranean depths. "Great. Now I owe my life to Patrick Adams."

"Hey, it's better than being dead." Angie didn't sound completely convinced.

I wasn't either.

We shared two bottles of wine and I finally drifted off to sleep in her couch—and woke up when I heard something moving furtively in the room near me.

Naturally I screamed.

Naturally Angie screamed too.

It was she, of course, getting ready to do her nighttime job. Doing the goons, I hoped, because I swear I wasn't going to speak to her again if she decided to work the streets after what I'd just gone through.

She assured me that she would make sure she stayed close to the goons. Real close.

Too much information.

With all of the adrenaline I had going, I didn't get back to sleep until four, after Angie came wandering back in, hair a mess, but a big smile on her face and a big wad in her wallet.

"I could get used to having a bunch of overpaid muscle living in the park," she whispered to me when she saw I was still awake.

I shook my head. There had been a time when I would have given just about anything to have the complex full, but nearly getting killed had put things in perspective. I wanted the goons gone because we'd fingered the killers and they were safely in jail. The sooner, the better.

* * * *

Andy was with Kevin Franklin again when I dropped in at his office.

"Hey Tina,"

Franklin was in a backslapping and jovial mood. I stepped away quickly before I got my own back slapped.

"I owe you bigtime for what you've found. Got the word from our lawyers. They think we have a case against the auditing firm. And best news, the auditors actually have some money, even after all the other lawsuits they've been through. I may be able to pay off some of my creditors yet." He pretended he hadn't noticed me moving away from him.

"Great, Kevin. Have you found anything else about mob involvement in your accounting department?"

Franklin got serious. "That's one of the reasons I was talking to Andy. After what's happened, I don't trust my own human resources team any more. They were the ones who vetted Sam, after all. So I'm asking Andy to run a background check on everyone left in my accounting group."

"Good thinking," I admitted.

"Yeah." He stepped closer, backing me into a corner and giving me a 'just guys' slug on the shoulder. "I'm not going to forget that you were the one who puzzled this one out, Tina. Anything you want, just let me know. And I mean anything."

"Sure, Kevin."

Franklin gave Andy a slug too and then punched the elevator button. The man was a fighting machine this morning.

Andy, on the other hand, looked like something the cat had dragged in.

"You look like hell," I told him.

He rubbed his eyes. "Good. I'd hate to feel this way and not have anything to show for it."

"Police still giving you trouble?"

He nodded slowly. "Pelcovitz tries to keep them busy, but they seem to have my schedule down. Whenever I've got an important customer meeting, they show up and drag me off, supposedly for more questions. I tell them I can't talk without my lawyer, so we sit at the police station and wait for Pelcovitz. When he shows, they let me go. I suppose it's their routine to break a suspect down and make him confess. I'm not going to confess anything, but it's definitely wearing me ragged."

I nodded. I could empathize with wearing ragged. "Thanks for coming last night."

"Hey, we're friends, right. What else would I do?"

That was a good question. I know a lot of divorced women and I couldn't think of even one of their exes who would have stopped by to check on them if their trailer had been mauled. Unless they thought they might be able to steal some of the silverware or something. Which made Andy exceptional. Normally, exceptional is good. Except when the police theory is that Andy had an obsession with me, I wasn't so sure this was a positive.

"I'll be living with Angie for a couple of weeks until I figure out what to do," I told him.

"You could move back into my place," he offered again.

I didn't want to believe Andy could have anything to do with the killings, but when he talked like this, I couldn't help just that fraction of doubt.

"Um "

"What's up with you and Franklin?" he asked before I could finish thinking up what I was going to say next.

"Me and Kevin?" I was mystified. "Nothing. Except I let him know about the mob involvement in his accounting." And even if I had been interested, I wouldn't have told Andy. I was almost completely certain he had nothing to do with the murders. But almost isn't the same as all the way. I didn't want another dead body on my conscience and Kevin Franklin was a nice guy even if he didn't do much for me.

"Hmm." He looked at me closely. It was the look he uses when he has something to tell me and doesn't think I'm going to like it.

"I hate it when you do that. What have you heard?"

He shrugged, but his heart wasn't in it. "I've heard from a couple of people that Franklin is seeing you in a new light. In an interesting light."

"Well, he certainly hasn't asked me out."

"Would you go if he asked you?"

"You're way over the line now, big guy," I told him. "I'm all grown up and nobody voted you my new mommy."

Andy's smile barely made it to his lips. "Be careful, Tina. I can't tell you how much last night scared me. If that pervert hadn't been watching you, all the guards in the world wouldn't have made any difference. And yet you're still charging ahead, getting involved, and putting yourself in danger."

"Thanks to me, we've got a lot possibilities for the cops to worry about besides you," I reminded him. "So it isn't like I'm just spinning my wheels. And besides, I'm going to be better with the bodyguards. Last night, I made a mistake. But other than that, I haven't been out of their sight for the past couple of days."

"Why doesn't that make me feel more confident? You've got to stop trying to take care of me, honey. I've got Pelcovitz for that. Just back off and let the professionals handle this case. You've done great, but it's past time for amateurs now."

I got up and walked out without saying anything. First he'd gotten jealous about Kevin Franklin of all people, and then he'd gone and told me to mind my own business.

A terrible thought crossed my mind. Maybe the police only had a part of the story down. Could Andy be involved with the mob too? Maybe that was why he was so reluctant to let me pursue the case. He'd rather let the police chase him for a weird motive than for them to understand what was really going on.

I tried to dismiss the thought, but I couldn't get it completely out of my head. The whole case smelled like roadkill left to rot in the sun. The way Kevin Franklin trusted Andy, looked up to him as a mentor, it would have been easy for Andy to insert crooked people into Franklin's organization. And the amount of money that had been taken from Big Cat Telecom made Andy's investments in the company look like small change. Like a cover, in fact.

* * * *

One of the goons had driven me to Andy's place and I let him drive me back to the trailer park. My attempts to hide the bodyguards hadn't worked, so I'd decided to put them to good use.

Angie had adopted that approach days earlier, but Angie always was more direct than me.

"Want to go out for a burger?" the goon asked me when we went past the last Jack in the Box before getting to the park.

"Last guy who took me out got killed," I reminded him. I was on my new no-mooching kick.

"Oh, yeah. Guess I'll take a rain check, then."

Who said there weren't advantages to being stalked? I had a handy excuse to turn down unwanted dates now. And unwanted dates were the only kind I was being asked out on.

We pulled up to the park just in time to see an older man, overdressed for the heat of a Texas summer in a wool suit and expensive-looking silk tie, step into the ruins of my trailer.

I thanked the goon for the ride, got out, and followed the man, being careful to stay well back.

"You with the insurance company?" I demanded.

"Ms. Tina Anderson?" He had a trace of an accent and one of his front teeth had a gold rim around it. All of a sudden, I wasn't so sure he was the insurance guy.

"I'm Tina Anderson."

"I see. I need to have a discussion with you."

"If it's about my insurance premiums, I'm pretty sure that I'm up to date," I lied. "Just, with all the mess, I can't put my hands on my paperwork." I looked around but the bodyguards seemed to have vanished.

"I'm not with the insurance company, Ms. Anderson. But we do need to talk. Ten minutes would be enough."

"Last guys who wanted to have a conversation with me tried to kill me," I said. "So I'm a little hesitant to just hand out appointments."

"That was a mistake," he said, his accent a bit stronger as he put a bit of emotion into his voice. "A mistake I wish to remedy."

Uh-oh. Unless I completely missed my guess, this was the godfather, or whatever the Russian mob called their leaders.

I backed up quickly. "I have guards all around the complex," I threatened.

"Of course, Ms. Anderson. Very wise of you, in fact."

He was not especially tall and he had to be pushing eighty, but now that I had a closer look at the old guy, I could almost see the power and danger radiating from him. He was even sort of sexy in a way-too-old sort of way.

Out of the corner of my eye, I saw movement and panicked, certain that the mobster had just distracted me while his killer had snuck up on me.

Without thinking, I dove to the ground, rolling toward the motion I'd seen. Maybe I was trying to bowl him over. Maybe not, I don't know. I was tired and having trouble processing.

If it had been another mobster, I would have looked like a genius and probably ended up saving the day and getting on the front page of the *Dallas Morning News*. Naturally it wasn't another mobster.

It was, in fact, my chicken, Charlaine, returned from the river and now quaking with fear at the giant woman rolling across the dirt toward her.

How she'd crossed three miles of south Dallas to return to my trailer, I'll never know.

"Very touching," the mob boss observed when I picked up the terrified bird and stroked her, cooing reassuring words into her little chicken-ears.

"Well, I'm not sorry about my involvement in the chicken rescue," I told him.

He waved his hand. "Mr. Vorobev misunderstood my feelings about your efforts. We're quite grateful, you know."

That surprised me. "Look, are you here to kill me, or can we sit down somewhere. Poor Charlaine is worried and I need to get her out of the sun."

"I raised chickens when I was a young man in Russia," he told me. "They don't mind the heat as long as they have access to water." He shook his head. "But I am being rude. Please allow me to introduce myself. I am Mr. Fomin." He gave me a rueful smile. "Sounds like an enemy in English, doesn't it. Foe Man. Let me assure you, though, that I have no wish to be any foe of yours. In fact, I hope to be your friend, Ms. Anderson."

Great. Just what I needed. Another mobster friend. "Trying to kill me last night hardly seems to be a friendly thing."

He shook his head gravely. "Again, I need to apologize for my associates. In the heat of the moment, they made a poor decision. They were sent to warn you to be careful, not to kill you."

Charlaine nipped at me and I made a decision of my own. Probably a lot dumber decision than the one Vorobev had made. "All right, Mr. Fomin. Let's sit down and discuss things. But outside where my bodyguards can see us."

He nodded gravely, then followed me to the picnic table I had installed in the trailer park in a moment of weakness when I'd thought that maybe Sam and Emily and I could have family moments. It wasn't much, but it was under a big live oak tree so it was shaded, at least.

Fomin sat across from me, his blunt hands on the table in front of him. Empty. His pale eyes were partially hidden behind bifocal glasses and a small hearing aid protruded from one ear. He should have looked harmless. He didn't.

One of the bodyguards wandered by, glanced at the old man, then shrugged. Clearly he didn't see what I saw.

I appreciated Fomin's act of putting his hands on the table but knew it was only a gesture. I'd seen the lump in his suit-jacket pocket. Unless he had a strange growth there, I was pretty sure he was carrying a gun.

"Talk," I told him.

"Of course." He paused to arrange his thoughts, then nodded.

"First, let me compliment you on your chicken stunt. We had a number of clues that the so-called Chicken Rescue League was up to something, but we were shocked by the scale of your operation and thought it was going to happen weeks later."

"Not that I'm admitting any involvement, but I think that was a pretty good raid."

"In case I am wired?" Fomin laughed. "We could use someone smart like you in the operation. Many of my associates are like Mr. Vorobev. Full of energy and purpose and not stupid so much as willing to switch their minds completely off for long periods of time. Mr. Vorobev is having the opportunity to rethink his poor decisions now. Perhaps he will learn from the experience."

Charlaine pecked at my hand again, got off the table and started chasing after locusts.

Good. Those bugs can make more noise than a low-flying jet.

"Your raid has quite disrupted our operations," Fomin continued, giving me a smile to let me know that we were still good buddies. "And, as you no doubt intended, it created a bit of police interest in our activities."

"I'm glad to hear it," I told him.

He laughed, with a small wheeze and a catch at the end. Too many cigarettes over his lifetime.

"I came to your country as a student, many years ago," he explained. "Many, many years ago. I learned little in University, but one thing I remember is called the law of unintended consequences. What you want is often the opposite of what you get. You learned this at Texas A & M University perhaps?"

Fomin had done his homework. I certainly hadn't mentioned my alma mater to Vorobev. Maybe in the software proposal I'd sent to Vorobev.

"Never heard of it," I told him.

"Ah? Well here is a fine example. You wanted to destroy our operations and fill people with horror about cruelty to the animals, no?

Instead, you create an interest in our business from people who have been unaware of the popularity of our sport. So now we have fewer birds, but bigger audiences. In this case, better for everyone."

It was interesting, but in a bad way. "So you came to gloat?"

Fomin blinked. "After what happened last night, I'm not surprised that you think the worst of us, Ms. Anderson. I'm merely trying to explain that I'm not angry with you, even though some of our lower level operatives might be."

"Well, that's a relief," I told him.

"Is it?" He reached into his pocket and I froze. Behind me, I heard the distinctive click of a shell being chambered. I guess the guard hadn't been quite as nonchalant as he'd acted. Pelcovitz had given the goons a good reaming the previous night so they weren't going to be caught with their pants down again.

Fomin slowly removed a pristine white handkerchief and wiped a drop of sweat from his forehead.

"Even after sixty years of living in Texas, I find the heat," he searched for a word, "disconcerting."

"Very interesting," I said. "But I'm still not sure why you're here. If you want to apologize for the attack last night, I think you have a lot of nerve. If one of my tenants hadn't been vigilant, I'd be dead right now."

Fomin's laugh was a soft of throaty whine. "Mr. Patrick Adams. Such an entrepreneurial young man. And quite enamored with your beauty, Ms. Anderson. He was most artistic in portraying your every movement before his on-line shrine abruptly vanished last night."

Had everyone in the world seen those naked pictures of me? This was more than a little embarrassing.

"Patrick is a peach all right," I agreed. "Is there anything else?"

"But yes." He started to move his hand and the handkerchief back to his pocket and stopped. "I'm going to bring something out. It isn't a gun," he announced to the goons behind me.

It was an envelope. A fat envelope that hit the picnic table in front of me with a substantial thud.

"What's this? Printouts of my dirty pictures?"

"I suspect you would hardly welcome photos of your naked figure, fine though it is," Fomin said. "This is a retainer. We wish to hire you."

He could have knocked me over with a feather. "You mean that restaurant management program was for real?" My computer was totaled, but maybe I could salvage the hard drive. It's the code that matters, after all. Hardware is replaceable.

Fomin shook his head. Rather sadly, I thought, as if sorry to disappoint me again. "That was Vorobev's idea. A rather clever one, I think. Despite his porcine appearance, the man is rather intelligent when he bothers to engage his brain. And perhaps you should try to persuade him to complete the purchase."

Yeah, right. I was so sure that making sales calls on the man who'd tried to kill me was going to be a happening thing.

"What do you want me to do?" Maybe this really was all about Patrick's website. Well, they'd have to come up with more money than would fit in one envelope before I'd agree to have my house wired again.

"We want you to continue your investigations. To find out what happened to our money."

He'd stumped me again. "What money?"

"Ms. Anderson. You've already persuaded me that you're an intelligent woman. If you think about it, you'll know exactly what money we're talking about. The money that your boyfriend, Sam Goodwin, alias Sam Katz, plundered from Big Cat Telecom, for us. One billion, three hundred million dollars, Ms. Anderson. It is," he coughed discretely, "a substantial sum."

Yeah, one point three bill was a substantial sum. Enough to buy my entire trailer park and then a thousand more like it.

"You think Sam stole Big Cat's money and kept it?"

"Several colleagues and I invested heavily in Big Cat Telecom. Our investments gave us a certain sway in hiring decisions. And insight into what was happening within the organization."

Fomin was talking carefully, as if he was concerned that I might be wearing a wire myself. But if I was to believe him, the mob planned the embezzlement, but they hadn't ended up with the money.

No wonder Vorobev had been after me when I'd told him I had Sam's stuff. He probably thought I was gloating about the missing money.

"I don't believe you," I told him. "Everyone knows that the mob took the money or Sam gambled it away. Sam was researching the mob to find an angle, some leverage. That was his interest in the CRL."

"There is no leverage worth one billion, three hundred million dollars." His words were still controlled, calm. But they carried an underlying sense of power-and truth. "None."

From what I knew of organized crime, Fomin was right. Friendship, embarrassment, years in jail, all would pale compared to that shower of wealth.

"But-"

"The envelope before you holds ten thousand dollars. Think of it as a simple thank you for the work you have done until now. And as a little incentive to keep looking. If you find more, we will pay you more."

"I can't take your money, Mr. Fomin. If I find anything, I'll report it to the police." Or to Pelcovitz and Andy.

Except I wasn't so sure about them any more. Big Cat didn't have the money. Sam didn't have the money. And if I was to believe Fomin, the mob didn't have the money. Which left my ex-husband, Andy, as the last man standing. Andy, the one man Big Cat's president ran to every time he needed to make a decision. The man Kevin Franklin used to vet his hiring decisions. The only man who had known that Sam Katz was really Sam Goodwin before Sam was killed.

"Your scruples do you credit, Ms. Anderson," Fomin told me. He shrugged. "I don't understand them, but I admire them nevertheless. However, I am not asking you to find our money for us. I'm simply requesting that you keep after the murders. Sam was one of us. You've already been able to learn more than my associates. Perhaps because you run in rather different circles. It is unlikely that I will ever see the money I worked so hard to earn, but I would like to see that whoever stole it from me is uncovered, exposed, and" he looked at me, letting his voice trail off.

Despite the Texas heat, an absolute chill ran down my spine. Fomin's pale blue eyes had looked watery and vague behind his bifocals. But when he spoke about his money and whoever had stolen it from him, they hardened until they shone like steel.

"Punished," he finally concluded as if he hadn't ever stopped.

"I see."

"As I said, this envelope is merely a reward for what you have done so far. For your inconvenience. You may think of it as full payment for the software project you did for Vorobev if that would help your ethical dilemma. There will be more money if you actually find the killers. More yet if you happen to mention their names to me before you engage the police."

A part of me wanted to tell him to stick his dirty money where the sun didn't shine. It was a small part of me, though. A bigger part couldn't help noticing the gaping hole in my trailer and reminding me that ten thousand big ones would let me make the down payment on a new one. Even though Patrick had done the damage, Fomin's hoods were responsible. He did owe me.

"I'll take the money," I said. "But I'm not making any promises."

"I didn't expect any promises from you, Ms. Anderson," Fomin told me. "I came to make promises to you. And the last promise is this. If you find who stole my money, you'll get another envelope. But this one will hold ten times ten thousand dollars."

I shrugged. If I'd been the greedy and money-grubbing sort, I would have gone after Andy for a big division of property. A girl has to eat, but I want to earn my money-or mooch it fair and square. I figured I'd earned the ten thousand for sitting there while Vorobev slid his knife along my ribs. I really, really didn't want to earn a ten times as much the same way.

"I appreciate you giving me so much of your time." Fomin stood, then held out his hand. "Again, my sincere apologies for the excessive actions of my associates."

I could have left him there with his hand hanging out. I thought about it, but only for a second. It wouldn't be smart, of course. Insulting mob leaders isn't a sign of intelligence. But that isn't why I shook his hand. I shook his hand because all of a sudden he reminded me of my grandfather.

Call me maudlin.

"With your aggressive guards watching, I won't risk reaching into my pocket a third time," Fomin told me when I released his hand. "My card is in the envelope, however. Feel free to call me if you have any questions that I, or any of my associates, could answer. Or, of course, if you learn any information you'd like to share with us."

I nodded. Then I couldn't help myself. "You seem like a smart businessman, Mr. Fomin. How come you decided to become a criminal?"

He gave me another of his wheezy laughs. "I am a Russian, as you see. Growing up in the Soviet Union, you were criminal or you starved. Looking for the trick, finding the right man to bribe, it all becomes a habit. A habit that can be hard to break when you're good at it. I became very good at it."

An oversized BMW pulled up as Fomin stepped away from my picnic table and into the parking lot.

A brute who could have been Vorobev's twin jumped out and opened the back door for Fomin, then rushed around and got in at the other side.

Fomin gave me a little salute just as his door closed and the mirror glass cut off all sight of him.

* * * *

Charlie, the goon leader, grabbed the envelope at the same time I put my hand on it.

"Hey, that's mine."

"We've got to check it for bombs."

"Mr. Fomin wouldn't bomb me, he likes me."

Charlie laughed. His laugh had a sort of tobacco wheeze to it, but that was the only similarity between it and Fomin's. Fomin seemed to get a certain enjoyment out of life. Charlie just mocked everyone around him.

"Fomin is on the FBI most-wanted list. He'd kill his mother for twenty dollars."

"So go arrest him, but leave my money alone."

He rolled his eyes. "It isn't my job to arrest people. My job is to protect you. And letting you blow yourself up with an obvious bomb wouldn't be doing my job."

"But stealing my ten-thousand dollars would, right?"

"You don't know that there is money in there. I find it highly unlikely."

Charlie had heard every word Fomin said. He knew as well as I did that the envelope was full of money. And I knew that if Charlie took the envelope, the only way I'd ever even get a chance to look at the money was when Angie flashed it around after she'd earned it on her back. Charlie would have a story on how the envelope really was a bomb or maybe filled with counterfeit. Neither one would help me with my new trailer.

"You say protecting me from this envelope full of money is your job."

"We don't know that there is money there, but yes."

"Well, guess what? You're fired."

My reaction sort of popped out. Once it had, though, it made sense. I'd asked for the goons because I'd wanted to smoke out the mob and not get killed in the process. Not getting killed had been a close call, but between visits from Vorobev and Fomin, we had definitely smoked out the mob. So, why did I need them glomming around my complex, annoying the neighbors and keeping Angie in a state of happy (and affluent) exhaustion? Answer: I didn't.

"You can't fire me."

I snatched my money out of his hands and dialed 9-1-1 on my cell. "Watch me."

The police aren't especially responsive to calls from trailer parks, but they eventually sent out a couple of units.

I told them that Charlie and his goons had refused to leave the complex and the cops escorted them off, warning them that they'd be in trouble if they came back.

Then I counted my money.

Fomin hadn't lied. Ten thousand bucks is a lot of money.

Chapter 15

Pelcovitz came by the complex a couple of hours later.

He looked pissed when he arrived, especially when he bottomed out his mid-life-crisis red Thunderbird convertible on one of the trailer park speed bumps I'd installed.

"Are you absolutely insane?"

I was busy cleaning out the mess the goons had left in Sam's trailer when he pulled up and pretended I hadn't noticed him coming.

"Did you say something, Pelcovitz?"

"My god, Tina. Last night you were almost killed and today you decide to send away your bodyguards. What were you thinking?"

He stood too close to me, trying to overwhelm me with his height. Probably a lawyer trick, I thought.

I heaved a couple more empty beer bottles into the trash. "I had the cops toss your goons off the property. I can have you tossed off too if you don't calm down and talk to me like I'm an adult."

"Andy owns this complex, not you."

I just looked at him. "Oh? You don't think Andy would back me up?"

That would be an interesting test. No matter how reluctant I was to admit it, I was being pointed directly at Andy as the lead suspect in the entire mystery. And Pelcovitz was as much an extension of Andy as Andy's arm.

"Not if he thought you were making a serious mistake," Pelcovitz answered carefully. "But I apologize for my outburst. Blame it on distress if you would. I certainly didn't intend to treat you with anything but respect. I simply wonder if your temper might have pushed you into making a decision that your further consideration might find to be unwarranted."

"The way you lawyers talk just sends shivers up my spine," I told him. "Sort of like when ol' Miss Chadham used to squeak the chalk on the board in school."

"I'm deadly serious, Tina," he told me. He physically backed off, though, sitting himself down on Sam's couch and giving me some personal space back. "If any of the bodyguards got out of line, I'd be happy to request a replacement. But you're in danger and need protection."

"We agreed to a guard while I was flushing out the mob," I reminded him as I'd reminded Charlie-the-goon. "Between Vorobev last night and Fomin today, I think we'd all agree that the mob is pretty thoroughly flushed. They don't want to hurt me now. So, that's that."

"Do you seriously think they'd tell you if they meant to kill you?"

"I don't think they'd send the old man here to give me money. Besides, I believed him when he said that they don't know who killed Sam."

Pelcovitz argued for a while, but his heart wasn't really in it because he knew he wasn't going to win.

"Perhaps you should move back in with Andy for a while," he suggested, beating a tactical retreat. From his expression, though, I figured it was a retreat to a carefully prepared position.

I didn't let him off that easily. "Is that your idea, or his?"

"Mr. Anderson did suggest that you might be safer where he could watch over you," Pelcovitz admitted.

My skin crawled. I'd made out with Andy just a few nights earlier. He was one man I'd always trusted, always believed would protect me. But if Andy was the killer, I wasn't safe. And none of the bodyguards, paid for by Andy, and nothing else, could keep me safe.

On the other hand, if I wanted to find out what was really going on, why not step into the lion's den?

"I'll have to talk it over with Angie."

Pelcovitz shouldn't have been surprised about my reinforcement, but he was. "Uh, I'm sure that will be satisfactory."

Had he thought I would head into the lion's den alone? Angie had done even more in the chicken rescue thing than I had. We were in this together. For better or worse, we needed to guard each other's backs.

I figured I would appeal to her Nancy Drew complex. Or Nora Charles if she was still on that kick. One thing for sure, I didn't want to do this alone.

Pelcovitz waffled for another ten minutes, trying to get me to agree to let the goons back into the complex or to leave for Andy's immediately, letting Angie catch up whenever she could. After a while he started to repeat himself, so I got back to cleaning.

I'd had no idea how big a mess half a dozen bodyguards can make in a trailer. They'd been there for less than a week, but I must have found a hundred condom wrappers, fifty sacks each from the various fast-food joints around the 'hood, and enough beer bottles to float a navy. If I'd been worried about them, it would have been reassuring to know that they had made themselves so comfortable. But I wasn't their mom and I was pissed that I had to pick up after them.

I won't say that I wasn't being a little irrational here. After all, I did have the cops escort them out of the park without giving them a chance to neaten up before they left. But I didn't think they'd bothered even throwing anything away the whole time they'd spent there.

There are times when I think I'll swear off men entirely.

* * * *

Angie was overjoyed that I'd fired the goons.

She'd been as sick of them as I was, and she'd had some really good reasons.

"They're a bunch of perverts," she told me. "What's wrong with good old-fashioned sex, anyway?"

As far as I knew, there was absolutely nothing wrong with sex, except I wasn't getting any because someone kept killing my boyfriends, but that was a whole different issue.

"You really think Andy is the killer?" she asked me when we got off the subject of sex and onto the subject of murder.

That was the stumper, all right. We'd both known Andy all of our lives. As far as we knew, he'd never tortured cats, pulled wings off of flies, or burned bees with a magnifying glass. According to the true-crime shows Angie was addicted to, those were the sure signs.

"He did beat up those guys from Sunset High that one time," I reminded her.

"Because they were insulting you for wearing out-of-style clothes."

What I'd worn to high school had been what I could find, shoplift, or pick up at the Good Will Thrift Store. To say that I hadn't been a fashion plate would push understatement to a new level.

"That's my point," I reminded her. "He can be violent if he's motivated. And what better motivation than staying out of jail?"

"But that's assuming he was behind the embezzlement in the first place. He doesn't need money. Why would he rip off Big Cat?"

I had a theory and I tried it out on her. "He could have found out about the mob's plan. He could have thought it would be better to divert the money to himself rather than just let the mob make off with it. Especially with all he'd invested in Big Cat."

"Why not just tell Kevin, then? Head the whole thing off."

It was a good question. One I didn't have a good answer too. So I didn't try. Instead I pulled out the big guns.

"Every time I start to think it could be Andy, I come up with some excuse for him, some justification why it couldn't be him," I reminded her. "But every time I do that, the evidence points me right back at him. So this time, I'm going to assume that he did it. If I can clear him, so much the better. If not, wouldn't you rather we know the truth?"

She thought about it. "Maybe."

I felt a little ambivalent about finding out for sure too. If it had just been the embezzlement, I would have figured that Andy had his reasons. But killing my boyfriends had to be over the line no matter how generous I was. I didn't want Sam's killer to get away with murder—even if his killer was the one man I'd truly loved.

"So are we going to move back in with him?" she asked. We were sitting in her kitchen, drinking more of her wine.

This could get to be a habit if I wasn't careful. I didn't want to get used to drinking better wine than I could afford. And, even with Fomin's ten thousand, I wasn't exactly flush. At least I wouldn't be once I made the down payment on a new trailer.

I nodded slowly. "That sounds like the best way I can think of to finally learn the truth."

"Not to mention putting ourselves in danger again."

I laughed. Too much wine and too little sleep, I guess. I can't think of any other reason I would think that was funny.

"Two questions," Angie said.

"Shoot."

"First, are you sure you can trust this Fomin guy?"

I couldn't tell her that he reminded me of my grandfather. For one thing, Angie is a lot more cynical about people than I am. For another, I think my grandfather had once had a thing for Angie.

"I'm going with my gut here, but I think if Fomin had wanted me dead, I would be dead and the goons wouldn't have been any the wiser. He wasn't like Vorobev. You know, impatient and looking for a shortcut. He was hard and focused."

Angie shook her head slowly. "And you're going to accuse your husband based on that?"

"Is that your second question? And he's my ex-husband."

"Huh-uh. My second question is what are we going to do with her?"

Her, in this case, referred to the little bundle of feathers I held in my arms and stroked while we talked. It was Charlaine, of course. The chicken had tagged around after me all day, not wanting to let me out of her sight. Probably she was worried that I'd dump her down at the river again.

"She's coming with us," I insisted. "It's too dangerous here for a chicken alone."

I didn't think I was being funny but Angie cracked up. "Anyway," she finally gasped when she had her breathing a little under control, "Karen is going to have an absolute fit. How delightful."

* * * *

176

Andy was happy to see us.

I'd finally gotten my car out of hock and it drove better than it had in a long time. I suspect Andy had gotten the garage to do something to it without telling me because they only charged me eight dollars for a battery charge. The Storm even looked better. Maybe I had waited too long between car washes.

We pulled up into the circular driveway in front of Andy's house at about nine in the evening. Angie was drunk and making baby noises at my chicken and I was trying my best to think of Andy in suspect mode.

It wasn't easy.

He didn't look like a killer, standing at the doorway in khaki slacks and a black t-shirt that showed an abundance of muscle.

"Mom moved out when she heard you were coming," he told me. "I think she moved in with her Tai Chi instructor. I figured there was something going on there." He gave us a big grin about that.

"I'm pretty sure this whole thing will be wrapped up in a few days," Angie told him. "Then we'll be out of your hair and your mom can come back."

We'd planned this out. Angie was a better actor than me so I'd given her the good lines. My job was to watch Andy.

Andy is easy on the eyes, so looking at him wasn't very tricky. The tricky part was to keep looking at him as a suspect rather than thinking about him as the sexy guy who'd taken my cherry, beat up the guys who bothered me, and married me when we'd gotten out of college.

"Oh? Is there anything new on the case?" he asked.

"You heard about Fomin dropping in on Tina, right? With what he had to tell her, things really fell into place. We've got an appointment with the police tomorrow." Angie was burbling along as if this was the most natural thing in the world. "We figure that even the Dallas Police Department should be able to take it from here."

Trust Angie to get in a dig at the boys and girls in blue. Dallas's finest had a hard-earned reputation for bungling. Most of that, though, was drug related. Drugs, Federal rewards for snitches, and just the sheer financial stakes the narcotics guys play with, have corrupted even the best police forces.

From what I'd seen on the murder side, the Dallas Police detectives knew their jobs and weren't any more incompetent than anyone else. It's just that they were so busy that they generally grabbed onto the first available suspect and ran with him. Embarrassingly, in this case, it looked like they'd guessed right and I'd been wrong.

Andy leaned forward, interest obvious in his suddenly more rigid posture. "Really? Pelcovitz didn't mention new information. This is great news."

Great news because he thought we were close to solving the case? Or maybe he thought it was great news because we hadn't gone to the police with our information yet, putting ourselves in his hands.

"Right," Angie effused. "The whole mob thing was a red herring all along. We figure Sam thought he got double-crossed by the mob cutting him out of his share, so that's why he was investigating chickens. He wanted to get his revenge. But the mob didn't know or didn't care. Until Sam stumbled across the real killer, or the real killer stumbled across him."

That was the best theory I'd been able to come up with anyway. If I was to believe Fomin, the mob hadn't gotten the money, but I was positive Sam didn't have it either. So, if he was checking out the mob, he hadn't realized who had taken the money. Unless he just developed a fondness for chickens. I gave Charlaine a little pat. I could understand people liking chickens better now that I had one of my own.

"I guess that makes sense," Andy agreed, his voice indicating that he wasn't positive. "What about Halprin?"

"Our theory on Halprin is that he just wanted to impress Tina," Angie told him. "He knew he wasn't getting anywhere with his Men's Virility Magazine stunt but he figured that Tina would, for sure, be interested in a guy who could figure out a mystery like this. So he did some digging. Since Tina had persuaded him that the mob was behind the murders, he probably called up the actual killer looking for information-and asked the wrong questions at the wrong time."

Andy nodded. "You guys have really been getting the scoop. I appreciate you going to bat for me on this, Tina. You too, Angie. When the police let word out that they suspected me, Anderson Software took a beating in the stock market. Not to mention the bills that Pelcovitz has been ringing up. It will be great to put this behind us."

"That's the plan," Angie said.

"But who is the real killer?" he demanded. "If it isn't the mob and it's someone who Halprin knew, that has to narrow it down."

I nodded happily. This was where I came in. "We figure about three minutes reviewing alibis and the police should have it. Halprin is the key, and the killer's big mistake."

"So you don't actually know the murderer's identity yet?"

Had Andy put a strange inflection on his question? I wasn't sure. Heck, I wasn't sure of much right then. Maybe I shouldn't have had the second glass of wine that Angie had forced on me.

"Don't worry," I assured him. "We're close enough to touch the answer."

I liked that one. Andy could think about it, worry whether I'd dropped a hint that we knew it was he, but I hadn't actually named him. I hoped it would keep the pressure on, make him do something stupid. Which, when I thought about it, would be only about the second dumb thing I'd known him to do in his life. The first being the entire embezzlement/murder situation. Unless you count falling for trailer-trash Tina. I didn't count that.

"Anyway, I'm glad you guys are here," Andy said. "Who's for a glass of wine?"

I didn't need anything more to drink and said so. When Andy told Angie he'd gotten a new shipment of wine from Australia, though, they tromped down to his wine cellar to take an inventory.

I borrowed Andy's laptop, theoretically to check my e-mail since my computer was still buried under a couple tons of aluminum, but really so I could start to snoop.

Andy was at least as good a programmer as I was, so I didn't think he'd leave things lying around obvious, but it's surprisingly hard to clean up evidence of anything that's ever been on your computer. It didn't look like Andy had defragged his hard drive in a while, let alone done a low-level format, so I knew that anything he'd deleted would still be sitting around on the hard drive in unallocated memory space, headers missing, but just waiting for me to recover it.

Of course, searching through data blocks on a hundred-gig hard drive is a lot like flipping through the phone book looking for someone you only know by their first name. You could spend a lifetime and never notice.

I installed a little search program, based on a virus detection routine I'd once written, and let it wander through Andy's drive for me. Then I really did check my mail.

The good news was, Vorobev hadn't filed a complaint on the thousand dollars he'd sent to me through Paypal. I withdrew the money, giving my bank account its first four digit balance since I didn't know when. The bad news was, I had an e-mail from Detective Dikens insisting that I get in touch with her immediately.

So I wasn't a liar, exactly. It turned out that we really were going to meet with the cops tomorrow, as I'd promised Andy. The only thing was, the killer I needed to finger was the one they'd been looking at the whole time. I didn't think that was going to earn me a whole lot of thanks.

* * * *

Andy didn't murder us during the night.

I'd left a bunch of pillows in my bed and slept on the floor just behind where Angie's door would bang into if someone decided to open it during the night. Charlaine lay next to me-my own watch-chicken.

Other than Angie tripping over me, twice, when she went to the bathroom to get rid of some of the wine she'd drunk, I didn't have any problems.

I was stiff and sore when I got up that morning. I felt even sorer when I checked on my bed and saw that it hadn't been slashed up or anything. I could have had a comfortable night in a real bed.

"You doing okay this morning, Tina?" Andy asked me when I wandered into his kitchen and poured myself a cup of coffee. "You look like something the cat dragged in."

I didn't think he'd poison me, but right then I didn't really care. I needed my caffeine fix in the worst way.

"Ugh."

"Oh. I talked to Pelcovitz. He suggests that you take an attorney with you when you meet with D.P.D. this morning. He's got a couple of guys lined up."

I shook my head. "If we need a lawyer, we'll hire our own."

"I guess you're not really suspects anyway." He grinned. "Unlike me."

Yeah, Andy. Unlike you.

We took the light rail down to Lamar and walked into the police station.

"I can't believe I'm coming here voluntarily," Angie whispered as we sighed in at the front desk.

"No kidding." Angie had spent plenty of time in the local lockup. Just about every election season, the City Council decided to prove how tough they are by trying to get prostitution off the streets and badgered the Police Chief until he mounted a series of headline-generating raids. Once the election is over, everyone was let out and the charges were dropped or converted to something like loitering which has a hundred-dollar fine. Still, Angie gets to spend annoying nights in jail, hobnobbing with some of our city's less desirable residents.

I've suggested to her that she take election season off, but she just laughs. For her, it's all part of the game.

Dikens kept us waiting for half an hour, then bustled out.

"You guys want coffee?"

I'd drunk cop coffee before. It constitutes cruel and unusual punishment.

I pointed to the mugs each of us had brought from Andy's place.

"We prefer something that actually has coffee as one of its primary ingredients."

"Oh. Well, come on back."

I was slightly reassured when she led us to her 'office' rather than one of the interview rooms. Her office was a small nook, surrounded by low partitions that she had covered with crayon pictures.

"You've got a talented kid," Angie complemented her.

"Yeah. She's growing up so fast."

I wouldn't have been able to tell whether the crayon drawings showed talent or not, but then, I'm exercising my maternal instinct on a chicken, so what do I know?

Still, it let me see Detective Dikens in a new light. She wasn't just the African-American Barbie princess of the D.P.D., she was a single mom, trying to make ends meet, trying to spend quality time with her kid, and working a job that could be, quite literally, a killer.

Angie and Dikens spent the next fifteen minutes talking girl things while I twisted in my chair, sipped my coffee, and wished I'd brought a book. I mean, who really cares that one of the uniformed cops is a Mary Kay lady and is giving free facials?

"You called this meeting," I reminded Dikens when I could finally get a word in edgewise."

Dikens nodded, her face settling into an aggressive bad-cop look. "I understand you had a run-in with a Mr. Fomin yesterday."

I should have expected she'd find out. As always, I figured the best defense was an attack. "Who told you that?"

She shrugged, her boobs jiggling with her movement. "I have my sources."

"Probably one of the goons," Angie volunteered. "Bunch of wanna-be and has-been cops there."

"My source of information isn't the issue," Dikens sounded a little cranky. "What is the issue is that you have been running around interfering with a police investigation. And that has to stop."

"I'm a suspect and my ex-husband is a suspect and you want me to just sit here?" I asked. Here I'd been having positive feelings toward her because of those pictures on the wall and now she had to go spoil it all. "You've consistently claimed that my stories of mob involvement were fictions. So what's changed?"

"No one has accused you of any crime, Ms. Anderson. Other than possible obstruction of justice. Or do you have a guilty conscience?"

"If I'm not a suspect, then what am I?"

"I guess we'd refer to you as a person of interest," she told me.

"One of those where you don't actually bring them to trial, you just ruin their lives?" Angie suggested brightly.

Detective Dikens had been hanging around with the guys too long. She clenched her fists until her knuckles popped. "I don't like your attitude."

Which got me mad. Getting mad at the cops wasn't one of my brighter ideas, especially since I would want the cops backing me up once I got the evidence I needed against Andy.

"I met with an old man who said his name is Mr. Fomin. For your information, Fomin is one of the more common Russian last names. So I couldn't say for sure if this particular Fomin has any relation to the Mr. Fomin the goons claim the F.B.I. is looking for. But if it is, maybe they should just go and arrest the old man rather than have you hassle me."

"If Mr. Fomin is involved, this gives a lot more credence to the mob scenario you outlined several weeks ago, Ms. Anderson. I'd think you would want to get to the bottom of this."

"Believe me, I do."

"My sources indicate that Mr. Fomin gave you something. We have reason to believe that this could be evidence."

I should have seen that coming. Rent-a-cop Charlie had been pissed because I hadn't given him the money so he'd flipped me to the police.

I wondered if they still had that reward program where they pay informants a percentage of whatever they find, so I asked Dikens.

She blustered, accusing me of completely missing the point, so I took that as a yes.

"I no longer believe that the mob was connected with Sam's death," I told her. "Of course, you're welcome to ask Fomin himself if you'd like. But there's no way you're getting your hands on my money."

"You're selling your husband out for ten thousand dollars?"

I wondered if Dikens was really shocked. If not, she put on a good act.

"I earned every penny of that money and I'm going to keep it," I told her. "Is there anything else you'd like to discuss? Because Angie and I have plans for the day."

Dikens muttered something about locking us up, which wasn't very smart on her part. Because when she asked me her next question, I said I wouldn't talk without my attorney present.

Dikens huffed a bit more, but she finally kicked us out. "I mean it," she said as her Parthian shot. "If you don't back off, I'm going to have you charged with interfering with an investigation."

"Just promise you'll come when we're ready to deliver the actual killer," I told her.

"Anderson, get lost."

On that note, we left.

Chapter 16

"That went well," Angie chirped to me when we got on the train for the ride back to Andy's house. "No question but the police will be bending over backwards to help us now."

I muttered something rude, then stared out the window, thinking.

As a programmer, I have to think ahead, connect the dots before I start writing code. But in this case, I'd been running around without really doing that basic work. It was late to get started, but I realized I'd been missing a huge clue.

"Who would Halprin have called when he decided to investigate?" I finally asked Angie.

She shrugged. "He was your boyfriend, not mine."

Okay, she was sulking. I couldn't really blame her after what I'd said to her. Besides, she had been bonding with Detective Dikens, just as we'd planned, and I'd done my usual bull-in-a-China-shop routine and messed things up.

"Halprin was a lawyer," I reasoned. "So, chances are, he would have called a cop or another lawyer."

Angie nodded cautiously, getting interested despite her sulk.

"We know he had a crush on Detective Dikens. So, if he'd called the cops, he would probably have called her."

"Unless he was too much of a chicken."

I considered that, then rejected it. Men's Virility had probably had articles on assertiveness.

Dikens had given me her card back at the beginning of the case so I looked up the number and dialed her from my cell.

"Yeah, Anderson?" I wasn't imagining the big sigh.

"I was wondering if Halprin called you before he got killed."

"I told you to stay away from the case, Anderson."

"I'd really like to know the answer to my question. I've been feeling guilty about his getting killed so quickly after our date."

Angie raised an eyebrow at me and I shrugged. My little whine hadn't made a lot of sense to me, either, but I was going for the sympathy vote, not the intellectual choice.

Dikens sighed again, not even trying to disguise it this time. "If I answer you, do you promise to give up this investigation?"

"Trust me, I don't want to have anything to do with the mob." It wasn't an answer but I hoped she'd think it was. I would hate to have to lie to a cop.

From the silence over the phone, I knew I hadn't fooled Dikens.

"Halprin did call me. I told him that I didn't have any reason to suspect mob involvement and that he'd be smarter to worry about his client rather than interfere with police business. Which was damned good advice. I wish he'd taken it."

"You didn't happen to mention that call to anyone, did you?"

"I'm hanging up now, Anderson. You need a cop in the future, call 9-1-1."

"Now we know he really was investigating," I told Angie. "It isn't just a theory any more. But I don't think Detective Dikens was the leak."

"So who?"

If not a cop, then another lawyer. And the other lawyer involved was —Pelcovitz.

We both said his name simultaneously.

Although we were already at Mockingbird station, we got off the train, turned around, and headed back downtown.

It seemed like every time I'd met Pelcovitz, he'd had Andy along with him. If we asked him out to Andy's house, or even gave him much warning, I suspected that he'd have Andy with him again. And he wouldn't answer anything that Andy didn't want answered. If we could get him alone, though, who knew what we might learn?

Pelcovitz's office was on the top floor of the Magnolia Building, just underneath the big red Pegasus that has been part of the Dallas skyline basically since before Dallas had a skyline.

His office suite filled the entire top floor, with dark wood, paintings that I suspected he hadn't bought from starving artists for five bucks each, and that indescribable scent of money wafting through the air.

We had to go through two levels of blonde before we even got to Pelcovitz's admin. In traditional old-Dallas fashion, Pelcovitz's offices seemed to define their status by the expense of the décor and the attractiveness of the staff. By that standard, they were on the top of their game.

His admin sniffed when we walked in. In her short-skirted black suit, the top unbuttoned to where we could catch just a hint of cleavage, she looked like something out of Vogue.

My shorts and t-shirt getup didn't fit the office style at all.

I thought Angie looked pretty good in a short skirt and crop top that showed off her pierced navel (we'd had ours done at the same time), but some people had no taste and the admin definitely didn't seem impressed.

"Perhaps one of the associates could help you," the admin suggested.

If she'd thought she would get away with it, she probably would have suggested the janitor.

"I don't think that Mr. Pelcovitz would be pleased to hear that you've blown off Mrs. Anderson," Angie said.

The admin consulted her notes, and her demeanor abruptly changed. She flashed an ingratiating smile. "Ah, Mrs. Karen Anderson. My apologies. You sound different over the phone. But your appointment isn't until this afternoon."

With any luck, we could be out of there a long time before that and I wouldn't have to risk running into my ex-mother-in-law.

"My schedule changed," I said.

"Mr. Pelcovitz is in a staff meeting now, but I could page him if this is an emergency."

It's funny how a little mistaken identity can change people's attitudes.

"If you don't mind," I said trying to sound magnanimous in a condescending way. Like Karen would.

"Of course, Mrs. Anderson. Perhaps you and your friend would like to have a seat in Mr. Pelcovitz's waiting room." She hopped up from her chair and opened a door to a room that looked like a living room, fireplace and all. "Can I get you coffee? Or a cold drink? And may I say that I thought you look much," she paused briefly looking for the right word, "younger," she finally decided, "than I thought you would be."

"Aren't you sweet," I said. "Coffee would be nice. If it's freshly brewed, of course. But please page Mr. Pelcovitz first. I have a great deal to get done today."

The admin showed us into the waiting room, then bustled out, a woman on a mission.

Angie collapsed into a chair and failed to smother an eruption of laughter.

"Quick thinking," I told her.

"I thought she was going to have kittens." Angie could hardly talk over her laughter. "Did you see the way her head snapped when I used the magical Anderson name?"

Angie pulled herself together just before the admin appeared.

The admin carried a tray that held dainty porcelain teacups for our coffee, and a china plate bearing a small mound of Pepperidge Farm cookies.

I would have preferred some Little Debbie Nutty Bars but I held my tongue, for once.

"Mr. Pelcovitz asked me to tell you that he'd be right with you," she promised.

I snarfed a couple of the cookies and pretended like I was used to fancy thin china, then settled down to wait for Pelcovitz.

"Mrs. Anderson, I'm sorry to keep you-oh, hi Tina. My admin must have-"

"I think we may have mislead her," I admitted. "But we needed to talk to you and your Praetorian guard was doing their best to keep us away."

Pelcovitz picked up one of the cookies, twisted it around in his hands, then set it on the coffee table. "Is this about Andy's case? I hope you aren't asking me to abuse client confidentiality." He laughed, as if he'd just told a big joke. Well, the joke was on him.

"Nothing about your client," I lied. "I'm checking connections on Halprin. I just spoke to Detective Dikens, but I wasn't clear on the exact timing of Halprin's call to you that night."

Pelcovitz smiled. "Ah, Tina. You've really got to let this case go. The police tell me that they've finally glommed onto the mob angle. Your plan worked. So why not follow through on the second part of the plan, which was to let the police do the leg work, tracking down alibis and turning up the evidence?"

I shrugged. "Believe me, Sid. There's nothing I'd rather do than sit back and let them do the work." And take the danger, I didn't add. "But I've got a personal stake in this," I continued. "My ex-husband is accused of murder, I've lost one boyfriend and one date. All in all, this case has put a real crimp in my social life. So humor me, will you?"

Pelcovitz looked like he was going to argue, until Angie did her little leg crossing and uncrossing trick.

The blood from his brain rushing lower into his body and all thought of argument abandoned his brain (all right, from what I could see, all thought of any kind abandoned his brain).

"I guess it wouldn't hurt to give you the details." Pelcovitz almost strangled on the words.

"Great. You talked to John after he got through with Dikens, is that right?"

"That's more information than Detective Dikens gave me," Pelcovitz conceded. "And Halprin didn't mention anything about talking to her."

That figured. Halprin hadn't been the world's best lawyer, but he was just dumb enough to keep quiet about a case that was going to get him killed. "He was working the mob angle but I hadn't given him much to work on and Detective Dikens would have given him less. So, did you point him anywhere?"

"It's been a while," Pelcovitz conceded. "Let me take a look." Pelcovitz pulled a Clio out of his suit pocket and clicked on it with the plastic stylus. And clicked. And clicked.

"Got it," he said when I was just about to grab that device from his hands and show him how to work it. How can anyone in the 21st century be so 19th century when it comes to technology?

"Got what?" I demanded when he got engrossed in reading his own writing. I wanted to be out of there before Karen arrived.

Pelcovitz gave me a paternal smile. "I take notes on this little machine when I get calls at home. When they seem relevant to a case, I let my admin Kathleen transcribe them. Halprin's call didn't seem to be leading anywhere so this is the only record I have. Good thing I didn't erase it, huh?"

"I don't know, Sid. Why don't you tell us what you wrote?" Grace under pressure I'm not.

"Oh, yeah. Good idea." Pelcovitz consulted his Clio again. "It looks like I told him I didn't have anything on a mob connection other than what you'd told me about the chickens." He looked up from the device. "This was early in the case, you remember. Before you'd really gotten involved."

I sighed. "I remember, Sid. What else did you talk about?"

"Hmm. It seems that I suggested that Halprin talk to Kevin Franklin about the possibility that there was a mob angle to the embezzlement thing. I figured that would be something Franklin could look into at Big Cat."

Bingo. If I knew Franklin, the first thing he would have done was run to Andy. Which gave us the connection. Andy found out about Sam's identity and Sam died. Andy found out that Halprin was investigating the mob angle and Halprin died. From a circumstantial basis, at least, the case had started to look ironclad.

But Andy knew that I'd been following the mob angle and he hadn't killed me. Which had to mean that Halprin had uncovered something definite. Something dangerous enough to Andy to make him kill.

Since I was pretty sure Halprin wouldn't have called Andy himself, he must have told Kevin Franklin something that Franklin had innocently passed along to Andy. Franklin wouldn't have recognized it for what it was, but Andy was smarter than Kevin Franklin. And he knew where the bones were buried. Whatever it was, it had to be something big. Big enough to make him jump to murder again, at a time when the police were already suspicious of him.

Once I learned what Franklin had told Andy, I figured that we'd have everything we needed to nail the case shut for good.

"Why don't we invite Kevin down here?" I suggested. "We could get him to fill us in on whether Halprin told him anything."

Pelcovitz looked like he was ready to balk, but Angie must have seen his expression as well. "Just to fill in the details," she interjected, her voice filled with the promise of sex.

"Oh, why not," Pelcovitz conceded. "I'll have Kathleen order up some lunch for us."

* * * *

During lunch, Pelcovitz showed how he got to be one of the top attorneys in Dallas by charming Angie into giving him a blow-by-blow of the great chicken raid.

Angie not only told him the raid story, she also told him about my new pet who was, I suddenly remembered, still hanging around at Andy's house.

I suspected that the maid would have had quite a shock that morning when she went to make up the beds. You just don't expect to see a pet chicken wandering around in a multimillion-dollar north Dallas mansion.

When he heard about Charlaine, Pelcovitz gave me this look that told me he understood exactly how a maternal instinct can go crazy like that. It should have been a condescending look, but somehow it worked. As I said, the man is smooth.

Pelcovitz could be an animal during cross-examination, but he was definitely giving us a look at the other side of the man-the side that kept clients believing and that let him get to the bottom of who-knew how many stories.

We'd just finished our lunch when Kevin Franklin arrived.

"Sorry I'm late," he told us when Kathleen ushered him into Pelcovitz's waiting room. "I should have taken the tollway. It seems like every time they finish working on one part of 75, they just find another to tear up."

"Can I bring you something to eat, Mr. Franklin?" Kathleen asked.

He considered. "I guess not. I've got a squash game with Andy in a couple of hours. He whipped my ass last week and I'm planning on making him eat that gloat." He leaned closer to me as if about to confide a secret. "I hired a coach to give me some pointers, Tina. Andy won't know what hit him."

What is it that makes men want to share their secrets with me? If any of their secrets were at all interesting, that would be one thing. As it was, though, they were mostly things only a male would care about.

"Good luck," I told him when he seemed stuck waiting for an answer.

"Hey, thanks, Tina." Apparently I'd given him the stroke he needed.

"Speaking of Andy, I thought I'd see him here," Kevin told us. "I mean, what is this, the Star Chamber or something?"

Pelcovitz laughed convincingly. "We think we've just about got everything we need to clear both Andy and Tina of any suspicion of murder."

"Hey, great."

I wasn't sure, but for just a second, it seemed to me that Franklin's enthusiasm was a little underwhelming. Since Andy was definitely the alpha male of the two of them, maybe a part of Kevin's subconscious enjoyed seeing Andy in trouble.

"We just had a couple of points to clear up before we turned the whole thing over to the police," I explained, not bothering to correct Pelcovitz's statement that Andy was off the hook. If I let that cat out of the bag, this meeting would be over in a hurry and Pelcovitz would dump us on our butts so hard we'd bounce.

"Outstanding. That's why I'm here, after all."

I nodded and took a sip of my Diet Coke. "First, we need to know what John Halprin told you that night when he called."

Franklin's tanned face drained of color. "Who told you I mean, how did you know I mean-"

I watched him writhe on the couch and it finally hit me. My instincts had been right and my logic had been wrong about Andy. He was too rich, too confident, and too basically honest to pull a scam like the Big Cat embezzlement. And if Andy had done it, he would have done it professionally, not leaving loose ends around that he'd have to clean up later, through murder.

Andy wasn't the killer.

Little tingles went up my spine as I watched Franklin sputter. One thing was obvious. If Andy wasn't the killer, and he wasn't, Kevin Franklin was.

He was already flustered, so I decided to go on the warpath.

"It was a pretty good trick bringing in a couple of mobsters and pointing the finger at them while you plundered your own company, wasn't it, Franklin."

I have to give him credit. He sucked it up and gave a game little laugh. "That's the craziest thing I've ever heard, Tina. Why would I embezzle money from my own company?"

"You mean Franklin did it?" Angie blurted. She wasn't usually late to the party but in this case, either she hadn't caught Kevin's hesitation, or she hadn't figured what it meant.

Kevin's argument was completely invalid, of course. There is a big difference between being a C.E.O. and actually owning a company. Andy wouldn't embezzle from Anderson Software because he still owned half of it. He really would be stealing from himself. But Kevin only owned whatever shares Big Cat had voted him-mostly options. And he'd been able to see the writing on the wall when the telecom industry collapsed. His options would be so far underwater that he'd never see any money at all.

A C.E.O. for a company like Big Cat may make upwards of half a million dollars a year, but that was a far cry from the billion-plus someone had plundered. That someone being the man sitting in front of us.

"It must have been quite a challenge," Pelcovitz had caught up fast and smoothly joined the discussion. "You conspired with Sam and Vlad to work the embezzlement, but somehow you diverted it all to your own accounts. Once you'd done that, you would have had to tell the mob that Sam and Vlad had made off with the money.

"Arranging their curious disappearances would have helped with the story, right?"

Kevin held up his hands as if surrendering. "When you're right, you're right. I thought I'd managed the perfect crime." He turned to me. "It was like your chicken raid, Tina. I mean, the mob was stealing the money and I caught them. I figured, hey, I'd just steal it from them and who would be hurt? I mean, who could they turn to? The police?

"And since I let Mr. Fomin know that his own guys had backstabbed him, he wasn't interested in coming after me." Franklin smirked as if he had gotten away with something really clever.

"Except Sam really did disappear," I said. "You must have been relieved when he turned up in my trailer park."

Kevin grinned. "I really appreciate you leading me to him, Tina. I knew he was hiding somewhere. He thought the mob had backstabbed him, but if they'd caught him, they would have gotten the truth out of him and I would have been in trouble. When Andy's Human Resources people contacted my staff for a background check, I knew I had to act in a hurry."

Kevin's big smiles were starting to wear on me. He should have been denying everything. We didn't have anything on him, really. Since he was bragging, that had to mean he didn't intend for any of us to talk to the police.

He'd killed at least two people already. Probably three. I suspected Amber was right about her brother Vlad being dead. I didn't think that Kevin would draw the line at a few more.

I glanced around the room as casually as I could, but the closest thing to a weapon I could see was a pile of Danish pastries that Kathleen had brought in for our dessert. Those fat pills might be killers, but they wouldn't do the job quickly enough to help us.

"Don't try anything stupid, Tina." Kevin's hyper-friendly salesman voice was gone. Now he sounded like the weasel I knew him to be.

"You'd be an idiot to do anything to us," I told him. "For one thing, the police already know everything. Murdering three more people would only reduce your chances of getting a jail term instead of lethal injection."

He shook his head slowly. "I don't think so, Tina. I think you were barking up the wrong tree and just happened to stumble on the truth. If I'd kept my mouth shut, none of you would be the wiser. And if I make sure all of you keep your mouths shut, I'll be able to continue on without any problems."

"If you kill us, everyone will know it was you," Angie reminded him. "If you start running now, you might be able to get away."

For a moment, Kevin seemed to consider her suggestion. He could tie us up, cut Pelcovitz's phone lines, and give himself a couple of hours of lead time to grab his money and head out of town.

If I'd been Kevin, I would have already had a fake identity set up, with most of the money squirreled away in a Caribbean numbered bank account. I didn't think I was a better criminal than Kevin, so he must have everything ready in case he had to run.

"Tempting, Angie," he told her. "But then, you always were one for tempting choices, weren't you."

"I'm thinking that super-jealous Andy discovered you and Angie doing a ménage à trois with Pelcovitz," Kevin mused. "Things got a little violent when he came in. Probably Andy hit Pelcovitz, like this." He slammed a fist into the lawyer's cheek, knocking him across the coffee table where we'd had our lunch and onto the floor. Diet Coke and the Danish splashed over Pelcovitz's expensive oriental rug.

"You son of a bitch," Angie said springing at him like a panther.

Franklin sidestepped easily, then grabbed one of her arms and accelerated her into the wall.

"He would have hurt you too, Angie. And blamed you for leading Tina into sin, because he knows what a slut you are."

Angie hit the wall hard, then collapsed to the floor.

"He's already killed two of Tina's lovers, but it hasn't stopped her from stepping out. So he's finally realized that the only way he can keep Tina from sleeping around is to kill her too."

Kevin was enjoying his sick fantasy too much. Escaping with his money wasn't enough. He wanted the money, respect, and to make his more successful friend pay the price. Just like he'd hung his supposed embezzlement partners out to dry when he didn't need them any more. It also looked like he had let murder go to his head. He actually liked inflicting pain.

A light knock on the door told us that Kevin's antics had been loud enough to disturb Kathleen.

"Is everything all right in there, Mr. Pelcovitz? Can I get you anything?"

"Call the police," Pelcovitz shouted from where he lay bleeding on the floor."

Kevin threw the door opened, grabbed Kathleen, and yanked her into the room.

"I didn't really get caught in traffic," he explained. "I thought you might know something, so I waited until your receptionist went out for a coffee break. That way, the only ones who saw me come in are in this room right now.

"So, welcome, Kathleen. I wonder if you were involved in the orgy too, or just happened to wander by while Andy was going crazy."

"Nobody is going to believe this stupid story," I told him.

He grinned, then pulled a small gun from his brief case, pointing it at me casually.

"Of course they'll believe it. Everyone wants to believe that the rich are more messed up than they are. It gives them a hint of satisfaction in their miserable lives. They believed it was Andy the first two murders and I didn't even bother planting evidence to point the police his way.

This time we'll probably have protesters worrying about how rich criminals manage to get out on bail to commit crimes again. A Texas jury will give Andy the death penalty before he can sneeze. Killing his own lawyer." Kevin shook his head in mock sadness. "Completely reprehensible. And to think that he was my friend."

He picked up Pelcovitz's cell phone and dialed. "Andy?"

He waited a moment.

"Yeah, it's Kev. Listen, I'm down at Pelcovitz's office. He's got some evidence that'll clear you for sure. You've got to get down here right away."

He pressed the power off button and smashed the phone into the floor. "That will make sure he doesn't have an alibi. Now, how should we stage this?"

"He won't have gunshot residue on his hands so the cops will know he didn't do it," Kathleen suggested. She must watch the same true crime shows that Angie does.

"Really? That's a very interesting thought. Thanks for your suggestion, Kathleen."

"Right. So you might as well put that gun away. Because we all know you aren't going to use it."

When she'd been snarling at Angie and me, trying to keep us from meeting with Pelcovitz, I'd thought she was a real bitch. Now, I was starting to warm to her. From the look on Kevin's face, the feeling wasn't mutual.

"No, I think the weapon is still useful. Want to see?"

Without waiting for an answer, he slapped his gun against Kathleen's perfect sorority-girl face.

The motion looked gentle. Almost a caress. That, however, was an illusion. Kathleen spun from the impact, joining Pelcovitz on the floor. Blood poured from her mouth.

Kevin seemed fascinated by the blood, or perhaps by the contrast between it and Kathleen's perfectly made up face.

It might be the only opportunity I was going to get and I took it. Moving as little as I could, I reached into my purse for the pepper spray I always keep handy.

Kevin brought his gun back to bear on me just as I pulled the spray out.

I wasn't sure that Kathleen was right about Kevin being afraid to use the gun, but I figured I would take the chance. He was planning on killing us anyway so there wasn't a lot of point in rolling over for him.

So, I yanked the spray out, pointed my hand in his direction, closed my eyes, and pushed the plunger.

Chapter 17

The pepper spray hissed out, blasting me directly in my own face. I'd been rushed, after all.

The stuff is seriously nasty.

Even through my closed eyelids, my eyes swam with tears. I forced them open and Kevin became a blur in khaki and lavender.

He coughed slightly. "What a charming idea," he told me. "Here I was wondering how to incapacitate you."

He stripped the spray can from my hand and pushed the plunger again.

From Angie's gasp, he'd hit her with it. The can really holds only one good spray but I'd stopped pushing when I got it in the face, so there was enough left to bother my friend.

The spray left a terrible stench in the air. I heard Angie gag and my adrenaline surge backed off enough to let me realize that I was sick in my own stomach.

Well, projectile vomiting isn't much of a weapon, but I wasn't in a position to be picky.

I pointed my mouth where I thought Kevin was standing and let nature take care of the rest.

"What are-oh, crap. That's disgusting."

Kevin yanked away from me and, from the sound of it, pulled a wad of napkins from the table and used them to wipe himself off.

I was still gagging, though. I'd inhaled a big dose of the spray and it didn't want to stay down.

Kevin backed away from me. "Tina, I really don't understand what Andy sees in you. I mean, he's got it all. But does he date high-class babes? No. He wants his little trailer park slut."

"At least he can get it up with a woman," Angie told him. Her voice was hoarse from breathing in pepper spray, but she had apparently survived the attack. Good.

I figured that if the two of us could rush him, maybe we could get him. Especially if he hadn't taken the safety off on his gun. Especially if Kathleen had scared him out of using the weapon. Unfortunately, Kevin wasn't going to let Angie and me plan out the attack and get our signals together.

I made a mental note to prepare better for the future. As if we were going to have one.

"All right, let's go outside," Kevin said.

That sounded promising. Once we got into the hallway, he'd have a hard time keeping track of all of us at once. One of us could somehow signal for help. I stepped toward the door.

"Not that way, idiot." He grabbed my arm and tried to smash me into the wall like he had Angie.

I may not be the brightest bulb, but I knew I didn't want that. Instead of trying to keep my feet and hurting myself, I just collapsed onto the floor-and wretched toward his expensive Italian tassel loafers.

He kicked me in my stomach.

It wasn't a great strategy because I wasn't really going to barf until he did it. As it was, I got messy all over those nice shoes. Good. If he was going to kill me, at least he'd have to buy new shoes afterwards.

As revenge went, it wasn't sweet, but it was better than nothing.

"Up," Kevin urged. He prodded me in the leg with one of those disgustingly messy shoes.

I got to my feet. My eyes were still tearing but I could sort of see again. "All right, boy genius. What's your plan?"

"Let's go upstairs," he said.

He chambered a shell into his automatic. The snick-ching cleared all remnants of pepper spray hangover from my mind. Obviously he'd decided that the police would just rationalize their way around the missing gunpowder residue if they had to.

"There is no upstairs," Kathleen told him. She seemed to enjoy goading him. It was a character flaw that I'd found annoying in the extreme when I'd been on the receiving end. A few minutes ago, I'd admired it. Now, after I'd gotten myself with pepper spray and gotten kicked in the belly, I wasn't sure I liked it so much after all. I'd like it a lot less if it made Kevin start shooting.

"On the roof, you idiot," he screamed. He was starting to lose it. If he hadn't been armed, that would have comforted me. As it was, it only made me more nervous.

"But-"

"Now. Move."

I helped Pelcovitz get to his feet. His eye was swollen mostly shut and I thought he might have lost a tooth. He also looked pissed as hell.

"Don't do anything stupid," I whispered to him.

"No whispering." Kevin's voice was almost a screech now. If Pelcovitz had any sort of normal office, someone would have noticed that something was wrong by now, and called the cops.

There are disadvantages to having soundproof doors and football-lengths of separation between offices.

Pelcovitz's office had private door access to the stairway.

Kevin urged us up.

Naturally the roof access door was locked.

"Told you we couldn't go this way," Kathleen taunted.

"Pick the lock, Tina," Kevin told me.

I laughed. I hadn't told anyone about my success with Amber's mailbox lock and I wasn't going to start now "If it was computer controlled, I might stand a chance. Against mechanical things I'm useless. But hey, you're the master criminal. You do it."

"Screw that." He fired a round into the lock. Yep, he'd decided not to worry about gunpowder residue all right.

I've seen commercials where locks stand up to repeated rifle shots. Obviously this wasn't one of those. The door almost flew opened.

"Out on the roof."

My eyes and my breathing were almost back to normal. Unfortunately, my stomach was still in a bit of a roil. The street looked like it was a million miles below and I've always had a nervous feeling about heights.

Instinctively, I moved away from the doorway toward one of the massive air conditioning units on top of the roof.

"Toward the edge," Kevin commanded. "Let's all take a look."

* * * *

When it was built, the Magnolia Building was the tallest in Dallas. Now, other skyscrapers loom over its modest twenty-nine stories. Even over the huge neon revolving Pegasus statue that stands atop the building.

I had a vague hope that someone in one of those buildings might be looking out their windows, might see us, might actually call the police.

I might as well have fantasized that Pegasus take off and fly us out of there. Dallas may be in the south, but people here have adopted the big city worldview. When in doubt, mind your own business and pretend that those crazy people aren't really there.

"Closer," Kevin urged.

We were already about five feet from the edge. A low ledge and a cable railing circled about three feet above it were the only things that separated us from a three-hundred-foot fall.

"You can shoot me if you want to, but I'm not getting any closer," I told him.

"Really. How about if I do this." He slammed a kick to Angie's knee.

My best friend collapsed, rolling closer to the edge.

I grabbed her and yanked her back, then realized that I'd done exactly what Kevin had wanted. My face was only about two feet from the drop.

"Now you two," he told Pelcovitz and Kathleen.

"Take me with you," Kathleen suggested. "I'll help you."

Kevin looked puzzled. "Why?"

"It'll be easier for you to escape if you're with a girl. Nobody will suspect anything."

Here I'd actually started to like the woman. What a two-faced weasel.

"Do I look like an idiot to you?" he demanded. "Why would I keep a witness alive?"

"I'll help push them," Kathleen volunteered. "That would make me as guilty as you. Then I couldn't gain anything from turning on you."

I'd read about the Stockholm syndrome before, but I'd never imagined it could kick in so quickly.

Kevin appeared to consider it. I didn't think he'd take her up on her offer, but I was pretty sure he would pretend to. Why not? Have her push us off, then push her off himself. If one of us fought back and pushed her off, then there'd be one less problem for him to deal with.

"I suppose I could use a partner," he acknowledged. "Let's start with the lawyer. Women don't worry me."

Kathleen looked at Pelcovitz, then back at Kevin. "Mr. Pelcovitz is a lot stronger than I am. I don't think I can help much with him."

She took a step away from the edge and toward Kevin.

"I thought you said you wanted to help."

Kathleen started to cry, big blubbering tears carving dirty trails through what was left of her carefully laid makeup. "You're not being fair."

It was enough to make a person gag. It also distracted Kevin. I wasn't sure whether that was Kathleen's plan or if she was just afraid to tackle Pelcovitz. I'd spent some time wrestling with guys in the back seats of cars and knew how strong even a nerdy-seeming type can be. Whether it was her plan or not, Kevin seemed distracted. The pepper spray had cleared from my lungs so I figured it was time for another stupid move.

I whispered to Angie that we should try to split up and carefully rolled away from the edge.

"Where do you think you're going?" Kevin demanded.

Kathleen's distraction hadn't worked very well.

"I'm afraid of heights," I told him, hoping that Angie would have the sense to keep moving.

"Afraid of heights?" He snickered. "I guess you're pretty smart to be. Some sort of psychic premonition, maybe. 'Cause this height is going to kill you."

"I don't mind pushing her," Kathleen volunteered. "Just don't make me push Sid."

Kevin gave Kathleen a big grin. "Right. Over she goes."

Kathleen moved toward me, her face grimacing with intensity. "It won't hurt," she encouraged me. "Don't resist."

"Or go ahead and fight," Kevin interrupted. "Things will go pretty fast once the first body drops and Andy won't get here for another twenty minutes. So we've got time to kill." He giggled. "Time to kill. That's a good one, isn't it?"

I didn't want to fight Kathleen. I wanted to kick Kevin in the face and knock out some of his teeth to match Sid's, then kick him in the stomach to make up for what he'd done to me, then slit his throat for what he'd done to Sam and John. These weren't very healthy attitudes, I knew, but then again, worrying about unhealthy attitudes at a time like that was like the firing squad victim turning down a cigarette because they cause cancer.

Kathleen stepped closer, her arms out like she was Godzilla coming toward me. I'd never been pushed off a skyscraper before, but something about this didn't feel right.

"Pretend to fight," she whispered. "But keep me between you and Kevin."

I clinched with her and tried to decide what to make of this. Was she trying to trick me into only pretending to resist, or did she really have a plan?

"Resistance is futile," she shouted as she shoved me toward the edge.

Shoved me oh-so-gently, however. Okay, maybe she was playing for time. But time for what? It wasn't as if Daniel Day Lewis was going to swoop up and rescue us.

I tried to think of some appropriate Borg counter, but came up empty. "Screw you, traitor bitch," I screamed as a cheap substitute.

She gave me a smile. "Good one."

Out of the corner of my eye I saw Angie watching. Watching us, not Kevin. It would be just my luck if she decided to intervene and ended up pushing all of us off the edge of the building.

"Come on," Kevin urged. "Over she goes."

Kathleen pretended to claw at my face and instead halfway ripped the top button from her low-cut suit jacket. She wasn't wearing a bra and had a more impressive figure than I would have guessed.

"I'll get you for that," she screamed. "That suit is practically new. My mother bought it for me from Neiman Marcus."

"Screw your mother and your mailman father," I shouted. I ripped the rest of her jacket off, leaving her naked to her waist. Under other circumstances, it would have been fun, actually. I'd been wanting to do something like that ever since she'd snubbed Angie and me while we waited for Pelcovitz.

"Hey, that's more like it," Kevin said.

Kathleen froze, looked down at herself, and slapped me, hard, across the face. "Bitch."

"Witch."

She grabbed my t-shirt and ripped.

I was wearing a jog bra, which was lucky because I'd worn one of my older tops and it practically disintegrated in her grip.

"Cool," Kevin breathed.

All right, we were acting out an adolescent male's fantasy. But Kevin seemed to be stuck in an adolescent world so that fit. More importantly, while we were doing this, we weren't going over the edge. Given the choice, I was happy with the one we picked. I just wasn't sure how long we'd be able to, uh, pull it off.

"Maybe you yank off my skirt," Kathleen whispered. "I'm wearing a thong."

I didn't think so. Kevin was distracted, but he wasn't stupid. He'd see through an obvious strip tease.

"Leave her alone!" Angie hit Kathleen from behind.

I hadn't realized she could move so fast or hit so hard.

Kathleen spun from me, letting me go so she wouldn't pull me off the edge with her. From the look in her eyes, she knew that she was going.

I reached for Kathleen, but missed.

She hit the cable, then tumbled over it.

* * * *

Kathleen draped over the edge of the building, hanging by her knees from the steel cable barrier. Sure enough, she was wearing a thong beneath her silky skirt.

"Yank her back up," I whispered. "I'm going for Kevin."

"You mean-"

I nodded. "She was acting."

"Crap."

Kevin probably hadn't realized he was getting closer to the action, magnetically attracted by Kathleen's peach-colored panties. But he was. He was breathing hard and his face was flushed.

Still, he wasn't totally distracted. As he stepped close to Pelcovitz, he lashed out a kick, striking the lawyer in the knee and dropping him back to the ground.

One ally out of the way.

"Let her drop," he ordered Angie. "She didn't come through for me."

By then I'd circled behind him. I took a breath and-

"Yoo-hoo. Sid? Are you up here?"

My ex-mother-in-law's voice froze the tableau.

"Karen! Run! Call the cops!"

I knew better. If I wanted Karen to do something, I should have told her to do the exact opposite.

"What are you doing up here with your clothes halfway off?" she demanded.

"What a screwed-up mess!" Kevin screamed out his frustration. He stepped away from the edge, reached to the stairway and yanked Karen up, then turned around, using her as a shield in case I was going to attack.

I checked to make sure that Angie had Kathleen safe, then took off across the roof. The Magnolia Building is big and has a lot of stuff to hide behind. If I could delay things, I could put a monkey wrench in Kevin's plan. Maybe.

"Going somewhere, Tina?" he demanded.

"What kind of game are you playing," Karen demanded. "This is supposed to be a lawyers' office, not some kind of cheap orgy."

She looked at Kathleen as Angie yanked her the rest of the way up. "And Kathleen. I thought you were a little classier than this bunch. To think that I told Andy he should take you out. What was I thinking?"

Kathleen covered her breasts with her arms and burst into tears.

The shadow of the turning Pegasus passed over my head, the whining machinery of that huge oil company logo-turned-civic- symbol blending with the scritch of Kevin's Italian loafers walking over the gravel on the roof. Walking toward me.

I ducked behind an air conditioning unit. If I could distract Kevin for long enough, maybe Angie could sneak free and call the police.

As if she'd read my mind, I heard the distinctive sound of Angie's high-heeled sandals 'sneaking' across the gravel.

Kevin fired a shot in her direction. "Don't even think about it," he ordered.

"You didn't even try to help me when I fell," Kathleen whined. "I thought we were partners."

"Don't be an idiot," Kevin said. "I don't need a partner. Especially not a backstabbing woman like you. Now shut up. I need to be able to hear. I need to think."

"But I wanted to be with you. I would have pushed her over the edge

if Angie hadn't butted in."

"Shut up." Kevin fired again.

I wondered how many bullets he had. If it had been a revolver, I would have guessed six. But with an automatic, I knew it was more. Even after wasting three shots, Kevin would have plenty to kill all of us.

The flying horse whined overhead again and I jumped up, grabbing the back foot as it came within reach.

My feet made a sound as I jumped, but this was likely to be my best chance. Kevin would be partially deafened by his own gunshots and the Pegasus's motor made enough noise to hide an airport.

"If you don't come out, I'm going to have to hurt Mrs. Anderson," Kevin warned.

My hands gripped the hot iron of the Pegasus's support frame and clamped down.

After about two seconds, I knew I had made a mistake. My arms felt like they were getting yanked out of their sockets and my shoulder blades ground together like millstones. Still, I held on for my life, wishing I'd been a little more active in my high school P.E. classes rather than always getting out of it by counterfeiting notes from my mom about having my period.

"This is all Tina's fault, isn't it," Karen said. "I don't have a clue what you're doing up here, but if you're trying to shoot Tina, I'd say she has it coming. Let me go and I'll see if I can spot her for you."

I knew that Karen didn't approve of me as a daughter-in-law, but this was a little extreme.

Kevin must have thought so too. "I trusted one of you women and look where it got me. You're staying with me, Mrs. Anderson."

"Humph. And I thought you were such a fine boy, too."

Keep talking. I concentrated all of my energy on sending the words to Karen. Keep talking. Distract him.

The horse continued its slow circumference of the rooftop and Kevin and Karen came into view. He was looking away from me. That was the good news.

The bad news was, Karen faced directly toward.

When she spotted me, she started and I waited for her to say something. I was a sitting duck up here and I knew it.

"Andy never should have married that Tina," Karen went on as if I was the invisible woman. "She's just trailer trash. Always was. I mean, a man like Andy, or like you, Kevin, can sow wild oats with her kind, but marry them? Really." Karen was getting into this now. "She probably killed those men herself, and blamed it on Andy. Her kind can't stand it when a man doesn't want to see her anymore."

I couldn't believe it. Karen was trying to save my life—all of our lives. For her it must have seemed like the perfect opportunity to say what she really thought and not get in trouble for it. Not that she kept much to herself, but usually I walked out before I'd heard much. This time, I was a captive audience.

My hands felt like they were welded to the sun-heated metal and I had to clench my teeth to keep from sobbing from the pain of just hanging on. My plan was, I'd kick Kevin in the back of his head as I swung by. The bad news was, the horse moved too slowly to put a good hit on Kevin. Despite my arms screaming at me, I started working on a pendulum motion.

"That's probably her gun you've got, isn't it, Kevin? I'll bet you grabbed it from her when you came up here."

I couldn't see Kevin's face but I figured he was probably processing Karen's words, trying to figure out if there was a way he could use her ideas. Killing Karen would make it harder to persuade anyone of Kevin's crazy theory that Andy had gone mad. Nobody would believe that Karen Anderson had been involved in some sex orgy gone bad.

"Just shut up," he screamed at her.

Franklin was losing it. Good. About time he joined the rest of us.

I had a good swing action going now, and the Pegasus had swung around so I was getting close to Kevin, except I suddenly realized that I had misjudged the horse's angle. I was going to end up about six feet to his right.

If I'd been Tarzan, I could have crept the six feet, hand over hand, along the horse's leg without even disturbing my swing.

But if I'd been Tarzan, I could have let Kathleen push me over the edge, gone in through a window on the way down, and rescued everyone. I wasn't Tarzan. I wasn't even Nancy Drew. As Karen Anderson had so graphically pointed out, I was only trailer-trash Tina, girl couch potato.

I promised myself that if I got out of this mess alive, I would start an exercise program.

Tarzan or not, I gritted my teeth and started edging up the metal pipe that supported the big flying neon horse.

And it was up. Because the steel bar was set at an angle, supporting the horse's rearing stance.

The good news was, if I made it, I would be able to drop on Kevin from a height of about twenty feet.

The bad news was, my hands were getting sweaty.

I caught myself with the first slip, gripping the bar with all of my strength.

Then my hand slipped again. I knew I was going to fall. And I wasn't close enough to hit Kevin.

For a fraction of a second, I hung there one-handed, my right hand scrambling to reclaim any sort of grip.

It's barely possible that I made a noise. A sort of groaning, wheezing, complaining noise. I'm not admitting I made it, just that it's possible.

Whoever made it, Kevin heard it.

He turned and fired.

I'd always thought that stories of feeling the wind from a bullet going by were mythical nonsense. I mean, a bullet is just a tiny piece of metal, after all. How much wind could it generate?

Quite a bit, as it turns out.

I'd lost my battle to hold on just as Kevin turned so I was falling when he shot at me. Luckily, it turned out. He couldn't have missed at that angle if I hadn't become a moving target. As it was, he missed me. He didn't miss poor Pegasus.

The neon horse exploded, electric sparks flying and glass sharding around me.

It was only about a ten-foot drop from where I fell. I figured I could keep my feet and keep moving.

Wrong, again, of course. My swinging had given me too much momentum. I fell and rolled.

Another bullet winged by me and I turned my roll into a summersault, heading toward Kevin. I didn't think I could get to him, but I was bruised, sore, and pissed as a son-of-a-bitch. I intended to give it my best shot.

I actually got close enough to him to let him kick me.

And Karen Anderson whirled into action.

She chopped at Kevin's hand, then grabbed the gun and twisted it, toward him.

He tried to yank away, but Karen tightened her grip on him, using both hands to twist his wrist until his baby finger was pointing at what was left of the flying horse. Then she dropped him.

I had her explain her Tai Chi moves to me later, but I'm still not sure I understand them. What happened, though, was that Kevin did a nose-dive directly into the gravel roof of the Magnolia Building and his gun skittered directly into Kathleen's waiting hands.

Kevin tried to get up, but Karen put her foot on his head and pressed it into the rocks.

"Kathleen, help me," he ordered. "Shoot them all. We'll take the money and head for the Caribbean."

"Are you kidding?" she asked. "Sid would fire me."

Chapter 18

I was still in the shower of my new trailer when the doorbell rang.

Just like a man to be an hour early for a date.

I pulled on an oriental-print silk bathrobe I'd bought myself in a rare moment of affluence and padded to the door to let Andy in. He could wait while I got ready.

I was so sure it would be Andy that it took me a second for my mind to re-compute.

"What are you doing here?" I reached for my pepper spray. The last person I wanted to see at my door, with the possible exception of Kevin Franklin, was Ivan Vorobev.

"Ms. Anderson. How nice to see you again. Please don't shoot."

I hadn't even noticed Mr. Fomin hidden behind Vorobev's bulk.

"Mr. Fomin," I said. It never hurt to be polite to the guy who gave you ten thousand dollars.

"Ivan wanted to apologize to you for the inconvenience he put you through," Mr. Fomin explained. "Right, Ivan?"

"Yeah, sure." He sounded about as apologetic as a hurricane.

"I understand," I said. I had less than an hour and I needed every minute of it if I was going to get beautiful for Andy.

Vorobev shifted from foot to foot, clearly uncertain about what to say next.

"You were going to tell me how sorry you were, right?" I asked. "And then you were going to disappear from my life. How would that be?"

Vorobev looked puzzled. "No. That's not quite it."

Uh-oh. I knew better than to ask, but I couldn't help myself. "Which part did I get wrong?"

"I didn't really want to kill you in the first place," he explained. "I was just going to warn you to back off, but then things got carried away. When Mr. Fomin told me that you were working with us, that you'd figured out who killed my brother, I figured, maybe, well, we could connect somehow."

If I'd been younger and more naive, I might have thought he was talking about a relationship. But this is the guy who had tried to kill me only a couple of weeks earlier.

This wasn't making sense. The only thing I could figure was that he'd really liked what I'd told him about the software project for his bar. "You want me to finish my software project after all?" My computer had been ruined with a cracked motherboard and destroyed power supply, but that the hard drive was recoverable. In the two weeks since Kevin had been arrested, I'd bought a used trailer, had it trucked to the park, and bought a new computer to install the old hard drive in. Fomin's ten thousand dollars was gone, but at least I had a life again. I hoped.

Vorobev wrinkled his forehead. "Oh, yeah. I forgot about that project. Do you have it? I mean, I'd really like to see it."

"Ivan, are you forgetting something?" Fomin looked a little nervous. I couldn't blame him. I was pretty sure my new trailer wasn't wired, but being on the F.B.I. most wanted list could make you paranoid.

"Right. I made you something. Hang on." Vorobev took off running back to the black Mercedes limousine parked in front of my trailer.

"I have a bad feeling about this," I told Fomin.

"You're doing all right? You have enough money now?" Mr. Fomin seemed ever so solicitous of my welfare. Maybe too much so.

"I'm hunky-dory," I told him.

"I don't know this expression."

"You've got to watch more Nick at Night," I told him. "Because nobody in America has used it in fifty years either. "It means I'm fine."

"I see." He nodded slowly, apparently finally realizing that he shouldn't use a low-class chick like me as his source for contemporary American slang. "Well, we appreciate what you did for us, Ms. Anderson. And want you to know that we'll be happy to return the favor when you need us. If anyone causes you trouble, we can help. Say that Mr. Patrick Adams decides to try his little trick again, for example. He can be made less troublesome very quickly." Fomin smiled. "And very permanently."

I shook my head quickly. Mr. Fomin's offer was just tempting enough to make me feel guilty. Patrick had saved my life after all. And he had taken my nude pictures off the net. But I would spend the rest of my life wondering who had seen them.

"I'll take a rain check," I told him.

"Here's Ivan with his contraption," he said.

Sure enough, Vorobev bounded up my trailer steps with some sort of a wooden box in his hands. He pushed it on me.

"What is it?" It looked fancy and well-constructed. Sort of like a project you'd do in wood-shop.

"I built it myself," Vorobev admitted.

"Great." I paused, hoping he'd explain.

Nothing.

"But why?" I finally asked him. "And what is it?"

"Your chicken," he told me. "She needs a place to live. It gives them comfort to have such a secure place."

Now that I knew what it was, it was obvious. There was a handled lid that could slide into place if you wanted to take your chicken with you somewhere, air holes drilled in an artistic pattern, and padding in the bottom of the cage that would make a comfortable nest for Charlaine to lay her eggs in.

Vorobev had found the one way he could cut through the fear and distrust he'd created when he'd tried to kill me. Thanks to Charlaine, I finally understood something about being a mother and how it can make the most irrational behavior seem perfectly logical. I'd even been able to understand my ex-mother-in-law, at least some.

"Thanks, Ivan." I kissed him on the cheek. It wasn't much, but it was a kiss. This for the guy who'd actually had a knife rubbing against my boobs looking for a soft spot between my ribs.

"Want to show me that software?" he asked.

"Maybe later," I told him. "I've got a date."

"A date?" He seemed overjoyed which was hardly flattering even if I didn't want to have him interested in me. "I thought you didn't have a boyfriend any more. I mean after-"

"He isn't exactly a boyfriend." He was something a lot more than a date-he was my friend.

If I'd just trusted my instincts and my best friend, I could have avoided that hellish hour on top of the Magnolia building. With what I'd already learned, we could have figured out that Kevin was the killer by putting our heads together.

I wasn't going to get back together with him. Not in the sense of being married and living together, anyway. Our worlds were too far apart. But they weren't so far apart that they couldn't do a little orbiting now and again.

"Well, that's great," Vorobev told he. He looked completely relieved. "I brought some passes to my bar. No cover charge for you or your friends. Ever."

"Thanks, Ivan." I took the greasy passes from him. Maybe, if I had an extreme deathwish, I'd dust them off and look at them sometime. For sure I wouldn't be using them.

"See, Mr. Fomin. She doesn't need me to take care of her after all."

I'd thought I had seen that coming from his relief at the word I had a boyfriend. So Fomin had blackmailed him into becoming Sam's replacement. I guess that indicated how both Fomin and Ivan thought about me-a hopeless project.

"Thanks for the chicken crate," I told Ivan. "Charlaine is going to like it a lot."

"Yeah, sure."

Fomin shook his head. "That's not good enough, Ivan. Tina says she doesn't have a boyfriend. A woman needs a man to protect her."

"Forget it, Mr. Fomin," I told him. "Besides, you don't owe me anything. The police wouldn't even have suspected mob involvement if it hadn't been for me."

He gave his tobacco-laden laugh. "That's why I want you to be grateful to us, Ms. Anderson. You're a menace, you know."

"All of her boyfriends end up dead," Ivan whined. "I'll come if she calls me, but I'm not going to date her."

I shook hands with both men.

"I'll call you if I need you. But I'm out of the Nancy Drew business."

Vorobev grinned and Fomin shook his head but both finally left and I went inside to show my chicken her new home.

THE END